Year of the Monsoon

Books by Caren J. Werlinger

Currently available:
Looking Through Windows
Miserere
In This Small Spot
Neither Present Time
Year of the Monsoon

Coming soon:
She Sings of Old, Unhappy, Far-off Things
Hear the Last Unicorn

Year of the Monsoon

— by —

Caren J. Werlinger

CORGYN
Publishing

Year of the Monsoon
Published by Corgyn Publishing, LLC.

Copyright © 2010, 2014 by Caren J. Werlinger.
All rights reserved.

eBook ISBN: 978-0-9886501-8-3
Print ISBN: 978-0-9886501-9-0

E-mail: cjwerlingerbooks@yahoo.com

Cover design by Patty G. Henderson
www.boulevardphotografica.yolasite.com

Book design by Maureen Cutajar
www.gopublished.com

Dedication

To my parents, Nancy and Ray.

Acknowledgements

There are many people to thank for their assistance in getting this manuscript at last into readers' hands. A sincere thank-you to Marty, Marge and Terry for reading early versions of this story and offering feedback and proofreading. To Beth Mitchum, for her editing skills. To Julie French of the Live Baltimore Home Center, for her assistance in researching Baltimore neighborhoods, and to Patricia Morill of the Art Gallery of Fells Point, for her generous time and assistance with my research of the Fells Point area.

And to my partner, Beth, for always being my first and gentlest critic.

Year of the Monsoon

Chapter 1

LEISA YEATS COUGHED A little as her first few breaths of cold night air hit her lungs. She pulled her scarf more snugly around her neck as she descended the brick steps of her front porch. From the sidewalk, she glanced back up at the dark window of the bedroom where she had so recently been sleeping in a warm, cozy bed next to her partner, Nan, with their corgi, Bronwyn, snuggled between them.

Shivering, she looked toward the Mini Cooper, thinking longingly of the heated seats. She sighed and unlocked her ten-year-old Nissan Sentra, tossing her backpack onto the passenger seat, and turned the ignition. She switched the heat on high and pulled away from the curb, her tires spinning a little on the compacted snow near the curb. A few of the neighbors in their Baltimore community of Arcadia still had Christmas lights up, but most of the houses on this mid-January night were dark and still. *The only good thing about being roused from bed at three a.m.,* she thought, *is that there's no traffic.*

By the time she pulled into the police station, the car was just getting warm. Her shoes crunched on the snow as she walked through the parking lot. She hurried through the sliding glass doors into the brightly lit lobby.

"Hey, Matt," she said to the young officer behind the desk as she retrieved her ID from one of the pockets of her backpack and clipped it to her jacket.

"Hi, Leisa," he answered, looking up from his computer screen. "You're on call tonight, huh?"

"Yup. The glamorous part of social work," she said, stifling a yawn. "What do we have?"

"Little girl." He swiveled the monitor so she could see the report. "Neighbors reported seeing her going through the garbage looking for food. Our guys said when they got there, she ran and hid in a closet. Found a female corpse in another room. Probably her mother. The M.E. thinks it was most likely an overdose, one, maybe two weeks ago. Won't know for sure until he does the autopsy."

Leisa grimaced. "Was it nasty?"

Matt shook his head. "No heat in the apartment. It's been so cold, the body was fine."

"How old's the girl?"

"Don't know," Matt shrugged. "She hasn't said a word. Looks like she might be five or six."

"Where is she?" Leisa asked, glancing around the empty lobby.

He jerked his head to the left. "Room 3."

"Alone?" she asked, displeased.

"There's a two-way mirror," he explained, pointing to a closed-circuit monitor next to his computer. "I've been watching her. It was the only way we could get her to eat anything. She wouldn't touch the food while we were in there with her."

Leisa leaned over the counter so she could see the image on the monitor. "So we don't have a name, either?" She watched the little girl get up from the corner where she was sitting on the floor, come get a drink of milk from a cup on the table and go back to her corner, leaving a half-eaten sandwich on the table.

"Nothing."

Leisa sighed. "Well, let's see what we can find out."

She went down the corridor to Room 3, knocked and opened the door. Without looking directly at the girl, Leisa could see her hug her knees more tightly against her chest, trying to make herself even smaller. Leisa took off her coat and scarf, draping them over the back of a chair and sat on the carpeted floor also, still not looking at the girl. Opening her backpack, she found a chocolate bar. Tearing the outer wrapper open, she broke off a chunk of chocolate and placed it on the wrapper on the carpet next to her. She pushed it toward the girl a few feet and left it. Ignoring the girl, she broke off another piece of chocolate and put it in her mouth. She set the remainder of the chocolate bar on top of her backpack and waited.

For nearly half an hour she waited, trying not to doze off. At last, the girl stirred from her corner and scooted closer until she could snatch the chocolate Leisa had left. She took it back to her corner and ate it, shoving the whole piece in her mouth.

"I really like chocolate," Leisa said as she took another bite. She placed another chunk of chocolate on the wrapper, not quite so far away this time.

It only took a few minutes for the girl to come and get the chocolate this time. Before she could scuttle away, Leisa held the rest of the chocolate bar in her open palm.

"My name is Leisa."

She looked at the girl for the first time. "What's your name?"

The little girl's greasy black hair was tangled. Her face and hands were filthy, her clothing stained and torn. She surveyed Leisa with dark brown eyes that were large and wary.

"What's your name?" Leisa repeated, holding the chocolate a few inches closer to the girl.

"Mariela," the girl murmured in such a quiet voice that Leisa almost couldn't hear her.

"Hello, Mariela." Leisa smiled, offering the candy bar to her. Mariela took the chocolate and this time stayed next to Leisa while she ate. Leisa glanced at her watch and saw that it was nearly four-thirty. "Tired?"

Mariela nodded.

Leisa spoke to the mirror. "Officer Wellby, could we have some blankets, please?"

3

Within a couple of minutes, Matt came in with three folded blankets. He winked at Leisa as he handed them to her and left.

Leisa spread one blanket on the floor beside her and placed a folded one next to her leg, patting it invitingly. Mariela laid her head down and Leisa covered her with the last blanket.

Mariela looked up at Leisa uncertainly, not sure whether this was a safe thing to do. Leisa smiled down at her. "Go to sleep. I won't leave you."

———

Was that night the trigger, the catalyst for everything that happened later? Leisa would wonder when she thought back. No, she realized. There had been no one cataclysmic event that had set things in motion. It had been so many little things, meaningless, or at least harmless at the time, chipping away at the foundation of their relationship, that by the time it was hit by something big – "our monsoon," Nan would have said – there was nothing left to hold it up.

"Hey." Maddie's round face, framed by a halo of frizzy hair, appeared over the partition around Leisa's cubicle.

"You do know," Leisa said, glancing up from the report she was filling out, "that using the door to my cubicle, like normal people, would be the polite thing to do. Just because you're seven feet tall –"

"Six two," Maddie cut in, ignoring the rest of Leisa's jibe. "How's Mariela doing?"

Leisa shrugged. "I'm not sure. I haven't had a chance to check on her today, but the residential staff said yesterday that she still hadn't said a word to anyone."

"She'll come around. What did Nan say about dinner on Saturday?"

"I didn't get a chance to ask her," Leisa said as she turned back to her computer.

Maddie's disembodied face frowned. "Everything okay with you two?"

"We're fine," Leisa reassured her. "She just got home late and I was already in bed. I'll ask her tonight."

"All right. Let me know."

Leisa stared at her monitor. "We're fine," she repeated to herself.

———◆———

Nan sat, feverishly typing a treatment note from three appointments ago. She closed her eyes and tried to remember. What had that woman been talking about? *Does it really matter?* she asked herself. *She's been stuck on the same issues for three years.* Her computer dinged that she had an e-mail and the little bubble appeared in the corner of her screen. It was from Maddie. *Dinner Saturday? Lyn's making chili. Hey, are you and Leisa okay?*

Nan frowned at the words. What was Leisa saying at work that would make Maddie ask that? It had been Maddie who introduced them, Maddie who saw what Nan couldn't, wouldn't see in herself. Like a child listening to a favorite bedtime story, Leisa had made Nan tell the tale of how they met so often that Leisa felt she had been there through all the maneuvering to get Nan to the party that evening, even though she hadn't. She knew this story inside and out – "most, not all," Nan would have corrected.

"Look," Maddie had said, making Nan sit down while Lyn went to make coffee for all of them. "Ever since we were in college together, I've watched you and the women you're attracted to. You always gravitate toward beautiful players who have no intention of settling down, or if they say they will, they end up cheating on you like Jenna did."

Nan colored slightly. "Thank you for analyzing my shortcomings, Dr. Oxendine," she said coldly.

Unperturbed, Maddie sat back and shook her head with a wry smile. She knew her friend far too well to be affected by the chill emanating from Nan's general direction. "I'm not analyzing your shortcomings, Dr. Mathison. I am analyzing your shortsightedness. There's a difference."

Nan crossed her arms defensively. "Relationships just don't work out for me."

Maddie leaned forward, elbows on knees, and said, "They don't work out for you because you sabotage them before they even get off the ground by the women you choose. You're still punishing yourself -" She stopped abruptly at the warning in Nan's eyes. Choosing different words, she continued, "You won't let yourself believe that you deserve someone good and loyal who will love you. Really love you." When Nan made no response, Maddie asked in frustration, "How can you see so clearly what your clients need and still be so blind when you look at yourself?"

Nan's face softened a little. "You don't know how lucky you are to have found someone like Lyn."

"Oh, yes she does," said Lyn, overhearing this last bit as she came into the living room with a tray filled with coffee mugs and a plate of cookies, "because I remind her all the time."

Their gray tiger-stripe cat, Puddles, followed her from the kitchen.

Maddie took Lyn's hand after she set the tray down on the coffee table, and pulled her over for a kiss. Lyn's long, wavy hair swung forward, obscuring them from view for a moment. Puddles jumped onto Nan's lap and began purring as Nan reached for a mug and waited while Lyn settled on the couch next to Maddie.

"Sometimes," Maddie went on, "you have to create your own luck. And yours could be about to change," she said with a pleased grin.

Nan's dark eyes immediately became guarded and suspicious.

"There's this new woman -" Maddie began.

"No!" Nan cut her off.

"No, wait," Maddie pleaded. "She just started working in residential. She's kind of quiet, but she seems really nice."

"Don't set me up," Nan groaned. "It never works out."

"You really didn't like me, did you?" Leisa said with a laugh later when Nan told her this story.

Nan shook her head. "I didn't want to like you," she corrected. It was too hard to fall in love. "You just set yourself up to have your heart broken," she might have added. Nan had stopped falling in love long ago, choosing instead to enjoy her lovers for as long as they stayed. It still hurt when they left, just not as badly. But her heart betrayed her the moment she met Leisa. She only remembered bits of the party that evening at Lyn and Maddie's.

She had found Lyn in the kitchen when she arrived. "Let me help you," she said.

"Oh, thanks," Lyn said gratefully, stirring multiple pans on the stovetop. "I lost track of time in the studio today. Working on a new landscape."

"I'd like to see it if you have time later," Nan said as she got out a knife and cutting board.

Lyn gave her a sideways glance, still keeping most of her attention on her steaming pots. "Is this your strategy to escape all evening? Help me in the kitchen and then go hide in the studio?"

Nan grinned and didn't answer as she began chopping onions. Within a few minutes, she was squinting with tears running down her face as she blindly continued chopping, hoping to keep the tips of all ten digits intact. She was startled when Maddie brought Leisa into the kitchen for introductions. She hastily wiped her streaming eyes on her sleeve and looked up to find Leisa looking at her with her head tilted to one side in a gesture that would become endearingly familiar. She took in Leisa's short, blond hair and slender build, but it was the gray-green eyes that captivated her.

"I hope it wasn't me," Leisa joked. "The tears," she added when Nan looked at her blankly.

"Onions," Nan said, holding up both knife and onion, and trying unsuccessfully to use her shoulder to brush back the small strand of hair that always pulled loose and hung along her cheek.

"Oh good," Leisa smiled, reaching forward to tuck the loose strand behind Nan's ear.

Nan felt her face get warm at Leisa's touch. Maddie continued Leisa's tour of the rest of the house, and Nan casually abandoned her plans of staying in the kitchen as she carried platters and bowls of Lyn's excellent cooking out to the dining room table. Nan mingled with the other guests, making small talk, but trying to keep an eye on Leisa's whereabouts. At one point, tired of the socializing, Nan slipped away to the studio to see Lyn's latest work and was startled to find Leisa there.

"Oh, hi," Leisa stammered apologetically. "I hope Lyn and Maddie don't mind, I just needed a few minutes of quiet."

Nan smiled reassuringly. "You don't have to explain anything to me. Besides," she said, gesturing around the room, "this is the most fascinating room in the house. I've known Lyn for years, and it still amazes me that she can turn a blank, white canvas into something this beautiful."

Together, they roamed the open space of the studio as Nan told Leisa about the various locations of the seascapes and landscapes Lyn had hanging or leaning against the walls.

"Maddie said you went to UNC with her," Leisa said.

"Yes," said Nan.

"Did you play basketball, too?"

Nan laughed. "No. I'm not tall enough or athletic enough. Especially for UNC."

"It's just... I saw some pictures of you two," Leisa said. "I almost didn't recognize her. Maddie was so –"

"Skinny?" Nan finished for her when Leisa stopped abruptly. She nodded. "She was. All arms and legs. Great for blocking passes and grabbing rebounds. We stayed at UNC for grad school, but then we came to Baltimore for post-grad and she met Lyn. Maddie calls it happy fat."

Leisa looked quizzically at Nan. "Do their families mind?"

"What? That they're with a woman? Or that the woman is a different color?"

Leisa blushed furiously. "Both, I guess."

"Lyn's family is fine, but I don't think Maddie's mother is thrilled about either," Nan said thoughtfully. "I went home with Maddie a few times when we were in undergrad, and I think her mother was suspicious of our relationship even then. Wondered why she was bringing this white girl home. Especially in their tiny town in southern North Carolina. I think I was the only white person there anytime I went. Maddie just lives in a different world than her mom."

Leisa turned to her. "So you two were never...?"

"Lovers?" Nan laughed at the thought. "No. Just friends. Best friends."

They continued their tour of the studio. Nan kept getting tantalizing whiffs of Leisa's scent every time she leaned close to see some detail in one of the paintings. Nan lost track of how long they had been in the studio, but realized they had come full circle to where they started. They could hear noisy laughter coming from the front of the house.

Regretfully, Leisa said, "I suppose we should get back before they wonder where we disappeared to."

"I suppose so," Nan murmured, wishing they could remain here alone.

For the rest of the evening, it seemed every time Nan looked in Leisa's direction, Leisa would feel it and catch her looking. It had been a long time since anyone's gaze had made Nan's heart beat faster.

Later that night, after all the guests had left, Nan stayed to help clean up. As she hung up her damp dishtowel, Maddie pulled her over to the kitchen island where they sat with a last glass of wine.

"So?" Maddie asked as she scooted her bar stool closer.

Nan's face broke into a reluctant grin. "I like her," she admitted.

Lyn came over and draped an arm over Maddie's shoulders. "Have you made plans to see her again?"

Nan's grin faded. "Not yet. I do like her. I want to take this slow. If there's a chance this could turn into something, I don't want to mess it up."

Maddie reached across the granite and took Nan's hand in both of hers. "You won't mess it up," she said confidently.

———

Maddie looked up at the ping of an in-coming e-mail. *Saturday sounds good.* She looked again as a second message followed. *Leisa and I are fine.*

Chapter 2

"IF YOU HAVE A heart, this job will break it more times than you can count," Maddie had told Leisa often.
"Why do you stay?" Leisa used to ask.
Maddie always shrugged. "I have to. If we don't care, who will?"
"How do you protect yourself?"

———————

The St. Joseph's Children's Home had been founded in the 1930s to take in Depression-era children abandoned by desperate parents who couldn't afford to feed and clothe them. Originally, the Home was a dormitory-style building affiliated with St. Joseph's Catholic School, both of which were run by the Sisters of Our Charitable Lady. This had, of course, created an inevitable rift between the "have-nots", who attended the school by virtue of the charity of the Sisters, and the "haves", whose parents paid tuition for their children to receive a good, Catholic education and felt their children deserved better classmates than the unfortunates who lived at the Home. Eventually, this prejudice drove more and more parents to send their children to St. Agnes ten blocks away. The Sisters felt this was God's way of telling them to expand the Children's Home, and so in the fifties, the upper floors of the school were turned into more dormitory space. However, during the seventies, the Sisters of Our Charitable Lady, like many religious orders, experienced such a significant drop in their numbers that they could no longer staff the Home and the school themselves. After much discussion, the Sisters decided to narrow their focus to providing a stable home environment for the children in their care. So, the children began attending public schools and the remainder of the school building was converted into offices and more dormitories. An interfaith coalition of churches and synagogues banded together to help keep the Home open, aided by grants and some public funding.

Maddie Oxendine had come to St. Joseph's when she and Nan moved to Baltimore right after grad school in North Carolina - "we will complete our doctorates, come hell or high water," they had promised each other. Maddie stayed through her doctorate - "which felt like hell and high water," she would have added; through cuts in funding and cuts in staff; she stayed when Social Services began calling, desperate for placement of some of their more difficult cases - kids who had gone through foster home after foster home. Five years ago, she became the director, reporting to the Superior General of the Sisters of Our Charitable Lady, but now with only a few of the nuns working at the Home. "Anyone who sticks around here long enough will eventually become director," she shrugged.

Maddie joked a lot - "It's the only way to stay sane," she often said - but her jokes hid a heart big enough for all the children who came her way; for eleven-year-old Allison, who had silently let her step-father use her every night for years to keep him from turning to her younger sister and who had watched in disbelief as her mother told the judge she would give up the girls so she could join the step-father who had fled to Florida; for Marco, an eight-year-old product of a rape whose mother had committed suicide when she could no longer cope with her family's shame; for all the others, abandoned, orphaned, deprived of any sense of self-worth. No matter how busy she was, Maddie made time every afternoon to go and sit with the children. Leisa often watched as Maddie sat on the floor, her arms and lap filled with little ones who had crawled up, the older ones gathered around, eager to tell her about their day at school.

———

"How do you protect yourself?"

"Find someone to build a life with," Maddie counseled Leisa when she first asked that question. "Thank God for her every day. And leave this place here when you go home to her. Give all you can when you're here, but let it go when you leave. Or it won't be long until you have nothing left to give. Believe me, this will still be here waiting for you tomorrow."

But "find someone to build a life with" sounded easier than it was, Leisa thought back then. She kept telling herself that things with Sarah were really over this time. And mostly she believed it. But she knew how easily Sarah had wormed her way back into Leisa's heart before. One look from those eyes, one kiss from those lips, and Leisa was hooked again. "Maybe she'll stay this time," Leisa would always tell herself. But she never did. And then she met Nan, and Maddie's advice didn't seem so impossible anymore.

Leisa's telephone rang, startling her from her reverie. "Someone from the coroner's office is here to see you," Sadie, the receptionist, announced.

"Be right there."

Leisa stood and stretched. She made her way upstairs from her basement office, climbing the wide marble stairs worn smooth from decades of children's feet running up and down them. When she got to the main floor, she could see a young man sitting on one of the wooden chairs in Sadie's office. He was holding an aluminum paint can which he almost dropped as he stood to greet Leisa.

"Miss Yeats?" he asked.

"Yes?" Behind her, Leisa could hear the soft clicks of Sadie's beaded cornrows and knew she was craning her neck, trying to see, even as her fingers tapped rapidly on the keyboard of her computer.

"I'm David Anderson. I'm interning with the medical examiner's office. I was asked to bring these to you," he said, holding out the paint can.

At Leisa's confused look, he said, "They're the ashes of the Gonzalez woman. It was pretty straight forward – a heroin overdose, but Dr. Bledsoe, the medical examiner, said it was probably a good thing. She had full-blown AIDS and was already dying. Maybe she even did it on purpose. All her other needle marks looked old, and this overdose was huge." He handed her the can. "I just need you to sign here," he added, handing Leisa a form acknowledging receipt of the ashes. "Good-bye," he said as he pocketed the signed form.

Sadie was watching her and eyeing the can with a repulsed expression. "What are you going to do with that?"

Leisa looked at the plain paint can in her hands, adorned only with a label printed with a name, case number and date of cremation. "I'm going to deliver it."

Florida Gonzalez' body had been identified by her fingerprints. She had an extensive police record – prostitution, petty theft, dealing drugs. Leisa had stared transfixed at the mug shots taken at each arrest. She had been a beautiful woman, but her face had transformed, becoming harder and more gaunt with each photo. A few photos showed her with blackened eyes and facial bruises. There was no mention of a child or pregnancy. Evidently, Mariela had been born between incarcerations, perhaps not even in Maryland since there was no record of her birth. The most recent arrest had brought a one-month sentence last year for prostitution. Leisa wondered who had taken care of Mariela during that time.

She found Mariela in the elementary common room, sitting by herself in a small rocking chair she had pulled into a corner. Even after two weeks, she hadn't made any friends, wouldn't talk to anyone. With her black hair washed and pulled back in a ponytail and wearing clean clothes, Mariela was a beautiful child. Her face looked fuller with a few good meals inside her.

Leisa pulled another chair up close and sat. "Hello, Mariela," she said. "Do you remember I told you they had to do some tests on your mother to be sure how she died? It was drugs."

"Never lie to them," Maddie always insisted. "Most of these kids have never heard anything but lies from adults."

Mariela said nothing, just rocked.

"These are your mother's ashes," Leisa said gently, holding out the can.

Mariela stopped rocking and looked up at Leisa. After a long moment, Mariela reached over and took the can into her lap and began rocking again.

"You are her family," Leisa said. "You can decide what to do with the ashes. Sometimes people keep them. Sometimes they have a funeral and bury them. You can think about it and let us know what you want to do."

She left Mariela rocking in her chair, hugging the can tightly and humming to herself.

———

Leisa hurried home later that day, anxious to get home to Nan. All afternoon, she'd tried unsuccessfully to shake the image of Mariela, sitting in her rocking chair, holding tight to her mother's ashes. A mother who hadn't taken care of her, hadn't protected her. None of that mattered to Mariela. Sitting in her car, stuck in rush-hour traffic, Leisa felt her throat suddenly tighten and tears sting her eyes. She reached for her cell phone and dialed her mother's house before she remembered she wasn't home. She and Aunt Jo were in New York all week.

"Mom, you really need to start doing things for yourself, taking it a little easier," Leisa had started telling her mother about six months ago.

Daniel Yeats had fought a brave but brief battle with prostate cancer five years ago. He had tried to keep working in his drugstore during his chemo and radiation, but it hadn't been long before Leisa's mother, Rose, had taken over the books. Luckily, Daniel's assistant, Ed, was able to handle the pharmacy counter by himself. Reluctantly, Daniel and Rose had decided to sell the store to Ed. Bruce Gallagher, Jo Ann's husband, drafted the legal agreement and the store changed hands, but Rose was the one who knew all the customers, so she stayed on, helping Ed through the transition. After Daniel was gone, she kept working because it gave her something to do, a schedule she had to keep. But this past Christmas, Leisa and Nan had conspired with Bruce to give Rose and Jo a gift of a train trip to New York City so that the two sisters could enjoy a week together, shopping, going to Radio City Music Hall and seeing some Broadway shows. They weren't due back until late Saturday night.

Leisa considered calling her mother's cell, but put her telephone down. "This is stupid. You don't need to talk to your mother," she muttered as traffic started to move.

When she got home, the message light was blinking on the answering machine.

"Hi, hon," came Nan's voice out of the speaker, "I'm sorry, but I had to re-schedule a late client. I should be home by ten. Love you."

Sighing, Leisa turned to Bronwyn who wagged her stump of a tail. "Looks like it's just you and me tonight, then," she said as she opened the refrigerator. She fed them both, and took Bron for a frosty walk in the winter darkness, remembering when it wasn't like this.

———————

"I don't want to work evenings anymore," Nan had said ten years ago when Leisa moved in with her. "I want to spend my evenings at home with you." Despite the advice from her accountant that it would negatively impact her income to lose after-work hours, Nan cut her schedule back to one evening a week.

Those days had been magical. They each rushed home to be together, cooking dinner, often with Lyn and Maddie invited over. Later, they would snuggle together on Nan's sofa to watch television.

"I've never seen you this happy," Maddie said to Nan one evening as she helped carry dishes into the kitchen.

Nan glanced back out to where Leisa sat at the table talking to Lyn. "I've honestly never been this happy," she agreed.

"It took you two long enough to figure it out," Maddie teased. "It's been what, eight months since we introduced you?"

Nan shook her head. "It wasn't me. I knew what I wanted almost as soon as I met her. She had... things she needed to work through." She lowered her eyes and smiled, embarrassed. "And she wouldn't sleep with me until she was sure she'd worked through them."

Maddie's eyebrows raised in surprise. "I knew I liked her, but morals, too?" She leaned closer and whispered, "Was she worth waiting for?"

Nan blushed and Maddie laughed loudly.

Leisa and Lyn both turned at the sound.

"What are you two saying in there?" Lyn asked suspiciously.

"Nothing," Maddie answered most unconvincingly, still laughing.

One of the biggest challenges for Nan in the beginning was meeting Leisa's family. "I've never... no one has ever wanted me to meet her family before," Nan protested weakly.

Leisa tilted her head and smiled. "A lot of things are going to be different from the way they were before," she said. It had not escaped her notice that Nan almost never talked about her family.

"Don't you do a lot of family therapy?" Leisa had asked, puzzled. "How can you do that if you can't talk to your own family?"

"Just because you're born into a family doesn't mean you're part of it," Nan countered. "Anyway, do you have any idea how many substance abuse counselors are alcoholics, from alcoholic families?"

"Well, you're invited to dinner on Sunday," Leisa said. "I've talked about you so much, they're starting to think I made you up."

"Isn't this what you always wanted?" Maddie asked when Nan called her in a panic. "Someone to build a life with? Someone who wants to include you in everything as her partner?"

"But what do I do when she wants the same from me?" Nan asked.

Her fears were allayed almost as soon as she met Leisa's family. The Yeatses and Gallaghers all welcomed her warmly, and soon began expecting her every time Leisa came home.

Leisa spent so much time at Nan's apartment, it seemed silly for her to keep her own. "I've never had anyone live with me before," Nan fretted, but Leisa blended into her life seamlessly and "I can't

17

remember what it used to be like for her not to be here," Nan admitted to Maddie. For months, they enjoyed the newness of their life together – a first for both of them, until "Don't you think it's time we started thinking about buying our own home together?" Leisa suggested.

If Nan thought meeting Leisa's family was cause for panic, it was nothing to the panic she felt now. "But this is... this is legal! I mean, this is serious," she said, practically gasping for air.

Lyn laughed. "If you mean, you can't just walk away, you're right. You've got to be ready for a real commitment and break all your old patterns, the things you did before. This is what normal couples do."

"But if you've never had normal, how do you know how to live it?" Nan asked more than once.

"We'll work it out as we go," Leisa said confidently.

"How do you do that?" Nan asked, bewildered. "How do you know?"

Leisa laughed, and said, "I don't know. No one does. But I believe." She placed her hands on either side of Nan's face and looked into her eyes. "I believe in you. I believe in us."

Within a year, Nan and Leisa bought a house together, and life settled into a blissful routine. "What's a home without a dog?" Leisa murmured one evening as she nibbled on Nan's ear. And so Bronwyn came into their lives, a tiny bundle of fur, stubborn and fiercely independent, even if her legs were only an inch long. Before long, vacations gave way to a new furnace and then a new roof.

One day after they'd been together almost three years, Leisa told Nan she was thinking of going back to school to get her master's in social work. "I could do so much more with that degree," she said.

Nan couldn't argue. She remembered how much her own master's and doctorate had meant, and she knew Maddie valued Leisa at St. Joseph's. So she began scheduling evening clients again to make extra money while Leisa attended classes, studied and worked nights and weekends. The nights Leisa was home, she was so tired she fell asleep as soon as her head hit the pillow. But even after Leisa had finished school and gotten her license, "we never got back to the way we used to be," Leisa mused as she and Bronwyn walked the dark sidewalks of their neighborhood.

They got home from their walk and tried to wait up, but Nan found them asleep together on the couch.

"Hey," Nan whispered, kissing Leisa on the cheek and giving Bron's tummy a rub.

"Hi," Leisa smiled, stretching. "Are you hungry?" she asked as she sat up.

"No. I grabbed a sandwich in between sessions," Nan replied as she took off her coat and scarf. "Why don't you go on up to bed? I've got to finish documenting my last couple of sessions, and then I need to watch a little TV and clear my head before I come up." She picked up her briefcase and gave Leisa a quick kiss before heading down the hall toward the den. "I'll be up soon. Love you."

Leisa stared down the hall at Nan's retreating back. She heard the study door click shut. Bronwyn pushed her wet nose under Leisa's elbow, squirming onto her lap. Leisa sighed and hugged her. "Not sure why we bothered to wait." She clicked the television off. "Come on. One more time outside, and then off to bed."

In the study, Nan opened her e-mail. There it was. She hadn't really had time to read this message carefully when she first saw it. Vaguely, as if she were observing someone else's behavior, she noticed that her fingers poised over the buttons on the mouse were trembling. She read the message through a couple of times before deciding to delete it. She made sure she deleted it again from the "Deleted Items" folder.

Chapter 3

NAN GAVE HERSELF A mental shake, hoping she hadn't betrayed her momentary inattention to her client. She tried to focus. Damn, it felt like this week was never going to end. And the tension between her and Leisa wasn't making time go by any faster.

Leisa had been a little cool this morning after Nan was so late getting home, and even through her own pre-occupation, Nan had picked up on it.

"I'm sorry I was so late last night," she apologized, coming over to where Leisa was waiting for the toaster to pop and giving her a hug from behind.

A smile tugged at the corner of Leisa's mouth. She never could stay angry.

"Tell you what," Nan continued. "Let's go down to Fell's Point this weekend. We can bring Bron and spend the day together, just us."

Leisa turned to hold Nan. "That sounds good," she said, her voice muffled as she nuzzled into Nan's neck.

"How has your week been?" Nan asked as they each finished getting breakfast ready.

"It's been kind of a weird week," Leisa replied. "You remember the little girl I had to go to the police station for? Well, yesterday –"

They were interrupted by the ringing of Nan's cell phone. "This is Dr. Mathison," she said. It was the ER of one of the downtown hospitals informing Nan that one of her clients had been admitted. Nan looked at her watch as she hung up.

"I'm sorry, hon, I'm going to have to stop by there on my way to the office," she said as she abandoned her cereal and filled a travel cup with coffee.

"But you haven't even had breakfast," Leisa protested.

"I'll grab something later," Nan assured her. "See you tonight. Love you," she said as she gave Leisa a quick kiss.

"Love you, too," Leisa said as she sat with her toast.

As Nan reflected back on that conversation, she realized Leisa never got to finish whatever she had started to say. "I've got to remember to ask her," she said to herself when, at last, she finished her last session of the day. She gathered up her things and hurried out to her car.

Why is Friday traffic always so much worse than other days of the week? Nan wondered as she drummed her fingers impatiently on the steering wheel, oblivious to the fact that the soothing Native American flute music playing on the stereo wasn't calming her in the least. When she finally got home, she parked quickly behind Leisa's Sentra and ran up the steps to the front porch. Inside, she could hear Leisa's voice coming from the family room. Something was wrong.

"I don't understand," Leisa was saying in a choked voice. When Nan entered the room, she could see that Leisa's eyes were filled with tears. Leisa handed the telephone wordlessly to Nan and collapsed on the ottoman.

"Hello?" Nan said cautiously.

"Oh, Nan," came Jo Ann's voice, "I'm so glad you're home."

"Jo, what's wrong?" Nan asked in alarm.

"It's Rose." Now, Nan could tell that Jo Ann was also crying. "She collapsed this afternoon. They rushed her to the hospital. They said it was a heart attack. She's dead."

—▶—

"Are you sure you'll be all right for awhile?" Nan asked the next morning, holding Leisa closely. Neither of them had slept for more than short bits and the little they got wasn't restful.

"Yes," Leisa sniffed.

"I'll be home as soon as I can," Nan promised, holding Leisa's face and kissing her tenderly.

A few minutes later, Nan jumped as the driver behind her honked his horn irritably at her failure to notice that the light had changed. She was on her way to the office to re-arrange her schedule for the coming week. Bruce had left immediately after Jo Ann called yesterday afternoon, insisting on driving to New York to pick her up and bring her home. "I don't want her coming back on the train –" He cut himself off before he could add "alone". They had gotten home sometime around four a.m. Leisa and Nan were going over to their house later to eat lunch and then go on to the funeral home. As Nan wove her way through traffic, she tried to figure out how to prioritize her caseload. Everyone seemed to be in crisis mode lately.

Going through her schedule at the office, she picked out the clients who most needed to be seen. When she looked at the list, she realized she could still put in half a week seeing them.

Nan shifted uneasily, recalling a conversation she'd had with Maddie before Christmas.

"Remember to take care of what's important," Maddie had said, refilling Nan's wine glass.

"What's that supposed to mean?" Nan asked sharply.

When Maddie didn't answer right away, Nan said, "You say something like that and now you're going to get all cryptic on me?"

Maddie swirled the wine in her glass, watching the ruby reflections on the granite of the kitchen island. "You're working a lot lately."

"So?"

"So it's work." Maddie looked at Nan. "You're a good therapist, but if you died in an accident tomorrow, your clients would find someone else to go to. Your work is not your life." She took a sip of

23

her wine, and asked, "Is there a reason you're working so many hours?"

"No," Nan replied emphatically. "No, it's..." But she didn't know exactly what it was.

"Don't you want to be home more?" Maddie watched her closely.

Nan lowered her eyes. "Nothing is wrong, exactly, we're just in one of those phases where we don't seem to talk anymore. I feel like I might as well be at work," Nan admitted.

Maddie reached out and squeezed Nan's hand. "Remember to take care of what's important," she repeated.

Sighing, Nan looked back down at her list of clients and decided to cancel the entire week. She couldn't remember the last time she'd taken a whole week off. "Leisa is the most important thing right now," she reminded herself as she reached for the phone.

A couple of hours later, she and Leisa were seated at the kitchen table at Jo Ann and Bruce's home a couple of blocks from their own house and from Rose's, all within easy walking distance of each other.

"Tell us what happened," Leisa said as Bruce laid out a platter of ham and turkey for sandwiches.

Jo Ann removed her wire-rimmed glasses and wiped her eyes with a tissue. "She was complaining of indigestion," she explained in a tremulous voice. "We thought it was all the rich food we'd been eating. We went back to the hotel to rest." She began to cry again. "I heard her fall in the bathroom. I did CPR, but the paramedics said she died immediately." She couldn't continue.

Leisa looked up, her eyes red and puffy. She studied her aunt's face, so much like Rose's that people often mistook them as twins. Their dark hair had gone silver over the last few years and they had defiantly refused to color it, declaring that they had earned every one of those gray hairs.

Leisa looked nothing like them, having been adopted, the only child of Rose and Daniel Yeats. Daniel used to tell her when she was little that they went to the baby store and picked her out, like picking a puppy at a pet store.

"Your mother and I walked around and around, looking at all the babies there, and we picked out the prettiest and smartest baby girl they had," he used to say, holding Leisa and rocking her with her blond head resting on his chest so that his voice rumbled in her ear.

"I think I was ten before I started questioning that story," Leisa would laugh.

Now, they all picked at their food as no one had much of an appetite. At last, Bruce looked at his watch. "We'd better be going."

At the funeral home, they met with Horace Spink, a pale man with large bags under his eyes that gave him the appropriately mournful expression of a basset hound. "We've been in contact with the New York City medical examiner's office, and they assured me that the deceased's remains would be available by Wednesday."

"What do you mean 'available'?" Leisa demanded.

"After they have completed the autopsy, of course," Mr. Spink answered with what he obviously thought was a reassuring smile.

"Oh."

He opened a desk drawer and pulled out a leather binder. "Perhaps we should start," he said, flipping the binder open, "with our casket selection."

It seemed there was an endless list of decisions to be made: arranging for the transport of the body, scheduling viewing hours, what to include in the obituary, choosing the floral arrangements, how many death certificates to order. Leisa had helped her mother with all of these things when her father died, but Nan had never been through this process. She felt helpless as she sat back offering nothing but her support.

Nan had often watched, a bit enviously, as Leisa interacted with her parents and with Jo and Bruce. It was abundantly clear watching them that Leisa was not just loved, but adored, something Nan could not relate to.

"We just don't have anything in common," she had said flatly when Leisa first asked why she didn't want to see her family more often. "Having them in Oregon and me here works out just fine."

Nan was the middle child of three, "the unspectacular one," she often said. Leisa had met Mr. and Mrs. Mathison once when they stopped in Baltimore on their way to Europe. "Let's be discreet," Nan had said.

Leisa cocked her head to the side and asked, "Are you ashamed of me?"

Nan flushed and replied, "Of course not. I just don't discuss my personal life with them."

Leisa laughed. "They're your family! How can they not be involved in your personal life?"

"You'd be surprised how easy it is."

"But," Leisa sputtered, "but you have a brother and sister!"

"Believe me, siblings are over-rated," Nan said sardonically.

"You wouldn't think that if you didn't have any," Leisa sighed.

———◆———

By Sunday afternoon, all the arrangements were made. Nan was lying on the couch reading while Leisa flipped through television channels from the recliner with Bronwyn snoring next to her. Leisa finally settled on a football playoff game. She turned the volume down and said, "I think I'm going to go to work tomorrow."

Nan slowly lowered her book. "Why?"

Leisa stared at the television. "I feel like I'd rather keep busy. I don't know what I'd do, just waiting for Friday to get here for the funeral."

"I took the week off to be with you," Nan reminded her.

"I can't remember the last time you took a week off," Leisa said.

Nan sat up, swinging her feet to the floor. "We could go somewhere for a few days if you'd like."

Leisa looked over at her. "I don't feel like going anywhere, and I don't want to be away if Jo needs anything. I just need to stay busy," she repeated. "It might be a good time to catch up on all the old files you never have time for," she suggested as Nan stood.

"Or it might be a good time for you to deal with your feelings," Nan said pointedly as she started to leave.

"Are you angry?"

Nan stopped, her head bowed as she said over her shoulder, "No,

I am not angry. I just think it's a strange time for you to be at work. And I bet Maddie will think so, too."

"Where are you going?" Leisa asked as Nan headed down the hall.

"To re-schedule some of the people I canceled."

In the office, Nan punched her computer keys with angry jabs, despite what she'd just told Leisa, as she entered her password to check her e-mail. Ten new messages. Clicking her way through them, she stopped abruptly at the sixth message. There it was again.

"Leave me alone," she whispered through clenched teeth as she hit the delete button.

Chapter 4

MARIELA SAT IN THE playroom, cutting shapes out of construction paper. She was singing to herself, using a glue stick to fasten the colorful bits of paper to the aluminum paint can. Leisa sat down next to her.

"That's really pretty," she said, brushing a loose strand of black hair off Mariela's forehead.

"They're flowers for my mama," Mariela said. As Maddie had predicted, Mariela had slowly begun interacting with people, occasionally playing with the other children, but still often preferring to be by herself. The paint can was always with her.

"That's a very nice thing to do."

Leisa looked up and saw Maddie watching from the far side of the room. Leisa went over to her.

"Should we do something?" she asked.

Maddie considered for a moment before she answered, "Not yet. This is probably the most normal relationship she's ever had with her mother."

They stood side by side watching Mariela continue decorating the can of ashes.

"Have you ever felt like you wanted to take anyone home?" Leisa asked tentatively. "For real, to adopt?"

Maddie looked down at Leisa. "Are you saying you feel that way about Mariela?"

Leisa shrugged. "I've never felt this way about any of the others. There's just something about her that -" Her throat was suddenly too tight to finish.

Maddie put an arm around Leisa's shoulders. "Come to my office."

Wishing she had kept her mouth shut, Leisa accompanied Maddie downstairs. Maddie closed the door of her office and sat behind her desk as Leisa took the other chair.

"How long have you been thinking about this?" Maddie asked.

Leisa plucked a loose thread off her jeans and twisted it between her fingers. "Actually, she's been on my mind pretty constantly since the night I was called out to get her."

"Leisa," Maddie said gently, "it's only been a couple of weeks..."

"I know that," Leisa said defensively. "I didn't say I was ready to do it."

"Have you talked to Nan about this?"

Leisa exhaled in exasperation. "I can't talk to Nan about anything lately."

"What's going on?"

"I don't know. I guess she's still angry that I came to work the week of the funeral."

Maddie frowned. "It's not like Nan to stay angry. Do you intend to talk to her about Mariela?"

———◆———

"Would you like to have children? Someday?" Leisa had asked Nan once as they were getting to know one another.

Leisa had always envied her friends who came from large families. Thanksgiving and Christmas had always felt as if something was missing with only her parents and Aunt Jo and Uncle Bruce. Her favorite television show growing up was old re-runs of *The Waltons*. She had no desire to get pregnant, but had always hoped she would meet someone who would be open to adopting two or three children. "Not just one," she insisted. "One is lonely."

"No. Absolutely not," had been Nan's unexpected reply.

Leisa was caught off-guard by the finality of Nan's response. Nan, who never saw anything in black and white, who always took the trouble to try and see every issue from the other person's side, was adamant about this.

Puzzled, Leisa asked, "Why not? Don't you like children?"

Nan's expression had hardened perceptibly. "No, I don't."

Leisa swallowed her disappointment. She knew she was already beginning to fall in love with Nan, but to give up her dream of a family....

Over the years, any hopes Leisa had that Nan might change her mind were dashed when friends began having children. Nan never held the babies or played with the toddlers. She often excused herself from get-togethers where she knew children would be present. Leisa had had to accept that Nan really didn't like being around children.

———◆———

"Do you intend to talk to her about Mariela?"

Leisa shook her head. "Not now. It's not the right time."

She couldn't help noticing that Maddie looked relieved. She knew Maddie most likely thought this impulse to take Mariela home was a reaction to Rose's death. And if Leisa were absolutely honest with herself, "there is a grain of truth in that" she would have had to admit.

Home was a very lonely place lately, but Leisa couldn't talk to Maddie about what was going on. She missed her mom so much it hurt. There was a constant emptiness inside, compounded by a sense of guilt that she had told no one about. That day in the car, when she had thought about calling her mother, but hadn't. "Why?" she kept asking herself. "Why didn't you call?" She knew the question didn't really make sense - "how could you have known?" argued a more logical side of herself - but she wished with all her heart she could re-do that day. Nan asked often how she was doing, and held her when she found her

31

crying. But as warm and solicitous as Nan was in regard to Leisa's grief, there was a distance in her recently that Leisa couldn't bridge. "It's nothing," she said whenever Leisa found her, brooding and taciturn, staring into space. As empty as the world felt without her mother in it, it seemed even emptier with Nan so far away.

———◆———

Leisa and Nan climbed into the Mini and drove to Rose's house, passing beautifully-kept Craftsman, Tudor and Colonial style houses. The early February sky was flat and gray, looking as if it might snow again. Leisa pulled into the driveway and sat there, her hands tightly gripping the wheel.

"Are you sure you're ready to tackle this?" Nan asked, reaching over to Leisa's shoulder.

Leisa hadn't been inside the house since Rose's death. Jo Ann and Bruce were the ones who had come over to pick out clothes for Rose to be buried in; Leisa hadn't been ready then.

"Gotta start sometime," Leisa answered.

Jo Ann pulled in behind them, and they entered the house together. "Where to start?" Jo asked, depositing a bag of groceries in the kitchen.

"Would you two be willing to start in the bedroom? I'll start in the office," Leisa suggested.

The third bedroom upstairs had been turned into Daniel's office, and Rose had continued to use it for that purpose. Leisa paused on her way down the hall, looking in on her old bedroom, still decorated with old movie posters from *Grease* and *Star Wars*. With Jo and Bruce being the only remaining family, no one had stayed here, even as a weekend guest, since Leisa had moved out. Rose had left it exactly as it had been. Leisa swallowed the painful lump in her throat and moved on down the hall to the office.

She switched on the desk lamp and sat in the old-fashioned wooden desk chair, swiveling around to look at the photos scattered about on walls and bookshelves. Turning back to the desk, she sighed. She wasn't really sure what to look for.

She pulled open the desk's deep file drawer and began leafing through the files there. She'd had the utilities switched to her name and had been paying the bills that had arrived over the past few weeks, so those files were familiar. She found financial statements for IRAs and other investments – presumably Rose and Daniel's nest egg to carry them through retirement. She had to blink back tears at the realization that neither of her parents had lived long enough to see the benefits of all their planning and saving. There was a file filled with medical and prescription receipts ready for the accountant for last year's tax return, another with receipts for the new gutters and roof that had been installed on the house. There were files with two life insurance policies – one had been Daniel's.

At the back of the drawer was a file marked "Will" and behind that another file which had no label. Leisa pulled these out and laid them on the desk. The will was pretty straightforward – Bruce's partner had drafted it, and Bruce had already told Leisa that she inherited everything except for a couple of bequests to charities that Daniel and Rose had supported. She flipped open the last folder and stopped short – her hand hovering in mid-air.

She was staring at her adoption certificate.

Of course there would be paperwork with any adoption. She knew that. She dealt with this stuff all the time. Why had her parents never shown this to her before? Why had she never asked? She turned to the next page in the file. It was a birth certificate, but not hers. Or was it? She scrutinized it. It had been issued in New York State. The birthdate and gender were correct, but the name was not. In the space for the name was typed Margaret Marie. Just a first and middle name. No last name. Not Yeats. Not anything.

She slid the birth certificate to the side and saw a different birth certificate. This one had her name, Leisa Ann Yeats. It was also from the state of New York, but the issue date was six weeks after she'd been born.

There was a baptism certificate for Leisa Ann Yeats from St. Vincent's Catholic Church in Albany, and some early immunization records.

The very last piece of paper in the folder was a hand-written note. It was written in pencil, faded and a little hard to read.

Margaret Marie likes her bottle not too warm. She likes to sleep with a fan blowing and one light blanket.

She is a good baby and will usually sleep through the night and hardly ever cries.

———◆———

"Aren't you curious?" Leisa's friends had always asked when they learned she was adopted. "Don't you want to find your birth mother?"

"No," Leisa always answered, laughing at their consternation. "I have two great parents. Why would I want to go hunting for the woman who gave me up?"

She suspected that most people didn't believe her, but she meant what she said. She'd never been curious about "the incubator," as she had come to think of the woman who gave birth to her. She felt only a sense of gratitude to the woman for carrying her, especially since abortion was a legal option by then. Leisa was actually grateful the woman had had the good sense to realize she wasn't prepared to raise a baby. She couldn't imagine more wonderful parents than Rose and Daniel Yeats. This was especially true after she began working at St. Joseph's.

Even Nan had been a little skeptical at Leisa's insistence that she wasn't curious. "You've really never thought about trying to find her?" she had asked.

Leisa thought Nan looked oddly relieved and joked, "What? Were you worried about having to deal with two mothers-in-law?" It was the first time either of them had talked in terms of a future together. It had just popped out.

———◆———

But this? Leisa ran her hands through her hair. She could feel her heart hammering in her chest.

"How are you doing in there?" Jo Ann's voice called as she came down the hallway.

Leisa flipped the adoption folder closed and stood up.

"I'm good," she said. "I think I found all the life insurance policies and investment accounts that will need copies of the death certificate."

Nan followed Jo into the office. "We got everything in the closet boxed up –" She looked more closely at Leisa's face. "Are you all right?"

"I'm... I'm fine," Leisa stammered. "I guess this was just harder than I expected it to be."

Jo Ann came over and hugged her. "I know, honey. It is hard." She let Leisa go and wiped her own eyes. "I kept remembering as we took clothes out of her closet, where we bought this and where we were when we found that."

"Is there anything you want?" Leisa asked. "Any jewelry, or anything of Grandma's you'd like?"

Jo Ann gave her a tearful smile and patted her cheek. "You are so good. But who would I give it to? You're the daughter I never had."

"Come on, you two, before you get me crying again," Nan said. "Let's get some lunch. Can Bruce join us?"

Jo Ann nodded. "He said to call him when we were done here."

They went downstairs to the kitchen where Jo Ann had left a bag containing rolls. "Leisa, would you get the soup from the refrigerator?" Jo asked as she reached for the phone.

"Hello?" came Bruce's voice from the foyer not long after.

"In the kitchen," Jo Ann called.

"Hi, girls," he said as he entered the kitchen. He removed his baseball cap from his balding head and took off his glasses so he could wash at the sink.

"I smell sawdust," Nan said as she poured water for everyone. "What are you working on?"

"A new hutch for the dining room," Bruce replied as he wiped his ruddy face with a paper towel. Woodworking was his outlet for the stress of legal work. "Someone keeps buying new china and we're running out of space to put it," he said, with a sideways glance at his wife. "As if this family is going to get any bigger."

35

There was an awkward silence. Bruce laid his callused hand over Leisa's in apology. "I'm so sorry, Leisa."

"It's okay," she smiled. "We're all going to have to get used to it."

Bruce looked around the kitchen. "Have you thought any more about selling the house?"

"I've thought about it," she admitted, "but I'm not ready to let it go yet."

There were so many memories attached to this house. Jo Ann and Bruce were just a few streets away, and all her life that she could remember, Leisa had called this house home. She had prayed Nan would agree to look for a house in this neighborhood.

"Are you sure you won't mind being this close to my family?" Leisa had asked anxiously as Nan caressed the carved oak newel post on the stairway of the house they were touring.

Nan pirouetted slowly in the foyer, taking in the stained glass window on the stairway landing, the built-in bookcases flanking the fireplace, the graceful arches separating the rooms and knew she could fall in love with this house. She looked at Leisa. "Are you absolutely certain they're okay with us?"

Leisa smiled. "For the hundredth time, they love you! I have to warn you, though, they'll expect us over for dinner at least once a week." Her expression became serious. "I know you're not that close to your family –"

Nan came to her and took her by the shoulders. "I love your parents, and your aunt and uncle. They are so unlike my family." She took a deep breath. "I can't deny there have been brief moments of panic," she said with a wry smile, "but I want us to have a home together. I've never been ready to take that step with anyone before." She looked at Leisa with a hunger that make Leisa's insides tingle. "I've never loved anyone this much."

Leisa stepped closer and kissed her, her lips soft and open, pressing her body into Nan's. "I love you so much," she whispered when they parted.

36

"Oh," Nan groaned as Leisa pulled away. "I suppose we should buy the house before we make love in it."

"Do you want to continue this next Saturday?" Jo Ann offered, snapping Leisa back to the present.

"Sure, if you're available," Leisa responded. "I really appreciate having help with this."

They quickly cleaned the kitchen and Leisa went to get the papers she needed, making sure the unmarked folder was among them.

Chapter 5

"DR. MATHISON? THIS IS Bill Chisholm. I know you've been receiving my e-mails," said the voice on Nan's office voicemail. "We need to discuss this matter. Please call my office."

Nan sat at her desk staring at the telephone number she had written down. She could hear Maddie's voice in her head, saying, "What would you tell a client who was putting off some unpleasant task they know is unavoidable?"

She glanced at her watch. She had nearly an hour before her next client was due. She might as well get this over with. She dialed the number.

"Mr. Chisholm, please," she said to the receptionist. "This is Nan Mathison."

She was put on hold while the call was transferred.

"Dr. Mathison."

She recognized the voice as the same one she had just listened to. "Yes."

There was a pause as Mr. Chisholm waited for her to say something more. "Thank you for calling," he said when he realized she wasn't going to offer anything further. "I understand this is probably an awkward situation -"

"It isn't really a situation at all, Mr. Chisholm," Nan interrupted. "A meeting, a relationship of any kind is out of the question."

Another pause, then, "I have dealt with many similar cases, and I do understand how difficult this can be."

"Do you?" Nan winced at the acid tone of her own voice.

"Could you and I meet?" Mr. Chisholm asked, undeterred by her iciness. "Just us, I give you my word."

Nan closed her eyes. Several seconds passed.

"Dr. Mathison?"

"I have to be in Williamsburg next month for a conference. Can you meet me there?"

"Give me the dates you'll be there and I'll be in touch."

A few minutes later, the conversation was over and Nan sat, staring at the wall.

———◆———

"What did she do to you?" Nan had blurted as she opened her apartment door to find Leisa standing there, crying. She took Leisa by the hand and led her to the couch. "What happened?"

Those days had been some of the longest of Nan's life, leaving her cursing herself for falling in love again. Leisa's old girlfriend, Sarah, had called, saying she needed to see her.

"Why haven't you told her how much this is hurting you?" Lyn had asked when Nan told her and Maddie what was happening.

"I can't do that," Nan protested, sitting at their island. "She has to decide for herself... If she goes back to Sarah, it doesn't matter that I love her, does it?" Nan's eyes filled with tears. "I told myself I was never going to do this again."

"What happened?" Nan braced herself for whatever might come out of Leisa's mouth.

Leisa wiped her eyes and said, "She said she misses me and wants to have me back in her life."

Nan's heart went still and cold. "Hasn't she said that before?" she asked, trying to keep her voice neutral.

Leisa nodded. "I've told you part of this story, but," She stood and paced, wringing her hands nervously, "there's more, and it's all twisted together in my head."

Leisa forced herself to stand still, but couldn't seem to look at Nan. "I told you that we got together in college. Even then, I caught her cheating on me. But she always came back, and I always let her. When we graduated, she laughed at me for thinking our relationship could last in the real world." She reached up and ran her hands through her hair and took a tremulous breath as she resumed pacing. "What I didn't know then was that she already had plans to get married. She never wore his ring at school, but she'd been seeing her boyfriend every time she went home. She was sleeping with both of us, and who knows who else, but I wasn't the one she wanted to take home to her family."

She paused her pacing and wrapped her arms around herself.

Nan hesitantly asked, "So, did she get married?"

"Yes," Leisa replied bitterly. "But now, she says she's realized that he can't love her the way she needs to be loved, the way I loved her. She wants me back."

She began pacing again. Nan's eyes followed her back and forth. "Has she left the husband?" Nan asked, although she was pretty sure she knew the answer.

"Oh no," Leisa laughed angrily. "She wants both of us."

Nan looked down at her hands, surprised to see how tightly they were clenched. "What did you tell her?" she asked quietly.

"This is the other thing I need to explain," Leisa said, but she paced for several seconds more, trying to choose her words. "There's no way I would go back to her, I mean, I wouldn't with the whole husband thing anyway, but, she... she knows me, knows how to get to me. She came close... it was... we kissed," she confessed. "She's bad for me, or I'm just really pathetic. She's like some kind of drug I can't kick." Leisa glanced sideways toward Nan. "You've probably never been with anyone who affects you like that."

"Oh, yes I have," Nan admitted. She wasn't sure she wanted to know the answer to her next question. "Did it stop with a kiss?"

41

"Yes."

Nan's initial relief was followed by confusion. "Then why were you crying when you got here? What is it you want?" she asked a little defensively.

Leisa turned to face Nan for the first time. "I want you," she said simply. "I've never been able to tell her no, and I don't know if I could have this time, except, I love you so much. I just had to be honest with you, even if it means you wouldn't want to be with me anymore after hearing what happened."

Nan stood at last and came to her. Leisa's eyes, as she drew near, reminded Nan of the turbulent gray-green surf off the stormy Oregon coast. "You haven't pushed me away," she said softly. "I love you, too."

"Even after this?" Leisa asked, her eyes reflecting her doubt.

Nan's answer was in her kiss, a kiss that was passionately returned by Leisa as they pulled each other close.

Leisa pulled away, breathing hard. "Please don't ever lie to me. I can handle anything you'll ever tell me, but don't lie."

Nan tenderly held Leisa's face between her hands. "I promise."

———

Nan wasn't sure how long she sat at her desk, staring at nothing. For ten years, she had kept that promise. Well, almost. She leaned forward and pressed her forehead against her hands. "What have you done?" she groaned.

Chapter 6

IN LATER YEARS, WHEN Mariela Gonzalez was grown, only a few recollections from her time at St. Joseph's stood out in her memory. The most vivid, of course, was the paint can. When her mother was alive, Mariela learned very early on how to read her mother's behavior. Sometimes it was safe to be around her; sometimes Mariela knew she had to stay hidden, unseen, especially when her mother had men with her. That was when she went to her secret place, the place no one else knew about, where she could hide or get out of the building without anyone seeing. Once her mother was in the paint can, it wasn't like that. Of course, the grown up Mariela realized how childish the memories were, but for six-year-old Mariela, the paint can came with a warm, soft bed, clean clothes and plenty of food, and no shouting or lying on the floor not answering when Mariela called to her.

In her six-year-old mind, all of these good things were tied to Leisa. Things got better after Leisa came for her. Mariela remembered other people as well – Miss Maddie with the wild hair who looked scary but was very nice, and the fat Latina lady who read her stories and put her to bed at night. There were others, but it was Leisa she watched for, waited for.

She remembered one day very clearly. Because she had never attended school, had never been taught numbers or letters, Mariela was being taught at St. Joseph's the first year to try and get her up to grade level so she could go to school next year. Her teachers, dubious at first that she could make up so much ground in one year, were delighted with her progress. She was proving to be extremely bright, and was absorbing all she was being taught with an insatiable capacity for learning. She was in one of the classrooms after her school day was done, practicing her writing as she copied from a storybook, reading aloud to herself. Leisa walked by and saw her.

"Hello, Mariela," Leisa said, coming into the classroom and sitting at the next desk.

"Hello," said Mariela shyly.

"How is school going?"

Mariela beamed. "I can read now."

"Can you? Read me story," Leisa said.

Mariela pulled her book closer and read a few pages about a lost puppy. She stumbled over a word she didn't know, and stopped reading, her head lowered, her hair hiding her face.

"It's okay," Leisa reassured her. "That was really good. Let's sound this word out. I want to find out what happens."

She helped Mariela sound out the letters in the unknown word and Mariela continued to the end of the story.

"Wow," said Leisa, giving Mariela's back a pat. "I had no idea you could read now. That was really good. And you're learning to write, too." Leisa scooted closer to see Mariela's paper. "That's very good." Her foot bumped something and she looked down. There sat the paint can on the floor at Mariela's feet, still decorated with the bits of colored construction paper. Before she could stop herself, Leisa was weeping.

Mariela put her book down and turned to Leisa. "What's wrong?" she asked worriedly.

Leisa struggled to control her voice. "My mother died a little while ago, too."

Mariela reached out and laid her small hand on Leisa's knee.

"Do you miss her?"

Leisa gave a watery smile and covered Mariela's hand with her own. "Yes, I do."

Mariela frowned. "Don't you have a can?"

It took Leisa a moment to realize what Mariela was asking. "No," she said, wiping her eyes. "We had a funeral for my mother... so we could say good-bye to her. She's buried at the cemetery."

Mariela thought about this. "But then, she's not with you."

"She's with me here," Leisa said as she laid her hand over her heart.

Mariela thought some more. "Could I bury my mama?"

Leisa looked into her earnest face. "Are you ready to do that?"

Mariela looked down at the can. "Yes."

Leisa brushed Mariela's hair back. "I'll look into getting a nice place for your mother," she said.

"Thank you," Mariela said. She looked up at Leisa again. "Are you an orphan like me now?"

Leisa's eyes filled again as she nodded. "I'm an orphan again."

"It was years and years before I understood what she meant by that," the grown Mariela would recall when she told Maddie about that day.

———◆———

Leisa paced back and forth in her cubicle, the papers from her adoption folder spread about upon her desk. Lying on top was the handwritten note. It still floored her that she'd had a different name, a different identity. It seems that for six weeks, her birth mother - she couldn't think of her as the incubator anymore - had kept her, held her, fed her. Maybe cared for her. Love seemed too strong a word. Leisa had always imagined that the delivery room nurses had taken her away immediately, that her birth mother had never even wanted to see her. But that obviously wasn't what happened. What else didn't she know?

———◆———

"If you ever want to search for her, you can tell me," Rose had said when Leisa was sixteen. They were on their way to Deep Creek Lake for the weekend, "just mother-daughter time," Rose said.

"I don't want to look for her," Leisa said, looking over at her mother from her new position in the driver's seat.

"Watch the road," Rose cautioned.

"There's no connection with her. She didn't love me. Why would I want to go looking for her?" Leisa asked matter-of-factly.

Rose was quiet for a few seconds. "It might not have been that simple. I know you feel that way now, but you may change your mind," Rose continued. "It's natural to be curious."

Leisa concentrated on a twisty section of road. "What about Dad?"

"Well," Rose sighed, "he feels a little more protective of you - I think it's a father thing. He wants to keep you safe from anything that might hurt you. After all," she laughed, "he did pick you out at the baby store."

———

"She was practically begging me to ask questions," Leisa realized now. "Why didn't I? Why did I just assume everything had been like some kind of fairy tale?"

It felt now as if her unquestioning belief that she had belonged solely and completely to her parents was as naïve as her one-time belief in the story about the baby store. She knew her parents had loved her; no part of her questioned that. But she had to admit that the discovery of these papers had changed her perception of her relationship with them - *it just feels different now* - and she felt guilty even thinking it.

It was like the summer between seventh and eighth grades. She and her best friend, Julie, had always been able to play make-believe, immersing themselves totally in the characters they made up. Their imaginations had seemed boundless. Then, that summer, Leisa could remember the very day they tried to play and couldn't. Leisa also remembered that that was the day she became aware of wanting to kiss Julie, and not in play. She could still feel the sadness, the awareness that something beautiful and innocent had gone forever.

She stopped pacing.

That was how this felt, she realized. The innocence with which she had always viewed her family, the simplicity of "we chose you" was gone forever. There had been hard choices and hurt and sacrifice. Only now there was no one to ask.

Almost no one.

She gathered up the folder and grabbed her jacket. She ran up the steps two at a time to Sadie's office.

"Sadie, I'm leaving for the day," she said.

Just then Maddie came in. "Everything okay?" she asked as she handed Sadie a file.

"Fine." Leisa pulled her jacket on. "Just something I have to take care of," she said vaguely.

It was almost four. She hoped Bruce would still be at the office. She needed to talk to her aunt alone. Pulling her cell phone out as she walked to her car, she called Jo's number.

"Please be there," she whispered. When her aunt picked up, she said, "Jo? I need to talk to you. Are you going to be home for a while? I'm on my way now."

She got there as quickly as traffic would allow. Remembering to bring the folder, she ran up the steps to her aunt and uncle's front porch. Jo Ann was waiting for her.

"Leisa, what's wrong, honey?" Jo asked as she closed the door. Leisa hung her jacket on the hall tree, not answering immediately.

"I need to ask you about these," she said, holding out the folder.

Jo led the way to the dining room where she sat down and opened the folder. Her face blanched as she leafed through the papers. She stopped when she got to the handwritten note.

"Your mother and father planned to talk to you about this," she said, looking over at Leisa. "Rose kept waiting for you to ask about her, but you never did."

"Can you tell me about this?" Leisa asked, tapping the note in her aunt's hand.

"She changed her mind," Rose had sobbed over the telephone. "All these months, we thought the baby would be ours..."

Rose and Daniel were living in Albany. They were devastated when they learned they couldn't have children. It turned out that both Rose and Jo Ann had such severe endometriosis that doctors felt successful pregnancies were impossible. Both sisters had had multiple miscarriages. When Rose and Daniel decided to adopt, the administrator of Catholic Charities gently warned them that the process would be lengthy and frustrating. They had been ecstatic when they got a call after just a couple of months telling them a young woman had decided early in her pregnancy to give the baby up.

"Why did she change her mind?" Jo Ann asked, feeling her sister's anguish.

"They said she asked to hold the baby, a little girl, and she just couldn't give her up," Rose explained, still crying. "I understand. Of course I understand. I know I couldn't do it. We're just so disappointed."

A couple of months later, they drove down to Baltimore with the tiny bundle in their arms.

"They said she kept praying, talking to her priest, trying to decide the right thing to do," Rose said, watching Leisa's perfect, miniature hand curled around Bruce's finger as he held her. "She finally decided this was best for the baby," she said, still not quite believing the baby was really theirs.

"They never meant to keep this from you," Jo Ann said to Leisa, reading her thoughts. "This was all part of what they wanted you to know."

"It just caught me off-guard to find it," Leisa said, slumping back against her chair and shaking her head. "And then when I did, they weren't here to ask." She looked up at Jo. "Were they really okay with me and Nan?"

Jo smiled knowingly. "With you and Nan? Yes. With you and what's her name from college? No."

Leisa blushed and laughed. "I can't blame them there." She tilted her head. "Did they always know I was gay?"

It was Jo Ann's turn to laugh. "I think they figured it out when you wrote a love poem for your sixth grade teacher and cut all your mother's roses so you could bring her flowers."

Leisa's face burned a deeper crimson. "Miss Davison," she said dreamily. "That was a serious crush. I felt really bad about the roses," she admitted sheepishly.

They were silent for a moment, then, "What are you going to do about this?" Jo Ann asked, tapping the note from Leisa's birth mother.

"I don't know," Leisa answered honestly.

———◆———

Leisa's office phone rang. "Hello," she said absently as she flipped through a folder on a new child referred to them that day.

"Hi," came Nan's voice. "Is anything going to keep you late tonight?"

"No," replied Leisa in surprise. "I should be done by five. What's up?"

"Nothing. I just feel like I've hardly seen you lately. I was thinking about cancelling my last two sessions so we could have dinner and a quiet evening together."

Leisa blinked. "That... that sounds really nice."

"Great." Nan sounded nervous. "Great. See you at home about five-thirty then. Love you."

"Love you, too. Bye." Leisa frowned in puzzlement as she hung up.

She glanced at a framed photo on her desk, taken last December at an anniversary party Lyn and Maddie had hosted to celebrate Nan and Leisa's ten years together. After Lyn and Maddie, who had been together for fourteen years, Leisa and Nan were the next in longevity among their group of friends. During the dinner, one of their friends had toasted them as "the perfect couple."

Leisa had thought of that evening several times over the past couple of months, as the distance between her and Nan had seemed to grow greater and greater. She wasn't sure why or even how the chasm between them had developed. "I can see it, I can feel it, but I don't know how to bridge it," she longed to say – to whom? Maddie? That would go over great if and when Nan found out about it. Plus it felt weird to bring personal problems to work. Lyn? Maybe. Sometimes Lyn was easier to talk to since she didn't have a history with Nan like Maddie did.

The night of the anniversary party, Nan had been more affectionate than she had been in a long time. When they got home, while Nan was taking Bronwyn out, Leisa lit candles in the bedroom, hoping to continue the romantic mood. When she emerged from the bathroom, Nan wasn't upstairs. Leisa went to the hallway where she could hear the television downstairs. She closed her eyes, listening for a moment, then went to blow the candles out before climbing into bed.

"What's going on?" Leisa whispered now, touching the photo.

———◆———

When Leisa got home from work that evening, she was surprised to see the Mini already on the curb.

"Wow," she murmured in surprise as she came in and smelled the aroma of pork chops cooking on the stove. Bronwyn raced to greet her, waggling her tailless rump and barking happily.

"It smells wonderful," Leisa said appreciatively as she entered the kitchen and Nan turned to her for a kiss.

"Hungry?" Nan grinned.

"I'm starving," Leisa answered. "What do you want me to do?"

"I've got all the food taken care of," Nan said, turning back to the stove. "Why don't you set the table and pour us some wine?"

Leisa's eyes narrowed suspiciously. "Wine, too? What's up? You haven't fed me like this since you were trying to get me into bed."

Nan laughed, and Leisa realized with a shock how long it had been since she'd heard that sound. She retrieved the corkscrew from a drawer and, with a small pang of guilt, realized that she had been so preoccupied with her grief for her mom and angst over the whole adoption thing that she hadn't even wondered if Nan's isolation was prompted by her own unhappiness.

"Well," Nan was saying suggestively, "maybe my motives haven't changed."

"I can only wish," Leisa shot back as she wriggled the cork out of the bottle. She closed her eyes. *Please mean it.*

While she poured the wine, Nan dished out pork chops, rice and green beans onto their plates. At the table, Leisa reached for Nan's hand before they started to eat and said, "Thank you. This is really nice."

Nan leaned over for a kiss. "You're welcome."

"How have you been?" Nan asked as they began eating. "I haven't really been available to you much these past few weeks."

"I know you've been busy at work," Leisa said. "I'm doing okay." She cut into her pork chop. "How about you? Difficult cases? Anything particularly troubling?"

"Oh, you know," Nan replied vaguely, but Leisa was used to this. Nan could never discuss specifics. "I'm grateful for all the referrals, but I think I'm working too much."

Leisa looked up at her. "Really? I haven't heard you say that since we first got together."

"I know. It's easy to slide into the habit of thinking work is more important than it is." Nan lowered her eyes to her plate. "There is something else I've been needing to talk to you about."

"I've had something I want to talk to you about, too," Leisa said.

"Why don't you go ahead," Nan suggested.

Leisa took a sip of wine before saying, "When we were cleaning out Mom's house, I found –"

She was interrupted by the telephone.

"How different might things have been," Leisa would wonder much later, "if we hadn't answered that phone?"

"Your grandmother died this morning," Nan's mother said as soon as Nan picked up. No preamble. No greeting. "You'll need to come home for the funeral."

Chapter 7

NAN SAT TENSE AND white-knuckled as the plane began its descent toward Portland.

"Are you nervous about landing?" Leisa asked, reaching over for her hand.

Nan gave her a quick smile that was more like a grimace. "Not about landing," she said darkly.

———◆———

"I would really like to be there with you," Leisa had argued to Nan as she made preparations for the trip to Oregon. "You were there for me with both Dad and Mom."

Nan turned to her. "I know, but my family is not like your family."

"Your parents were perfectly nice to me when I met them," Leisa pointed out.

"I know," said Nan again distractedly as she held up two different pairs of black pants, trying to decide which to pack. "But they were meeting you for the first time, on our turf. They could fool themselves that you're just a friend. My mother would never violate the law of polite first impressions, at least not to your face. It won't be

53

like that if they have to figure out what to do with you for what's supposed to be family time." She folded both pairs into her suitcase.

"Family time," Leisa repeated quietly, sitting in the club chair in the corner.

Nan recognized something in her tone and looked over. "Hey," she said, kneeling next to the chair. "Their definition, not mine."

Leisa just stared at her questioningly.

"Look," Nan said, taking Leisa's hand in both of hers. "We've never really talked about this but, I'm... I'm not actually out to my family." At Leisa's astounded expression, Nan hastened to explain, "You don't understand what it was like in my family."

"Then explain it to me," Leisa implored. "For as long as I've known you, there's been this wall when it comes to your family."

Nan pushed to her feet and went back to the bed where she fiddled nervously with a pair of socks. "There are some things you need to understand, things I've never talked about... to anyone."

"I can't understand if you won't tell me."

When she was sixteen, Nan began playing the piano accompaniment for the church choir. Her mother insisted on their going to church each week - not from any sense of piety, but because it was the thing to do - "if you don't want people talking about you," though Nan noticed it never stopped her mother talking about others. When Nan was offered the invitation to play for the choir, she jumped at it. If she had to be at church, at least this way she had an excuse for not sitting with her family.

The church had hired a new choir director, Marcus Oakley. He brought new energy, "and new music," Nan said enthusiastically. One evening, she was in the chapel practicing some of the new music before the choir's next rehearsal, repeating the phrases until they felt comfortable. She began singing along.

"Wow, you have a beautiful voice," said Marcus, startling her.

"I thought I was alone," Nan mumbled, burning a deep red.

"I mean it," Marcus said with a dazzling smile. He was young, just twenty-three, fresh out of college with his music degree, making the most of his first job. He was tall, handsome and black.

There had been a sudden surge in female choir applicants since he arrived, but Marcus showed no interest in any of them. "He must have a girlfriend back home," they whispered.

He sat down next to her on the piano bench. "Let's try something else," he said, picking another piece of music. He played so she could concentrate on singing. "Wow," he said again. "I'd like you to be a soloist."

"You're crazy," she protested. "Don't you know what they would say?"

The choir at Water Street Presbyterian Church was an elite – and elitist – group of mostly older church members, and Marcus had indeed been approached by several of them already, all telling him how the choir was to be run.

"Yes, I'm crazy," he agreed with a grin. "But I know good when I hear it." He became serious. "It would mean extra practice time during the week, though. Would it interfere with school?"

Leaping at the opportunity to become involved in something that was as different as possible from her brother and sister's activities of sports and cheerleading, the choir became Nan's sole focus outside of school. Marcus took her on as a sort of apprentice, tutoring her at a master level on the piano as well. He taught her about choral arranging and conducting and transposing. She took in everything he taught her, and though she and Marcus never discussed anything personal, he saw a lot.

He saw the disappointment in Nan's eyes when she sang magnificently, glancing toward her mother, hoping to see some sign of pride only to see her mother whispering to someone throughout her hymn, not listening at all. He saw the way Nan isolated herself, hiding behind the piano rather than socializing with the other choir members, and he found her in the church at all hours, practicing, always by herself.

Then one day, "Did you hear?"

"Wait till I tell you..."

Nan was revolted by the malicious delight with which the rumors were whispered and spread among the congregation.

Marcus had been attacked. What at first seemed like an ordinary mugging was soon revealed to be a hate-motivated bashing as Marcus left a gay bar one night. But the physical beating was only the beginning. Before he was even released from the hospital, a movement had begun, spear-headed by Linda Mathison, to have Marcus fired as the church's music director.

"You can't do that!" Nan argued. "So what if he's gay? He's the best music director we've ever had!"

Linda's face was livid. "He's despicable and vile!" she spat venomously. "To think we allowed someone like that into our church, let him work with our children. Those homosexuals don't deserve to live among decent people."

The day Marcus was released from the hospital, Nan told her mother she was going to the library.

"Nan," Marcus said, opening his door to find her standing on his stoop. "You shouldn't be here." But he stepped back to let her in.

"I had to come," she said, trying not to stare at his bruised face, one eye swollen shut with stitches along the brow.

He eased himself painfully onto his couch. Nan tentatively sat beside him.

"You can't stop this," he said, reading her mind.

"But I have to try!" she blurted out. "I have to stop her."

Marcus shook his head. "Even if you stop your mother, someone else will step in and follow her lead," he said. "I do not want you getting caught in the middle of this."

Nan's eyes filled with tears. "But I'm like you," she whispered.

Through his one open eye, he looked at her sympathetically. "I know," he said gently. "That's why it's especially important for you to protect yourself. And me. If you tell them about yourself now, they'll blame me for turning you gay. It will only make things worse for both of us. I don't want you to go through anything like that."

Nan hadn't even thought of it that way, but instinctively, she knew he was right.

———

"I didn't know you played piano and sang," Leisa said in astonishment, going to the bed where Nan stood, her arms wrapped tightly around herself.

"I don't anymore," Nan replied, her eyes focused on the past. "I did what Marcus asked. I kept quiet. I let them fire him. I let my mother think she'd won. For more than twenty years, I've regretted that decision and lived with that act of cowardice."

"What you did was necessary," Leisa said gently.

Nan turned to her, her eyes filled with angry tears. "It might have been necessary, but it doesn't make it any easier to live with. My only act of defiance to my mother was refusing to ever set foot in that church again."

She wiped her hand across her eyes. "I'm not ashamed of you. I'm not ashamed of us. But I would not want to put you through what I know my mother is capable of." She reached for Leisa's hand. "Both of your parents' obituaries listed me as a daughter-in-law. Even if my family got to the point of accepting you privately, they would never acknowledge you publicly. They're too afraid of what people might say."

Leisa reached up and laid a hand on Nan's cheek. She kissed her tenderly, her own eyes moist. "I'm not afraid of your mother, but I don't want to make things worse for you. If you want me with you, I will go."

Something in Nan's expression hardened. "Their definition, not mine," she repeated, more to herself than to Leisa. "Get your suitcase."

———

They were waiting outside the terminal at the pick-up area with their bags when Stanley Mathison drove up in his Lincoln. He looked much as Leisa remembered, tall and thin, with scant dark hair combed over to one side and dark eyes magnified by thick glasses. He quickly helped them load their suitcases into the cavernous trunk and pulled away from the curb, threading his way among the cabs and hotel shuttle vans.

"How was your flight?" he asked Nan, who was in the front passenger seat.

"It was fine," Nan answered.

"Leisa, how have you been?" he asked, glancing at Leisa in the rearview mirror. All she could see were his eyes, blinking at her through his eyeglasses.

"I've been pretty good, thank you," she replied. "I'm sorry about your mother-in-law."

"Yes, well…"

There was no further conversation as he drove home. Leisa almost burst out laughing from the back seat. How long could people sit in an enclosed space and say nothing to one another?

At length, they pulled into the driveway of a seventies-era brick ranch house. Linda Mathison came out to greet them as they climbed out of the car. She was thin also, all corners and angles in a slim-fitting sweater and pant set all in a matching shade of turquoise. She wore heavy gold bangles at her wrists and a heavier gold necklace around her thin neck.

"Mother," Nan said stiffly as Linda gave her a small hug. Nan closed her eyes as she picked up the scent of alcohol through the cloud of Chanel No. 5 that wafted about her mother.

"You remember Leisa," Nan prompted as Leisa emerged from the back seat.

"Of course," Linda said after the slightest hesitation, reaching a bony, manicured hand out to her. She had a smile on her face, but the expression in her eyes was inscrutable. "Stanley, get the bags," she said, leading the way into the house, passing a formal living room and dining room on either side of the foyer. Leisa had half-expected to see plastic covers on all the furniture. Everything was tasteful, impeccable – and utterly unwelcoming.

"Nan, you may put your suitcase in your old room," Linda said, pointing down the hall, "and Leisa may use Bradley's room," she added as they started down the hall.

Leisa caught Nan's eye. If Linda guessed the nature of their relationship, she was taking no chances on anything happening under her roof.

"Sorry," Nan muttered as they went down the hall toward the designated rooms.

"It's okay," Leisa assured her in a low voice. "You did let them know I was coming, didn't you?"

"Well," Nan stalled. "I told Dad. I'm getting the feeling he didn't exactly tell Mother."

Nan dropped her suitcase off and went back to Leisa. "We'd better not linger or they'll think we're tearing each other's clothes off," she said wryly. "Gird yourself."

They found Linda and Stanley sitting in the two wingback chairs in the living room, leaving the sofa for them. Nan sat tensely on the edge of the cushion, and Leisa did the same.

"Your grandmother's viewing will be this evening after dinner," Linda said, picking up a crystal tumbler from the end table beside her and taking a sip of the pale gold liquid within. "We're eating at the club. Bradley and Miranda will be joining us. The funeral will be tomorrow morning and the reading of the will is tomorrow afternoon," Linda said. "Then we'll all go to church on Sunday."

"We're flying home tomorrow evening," Nan said. "We can take a taxi back to the airport if need be."

"Won't they be insulted if we're only there for a little over twenty-four hours?" Leisa had asked when she looked over Nan's shoulder at the flight arrangements she was making on-line.

"They're going to be insulted by something, no matter what we do," Nan warned her. "At some point, my mother will get angry and give us the silent treatment. Just wait. You'll be ready to go. I know I will."

"That is simply out of the question," Linda said now, the ice in her glass clinking as she set it down hard, her lips pressed into a thin line. "What will people think?"

Nan kept her face carefully neutral. "What people is that?"

Leisa could see Linda's jaw muscles tense. "All of our friends, the people we socialize with. It's just not right."

"None of those people know us. They know you. What they think of us is not important."

"Of course it's important," Linda bristled.

"No, Mother, it isn't," Nan insisted with a forced calm. "What other people think only matters if you let it matter. So to me, what other people think really is not important."

"Obviously," Linda said icily with a half-glance toward Leisa.

Leisa could feel Nan's anger rising, and could feel her own face and neck flushing. She'd never sat through a confrontation such as this before. Defiantly, Nan reached over and took Leisa's hand. "I came for Grandmother, not anyone else. And we may as well clear the air right now. Leisa is here as my partner, not my friend. Once I've said my good-byes to Grandmother, we're leaving. We both need to get back to our work."

———

"Well that certainly created a warm and fuzzy atmosphere for dinner," Leisa giggled later that evening when she and Nan were finally alone. "I think for once, your mother didn't know what to say. And your brother and sister are charming."

"Told you."

Bradley and his wife, Tammy, arrived first at the country club with their two children. Bradley had retained his athletic build and good looks, but Tammy looked as if her plastic surgeon had supplied quite a bit of assistance. Leisa tried not to stare at the overly plump lips, the stretched skin between hairline and eyebrows or the impossibly prominent boobs. Their children, a girl of thirteen and a boy of eleven, were quiet, owing largely to the fact that they texted the entire time they were seated at the table, hiding their phones on their laps under the table cloth in deference to the club's no-cell-phone policy.

If they were surprised to be introduced to Leisa, they hid it much better than Nan's sister, Miranda, who responded with "Oh" when Nan made the introductions. Leisa could still see hints of the homecoming queen in Miranda's beautiful face, but it was a cold, haughty beauty. Leisa couldn't help feeling a stab of pity for Miranda's husband, Ted. Balding and pudgy, he seemed like a man who had made a deal with the devil to get a beautiful wife. Their daughter, also eleven, didn't bother trying to hide her earphones or phone, looking enormously bored to be there.

At the funeral home, Linda and Stanley were busy receiving visitors who had come to pay their respects, or, rather, Linda was receiving them as Stanley dutifully stood near-by.

Leisa couldn't help but compare the frigid atmosphere of this funeral with the warmth of Rose's only a few weeks ago. Despite the tragic suddenness of Rose's death, there had been hundreds of visitors at the funeral home and again at the funeral. Nearly everyone had a story of some kindness Rose or Daniel had done them over the years, and there had been more laughter than tears as people reminisced.

"Look at her," Nan whispered to Leisa. "You'd think she actually liked the old lady, the way she keeps dabbing at her eyes."

"Why are you even here?" Miranda hissed, startling both of them as she appeared from out of nowhere.

"Well, unlike you," retorted Nan, still whispering, "I'm actually here for Grandmother."

"And what is that supposed to mean?"

"It means that for all her crankiness, she was good to me," Nan said. "She was the only one who encouraged me to escape this place. I'm probably the only one who loved her, and the only one who doesn't care what she left me in her will."

Miranda's nostrils flared. "That's a terrible thing to say. You're not here - you don't come home for years, and then you have the indecency to show up with your lover at a time like this -"

"If you ever bothered to notice anything outside your own life," Nan shot back, her voice getting a little louder, "you would know that Leisa isn't my lover. She's my partner and has been for over ten years. Ten faithful years, I might add." Nan felt a little stab of triumph at the angry flush that colored her sister's cheeks. "And you wonder why I don't come home more often," she added scathingly.

Bradley came over at that moment. "Mom wants to introduce you to some people," he said, eyeing Leisa in a way that made her edge away from him.

She followed Nan as they all shuffled in Linda's direction. Miranda grabbed Ted by the arm on her way to her mother where

Linda introduced them to several older couples gathered near the closed casket. Linda turned, reaching a hand out to Nan when her eyes met Leisa's for a fraction of a second. She immediately turned her back on them, directing her friends' attention across the room to Miranda's daughter who was sitting sullenly in a far corner, still listening to her music.

Nan spun on her heel, taking Leisa by the hand and leading her outside. The evening air was misty and cool, refreshing after the stuffy warmth inside.

Nan closed her eyes and bowed her head as she leaned against the iron railing. Her hair fell forward, shielding her face from view.

"Are you all right?" Leisa asked softly, brushing Nan's hair back behind her ear. When Nan didn't answer, Leisa said, "I think this time at the funeral home is the only time I've seen your mother without a drink in her hand since we got here. Does she always drink this much?"

Nan nodded, still not looking at Leisa. "She never gets falling down drunk, or out of control. She just... No one wants to deal with it, certainly not my father. That was a big part of why my grandmother wanted me to get away. She saw everything, and knew it wouldn't change."

She picked her head up, swinging her hair back, and looked at Leisa, her eyes shining. "I'm so sorry you had to be subjected to this," she said. She took Leisa's hand and kissed it. "But I'm so glad you're here for me."

———

As Nan entered the church the next morning for the funeral, she stopped on the threshold of the sanctuary and took a deep breath. They took a seat in the pew with the rest of the family. Nan looked around, toward the choir loft. Leisa reached for her hand.

Nan blinked the tears from her eyes, looking down at Leisa's fingers wrapped around hers. Even as she dimly registered her mother's indignant huff of disapproval, she clung desperately to Leisa's hand, like an anchor holding her in the present, refusing to let the ghosts of the past pull her under.

Chapter 8

IT SEEMED THAT THEY had no sooner returned to Baltimore than it was time for Nan to pack again for Williamsburg. Leisa carried an armful of clean laundry upstairs to the bedroom.

"Here's some clean underwear and socks," she said.

"Thanks." Nan's voice echoed a little from the bathroom. Leisa was sorting clothes into piles on the bed when Nan emerged.

"Have you decided what –" Leisa began as she looked up. "Have you been crying?"

Nan didn't answer as she pulled open a dresser drawer and rummaged through it for sweaters to bring. "It's always so damned cold at these things."

Leisa went to her and took her by the shoulders. "What is it?" she asked, concerned.

"I just don't want to go to this conference," Nan replied moodily.

Leisa smiled in relief. "It's only for a few days." She pulled Nan to her and kissed her neck. "We could send you off with some good reasons to hurry home," she said suggestively, as her hands slid under Nan's t-shirt.

Nan grabbed Leisa's wrists and stopped her. "Not now. I've got too much to do," she said a trifle impatiently as she pulled away.

Leisa's face burned as if she'd been slapped. She turned back toward the laundry on the bed. Nan realized what she'd done and reached for her arm, saying, "I'm sorry."

"What is wrong with me?" Leisa asked, hurt tears welling up in her eyes.

"Nothing. Nothing is wrong with you," Nan insisted, pulling Leisa down to sit next to her on the edge of the bed.

"Do you know how many months it's been since we made love?" Leisa asked. "I try, and you don't respond. There must be some reason," she gasped as she started to cry in earnest.

"How did you expect her to react?" Maddie asked days later when Nan's world blew apart and she finally told Maddie everything.

"It's me," Nan said, trying to put an arm around Leisa's shoulders, but Leisa shrugged her away. "I just can't... I can't be that for you right now."

Leisa turned to look at her with tears streaming down her cheeks. "I don't understand."

"There's so much I need to tell you –"

Leisa stood suddenly, her eyes cold and accusing. "Is there someone else? Because if that's it, don't you dare give me this 'it's all me' bullshit."

"No!" Nan exclaimed. "There's no one else, I promise. Not... not like that. Please," she pleaded. "We need to talk. I tried before my grandmother died, but... I just can't get into it right before I leave. I'll explain everything when I get back."

Leisa's eyes remained distrustful. "Fine. Maybe when you get back, I'll sleep with you again. But not tonight."

She left the room and went down the hall, slamming the door of the guest room.

———

Friday afternoon found Leisa stuck in rush hour traffic on I-95 South. Jo Ann and Bruce were watching Bronwyn for the weekend so Leisa could drive to Williamsburg and surprise Nan.

"Are you sure surprising her is a good idea?" Jo had asked. "Isn't she going to be busy with her conference?"

"She's been there since Wednesday, and if I know her, she's probably been eating every meal alone in her room." What Leisa couldn't tell her aunt was that they hadn't spoken since their argument Tuesday night.

Traffic began to move.

"Come on," she urged, watching the speedometer needle creep up to forty.

The past three days had been hell. She'd barely slept. She and Nan had never slept apart out of anger, but even worse, she'd gotten up early Wednesday morning and left for work without seeing Nan off. Now she couldn't shake the guilt she felt. They'd never gone this long without speaking, but "I don't even know what to say to her at this point," she would have said because she was afraid to imagine whatever it was Nan hadn't been ready to tell her.

Finally, on Thursday, unable to stand it any longer, she'd gone to Maddie. "I need to speak with you if you have a minute."

"Sure," Maddie said. "Come on in."

Leisa closed the door and sat, clamping her hands between her knees to control her fidgeting.

"I'm sorry to bring personal things to work," she began.

Maddie leaned forward. "What is it?"

"I don't know exactly," Leisa admitted. "Nan... something is wrong and she can't tell me what it is. I thought maybe you might know what's going on."

Maddie frowned. "What makes you think something's wrong?"

Leisa shrugged. "Everything. She's been distant for months. She was working like seventy hours a week until Mom died. But even when she was home more, she wasn't there with me."

She blinked back the tears she could feel stinging her eyes. "We had an argument the night before she left. She said there was something she needed to tell me when she got back, but..." The tears spilled over. "I'm really scared," she said as she swiped her sleeve across her eyes.

"Hey," Maddie said, getting up and coming around her desk to sit next to Leisa. She laid her large hand gently on Leisa's shoulder.

"You're her oldest friend," Leisa said, sniffing. "Do you have any idea what's bothering her?"

Maddie shook her head. "I honestly don't. I've talked to her about working so much, but she hasn't said anything about any other problems."

"Why didn't Nan tell her years ago? When they first met?" Lyn asked incredulously when they finally knew the whole story. "And why didn't you tell me?"

"It wasn't my story to tell," Maddie mused. "I'm not really sure why Nan didn't tell her. I think it had a lot to do with the garbage Leisa's old girlfriend had pulled on her. Nan was afraid Leisa would walk if she told her the truth."

Lyn shook her head sadly. "And now Leisa may walk because she didn't."

———

By six-thirty, Leisa was getting off I-64 at Williamsburg. Nan was staying in the hotel where the conference was being held. Scanning the hotel signs cropping up amidst all the pancake houses offering cheap breakfasts, she spied the one she sought. She pulled into the parking lot and found Nan's Mini. She parked next to it and entered the hotel lobby, her heart pounding. She tried Nan's cell phone, but, as she expected, got her voice mail immediately. Leisa walked over to the registration desk.

"May I help you?" asked the young woman behind the desk.

"Yes, could you tell me what room Dr. Nan Mathison is in, please?"

The young woman stared at Leisa through smudged glasses, which she repeatedly pushed back up the bridge of her nose, only to have them slide down again. "I'm sorry, but we're not allowed to give out that information."

"No, you don't understand," Leisa explained. "I'm her partner."

She waited for this revelation to change the desk clerk's mind about giving her the room number. After several seconds and three more pushes of the glasses, the clerk said, "So, she should have given you her room number."

Trying not to lose her patience, Leisa said, "She would have, but her cell phone is turned off for the conference. Perhaps you could call her room and tell her I'm here," she suggested with exaggerated politeness.

The clerk blinked a couple of times. "I could do that." She started to reach for the telephone and stopped. "What's your name, please?"

"Leisa."

The clerk scanned a computer monitor and punched some buttons on the telephone. After several seconds, she hung up. "I'm sorry, but she's not answering her room phone." She pointed to the far end of the lobby. "You could wait for her at the bar if you want."

On her way to the bar, Leisa passed a couple of people sitting in chairs in the lobby. She quickly scanned the hotel's dining room as she went by, looking for any sign of Nan and seeing none. There were several people seated at the bar. She chose a small table set back in an alcove from which she could see the lobby and the entrance to the dining room. Her waiter had just brought her a Sam Adams when she saw Nan step out of the elevator across from the registration desk. Leisa was just standing to go to her when she saw Nan stop to greet one of the men Leisa had passed in the lobby. Nan shook hands with him as he gestured toward the bar.

"Damn." Leisa looked around quickly. The man was no doubt one of the other conference attendees, but she didn't want to be introduced and have to sit politely while he and Nan talked about whatever. Not with the tension between her and Nan right now. There was no way out of the bar without walking by them, but her table was next to the restrooms. Quickly, she got up and ducked into the women's room.

She took her time, and when she was ready to exit, she opened the door slowly to make sure she wasn't going to run smack into Nan. She couldn't see them anywhere. As she slid back into her seat, she heard Nan's voice coming from an adjacent booth.

"...how you located me, Mr. Chisholm," she was saying.

"It wasn't easy, Dr. Mathison," he replied. "It took some serious digging, and calling in a few favors from people with access to the records."

"That sounds -" Nan stopped as their drinks were brought. She waited until the server left. "That sounds illegal."

"Well," he said placatingly, "not so much illegal as unorthodox. It's why the family hired me."

"What do they want?" Nan asked. Even from where she sat, Leisa could hear the chill in Nan's voice and wondered why Mr. Chisholm wasn't backing up as fast as he could.

"To meet you. Or more precisely, Todd wants to meet you," he said.

"I told you over the phone, that is not going to happen."

"I remember. But I think once you know the circumstances you may change your mind."

"I doubt it," Nan said firmly.

There were a few seconds of silence, and Leisa held her breath, afraid maybe they were getting up from the booth.

"I brought a photo of Todd," Mr. Chisholm said. Leisa imagined he must have been offering it to Nan because a few seconds later he asked, "Don't you even want to see what he looks like? I knew as soon as I saw you that I had found the right person."

Nan said nothing.

"He has leukemia, Dr. Mathison. It's stage IV, terminal, the doctors say. His dying wish is to meet his birth mother."

Chapter 9

FUNNY HOW LIFE CAN change - one wrong word, one bad decision - and nothing is ever the same. This is opposed, Nan would ponder over the days and weeks that followed, to the big things - the planned things - that change life. It seemed unfair in a way that accidents, things that happen in a split second, can have the same impact as things that take time and planning. Like having a baby. Nine months for that life to develop, after only five minutes of drunken sex with someone she couldn't even remember at some party in college. Nine months to agonize about what to do. An abortion was never really an option. Not for Nan. It wasn't the baby's fault. Keeping the child was never an option, either. As it was, the birth would occur just in time for her to begin grad school as planned.

Maddie was the only person who knew. Not her family, no other friends. And after the adoption was arranged and the newborn baby had been taken away, they had never spoken of it again. But Maddie knew. Nan could see in Maddie's eyes when friends brought babies to gatherings that she alone understood why Nan had to leave the room. How could she hold someone else's infant when she hadn't even held her own? Hadn't even asked to see him?

"What kind of person could do that?"

Nan had asked herself that question more times than she could count, but it was Leisa who asked it aloud when Nan finally got to the house.

It had taken several seconds in the hotel bar for Nan to realize that the person who got up from the table behind them so abruptly that she knocked her chair over was Leisa. It had taken another few seconds to realize that Leisa had just overheard their entire conversation.

Nan leapt from her booth, leaving Bill Chisholm sitting there as she ran full-tilt through the lobby and out into the parking lot just in time to see Leisa's Sentra squeal away. It took another half hour to extricate herself from Mr. Chisholm's attempts to set up a meeting, pack her things and check out of the hotel. Leisa wouldn't answer her cell phone. That drive home was the longest four hours of Nan's life.

When she pulled up behind the Nissan, the house was dark. She let herself in the front door and set her suitcase and briefcase down. She could make out the shadow that was Leisa in one of the chairs flanking the fireplace. She was sitting with her knees hugged to her chest. The only sound was the ticking of the mantel clock.

Nan left the lights off, taking the adjacent chair, and saying nothing for several minutes. At last, she quietly said, "That wasn't how I wanted you to find out."

"No, I can't imagine it was." The calm of Leisa's voice frightened Nan more than any crying or shouting would have done. "I suppose this is what you wanted to explain to me when you got home?"

"Yes."

"I'm listening."

Nan took a shaky breath. She could feel herself shivering uncontrollably. "My senior year of college. There was a party at the end of fall semester. I was feeling sorry for myself because my girlfriend had just broken up with me to be with someone else. I got very drunk. He was someone I barely knew. It would sound better to say he was someone I at least cared about, but... it was a fuck in the crudest sense of that word. I don't remember much. I think he passed out afterward. I never spoke to him again."

Nan waited, but Leisa said nothing.

"Maddie was the only one I told. I didn't want to have an abortion and I didn't want to raise a baby by myself. She was with me at the hospital. The adoption was already arranged. They took it - the baby - away immediately."

"You never even looked at him?" Leisa asked. The appalled tone of her voice stung Nan who said nothing.

"Why didn't you tell me?"

It was Leisa asking now, but it could have been Maddie or Lyn or Nan asking herself that question a million times over the years.

"I was afraid," Nan whispered. "You were hurt so badly by Sarah, and so distrustful of any woman who had been with a man. And..." she paused. "I was so ashamed of that entire episode of my life."

She leaned her elbows on her knees, pressing the heels of her hands against her eyes. "I told myself at first that I would tell you if it looked like things might get serious between us. And then, when you told me about Sarah, I told myself I'd tell you when that hurt was less. And the longer I waited, the harder it got. Eventually, it felt like a bad dream, something I would never have to tell you about. But, a few months ago, that man, Bill Chisholm, started e-mailing me. He'd tracked me down." She sighed. "You heard the rest."

She sat with her head resting on her hands for a long time.

Finally, she heard Leisa's voice, still eerily calm, say, "I don't understand how you could lie to me for our entire relationship. What kind of person could do that?"

Nan stiffened, knowing what was coming. Her heart was beating so hard, she could hear the blood thundering in her ears, and she felt as if she couldn't breathe.

"I don't know you," Leisa said quietly. "If you could lie and hide something like this, what else might you have been lying about? I don't trust you anymore."

Nan could feel hot tears squeezing out of her eyes, still pressed against her hands.

"I think we need some time apart," Leisa continued. "I'm going to move into Mom's house until we can figure this out."

71

"Didn't you try to stop her?" Maddie asked.

"How could I?" Nan responded dejectedly. "Everything she said was true. And I don't know how to make it right."

She looked over at Maddie, sitting in the same chair Leisa had sat in. "How is she?"

Maddie shrugged. "About as you'd expect. She's angry with me, also. She sees me as part of the deception."

She looked at Nan, noting the dark circles under her red-rimmed eyes. "I'm worried about both of you, but you I can keep an eye on. Does Leisa have anyone else to confide in?"

Nan thought. "She's close to Jo Ann and Bruce, but I don't know that she could talk to them about this. Would Lyn try talking to her?"

"She already offered," Maddie said. "But she wanted me to tell you that if Leisa does agree to talk to her, she's going to keep Leisa's confidence. We're not allowed to ask."

Nan nodded as her eyes filled with tears again. "She must feel so alone."

A steady rain fell Saturday morning as Leisa sat cross-legged on the couch in her mother's family room, addressing an envelope. A New York State Adoptee Registration form lay beside her, already filled out and notarized. Adoption records in New York were still sealed, but the woman on the phone had explained that if both the adoptee and a biological parent or sibling registered, then the state would put them in touch with one another. She stared at the form.

She flipped open her adoption folder and pulled out the hand-written note yet again. Never had she struggled like this. Usually, she made decisions quickly and without second-guessing herself. This was a dilemma she had discussed with no one.

"I know you wanted me to ask questions," she said aloud to a photo of her parents on the fireplace mantel. "But knowing about her feels different from meeting her. Would you be okay with this?"

She glanced at the note. "You know, the other problem with meeting her is that right now, I can imagine her any way I want. If we meet, then I'm stuck with the reality of whoever she is."

Bronwyn raised her head from where she was curled up in her bed near the fireplace. Nan had suggested that Leisa take Bron since her work hours were more predictable. Leisa was secretly glad to have Bronwyn with her. She'd never lived in this house alone.

Leisa stared at the mantel, lined with family photos. Next to the photo of Rose and Daniel was one of her, Nan and Bronwyn that they had given to Rose last Christmas. As she looked at it, a shadow fell over her face. She folded the form and stuffed it into the envelope, sealing it before she could change her mind. She unfolded her legs and went to put the letter out in the mailbox for the Saturday mail pick-up.

"Oh, hi," she said in surprise as she opened the door to find her aunt standing on the front porch shaking off her wet umbrella. Leisa put her letter in the mailbox and said, "Come on in." She held the door open and, before Jo Ann could ask, added, "And no, I don't want to talk about it."

Jo Ann gave her that look, the one she used to get from her mother whenever she was being a smartass.

"Well, that's good to know," said Jo, "but that's not why I'm here. I came to see if you needed any more help going through the house." She bent over to pet Bronwyn who was dancing on her hind legs trying to get someone's attention.

Leisa narrowed her eyes suspiciously, thinking Jo could have called for that, but she didn't voice that thought.

"No, actually. Now that I'm staying here... for a while, I need the linens and kitchen things." Leisa led the way into the kitchen. "Want anything to eat or drink?"

"A cup of tea would be lovely. It may be March, but it's still cold out there, especially with the rain."

Leisa filled the kettle and put it on to boil. "Is Bruce in his workshop?"

"Yes," Jo answered as she sat at the kitchen table, one Bruce had made many years ago, and picked up the paper. "He'll probably be there all weekend, working on my hutch. He blames it on me, but if I didn't give him projects, he would drive me nuts."

Leisa smiled. It was true. She couldn't ever remember seeing Bruce sitting around doing nothing.

Within a few minutes, Leisa and Jo Ann were both cradling hot cups of tea in their hands as they read the paper.

"You do know," Jo Ann mused as she appeared to frown through her bifocals at something on the page, "that this is not the way to solve anything."

"Mmmm." Leisa also pretended to read the paper. All her life, any potential arguments or conflicts had been handled in this type of non-discussion. No one ever shouted or cursed. She had never seen her parents express anger toward her or one another. This was actually how she came out to them.

———

"So," Rose had said at the breakfast table as she picked up a section of the newspaper during Leisa's Christmas break her sophomore year of college, "how was your semester?"

"Oh, you know," Leisa answered noncommittally as she flipped through the sports section. "Grades were okay."

Daniel spoke up from behind the business pages. "Not really."

Leisa's only tell was a reddening of her face. "Oh?"

"Mmmm," Rose responded. "Funny. Your grades got here yesterday."

"They did?" Leisa stared at basketball scores.

"Mmm hmm." Daniel turned the page. "Anything going on?"

Leisa shook a crease out of her pages. "Well, I met someone."

"That's nice," Rose said, smoothing a wrinkle in her page. "What's his name?"

Leisa pretended to read for several seconds. "Her name is Sarah." Her hands were trembling so badly that her newspaper rustled. She set it down and folded her hands between her knees.

She kept her eyes glued on the small print in front of her, so she was never really sure what her parents' reactions were to that announcement, but there was a long silence before Daniel said quietly, "Well, you're going to figure out how to balance seeing Sarah with getting better grades, right?" He was staring at stock prices. He didn't own any stocks.

"Yes."

"Because if you don't," Rose said as she reached for the lifestyle section, "you will be responsible for your own tuition next year."

Leisa folded up the sports section. "Right."

———————

If Leisa had ever wondered which side of the family originated the non-discussion technique, she now knew because Jo Ann was good at it.

"Most people are not open books, even to their spouses," Jo said as she flipped a page.

"About little stuff," Leisa answered. She wasn't sure how much Jo Ann knew. Nan was not usually much of a talker, and Leisa hadn't told her aunt anything.

"Sometimes big things, too." Jo Ann held up her part of the paper so that it obscured her face. "Especially if it involved a mistake they would never make now. Something they're ashamed and embarrassed by."

"Mmmm," Leisa repeated. Okay, so Jo knew. It floored her for a moment that Nan would have gone to them and explained what was happening. If she had, she must also have told them why. "Like getting pregnant and giving the baby up for adoption? And somehow forgetting to mention it?"

Jo Ann lowered the paper, still pretending to read. "Like trying to do the right thing after making a horrible mistake. Thinking you've put the baby in a situation where he'll grow up loved and cared for, only to find out he's not going to grow up after all."

Leisa's hands gripped her paper more tightly. "I don't understand her. I don't understand how she could have a baby and never even hold him or look at him, even if adoption was the best thing for everyone."

Even as she said this, she thought about the struggle of her own birth mother, and realized maybe Nan's way was the only way she could have given him up, but she continued relentlessly, driven by her anger and her pain. "I feel like I don't know her anymore."

Jo Ann looked directly at Leisa for the first time. "Nan probably needs you now more than she ever has," she said quietly.

———————

"I don't know what's wrong with me," Leisa had confessed to Lyn earlier in the week. "My life is coming unraveled. I should be an emotional basketcase, but I can't cry. I'm too angry to cry. In fact, it's about the only thing I do feel."

Lyn glanced at Leisa as they walked Bronwyn. "Why are you so angry?"

"Everything I thought I knew, everything I trusted - nothing is the way I thought it was."

"Are we talking about more than Nan?"

Leisa didn't answer for a long while. "I just... I don't know what to believe anymore."

"I hope you believe that Nan loves you," Lyn said gently. "No matter what else has happened, she loves you."

Leisa kicked sullenly at an acorn. "I'm just not sure that's enough."

———————

"Nan probably needs you now more than she ever has."

Leisa looked at her aunt, unable to come up with a response to that. The doorbell rang.

Jo got up to answer it as Bronwyn barked and whined at the door. When Jo opened the front door, Nan was standing there, soaking wet. "Get in here," Jo Ann said, pulling Nan inside. She grabbed her umbrella. "I was just leaving. She's in the kitchen."

"Jo, no," Nan began to protest, but Jo Ann was already descending the porch steps. She bent to hug Bronwyn, and then went to the kitchen, unsure of the reception she would receive.

"Who was —" Leisa started to ask, stopping as she saw Nan standing there.

"Hi," Nan said uncertainly.

Leisa didn't respond, but went into the laundry room, emerging a moment later with a clean towel. She held it out, noticing the dark circles under Nan's eyes. "Would you like some coffee or tea?" she asked.

"Some hot tea sounds great, thanks," Nan said as she dried her hair and wrapped the towel around her shoulders.

"Great day for a walk," Leisa said a little sarcastically from the sink as she refilled the kettle, looking out the window at the steady drizzle.

Nan shrugged. "I hadn't really intended to go for a walk. I was just wondering how you are..." Her voice trailed off.

Leisa put the kettle back on the burner and turned to face Nan. Leaning against the countertop, she crossed her arms and thought about what Jo had said. "How are you?" she asked, choosing to avoid responding to Nan's half-phrased question.

Nan toyed with a section of the paper, flicking the corners. She had never mastered the art of the non-discussion, preferring to tackle things more directly. "That's what you get for marrying a psychologist," she would always point out.

"I'm not so good," Nan replied honestly.

There was a long and very strained silence, thankfully broken by the whistle of the kettle. Leisa busied herself making two fresh cups of tea, making Nan's the way she liked it, with a spoonful of honey.

Leisa sat back down at the table, staring into the smoky amber depths of her tea. "You were saying?"

"I've left you alone this week only because I didn't know what to say. I have no defense for what I did. I hope you didn't think I was playing some kind of waiting game with you."

"You've never played games," Leisa said softly.

Nan looked helplessly at Leisa who wouldn't meet her eyes. "It was so hard not to call or come over, to try and talk this out, but... There's no excuse, no good excuse, for not telling you about the baby, except that the longer I waited, the harder it became because I hadn't told you earlier, until it just felt like it was, I don't know, like some kind of cancer that was best left sealed away. Most of the time I could forget it. Until these last few months."

She gently swirled her tea in her cup. "It was almost a relief to realize that this would force me to tell you, except I was so afraid of having betrayed your trust..."

She sat with her teacup clenched in her two hands, waiting for Leisa to say something. But there was only silence. She closed her eyes, and whispered, "Can you forgive me?"

"It's not about forgiving you," Leisa burst out. She sat back, releasing an exasperated breath. "Everybody sees us as this perfect couple, but you haven't touched me or held me or kissed me - really kissed me - for months. We don't talk anymore. We sit in the same room and have nothing to say to one another. I've tried so hard and you just ignored everything I did. There are so many things I wanted to -"

She stopped and looked at Nan who had tears leaking from her still-closed eyes. Bewildered, Leisa felt herself grow colder at the sight of those tears rather than melting as she normally would have done.

"It's not about forgiving you," she repeated. "It's about trusting you. It's about feeling like I know who you are. Because right now, I don't."

Nan's eyes opened and more tears spilled over. "Do you still love me?" she asked in a strangled voice.

Leisa blinked and looked away, confused. "That's not a fair question right now."

"Yes, it is," Nan insisted, swiping her eyes with her towel and leaning forward. "Do you love me?"

"I don't know," Leisa murmured, her eyes still averted.

———

An hour later, Maddie held a sobbing Nan. During a brief period of calm, Nan reminded Maddie of the night she met Leisa. "I told you I was afraid I'd find a way to mess things up."

Maddie sighed. "Yes, well... I have to admit, ten years into the relationship, I thought we were past that little hurdle."

Chapter 10

MADDIE PEEKED INTO LYN'S art studio. "Hi."

"Hi!" Lyn beamed, setting her palette and brush down so she could give Maddie a kiss, her arms wrapped tightly around her.

Maddie nuzzled into Lyn's neck and sighed.

"What's wrong?" Lyn asked.

Maddie pulled back so she could see Lyn's face. "I hate to interrupt you when you're working."

"I'm not working on anything brilliant," Lyn laughed, taking Maddie by the hand and leading her to the studio's daybed where Puddles was curled up sleeping.

"I'm worried about Leisa," Maddie began as she gently shifted the cat over so they could sit back against the multiple pillows piled against the wall.

"Why?"

"I'm not trying to pry, but in your talks with Leisa over the past couple of weeks, has she said whether there's anything bothering her other than the situation with Nan?"

Lyn shook her head. "No. But I've had the same feeling that there's more going on. When I asked her, she just said she felt like

79

she couldn't trust anything right now – whatever that means. Why, what have you noticed?"

Maddie sighed again. "She's surly with everyone. She has pissed off more people in the past two weeks than I do in a year. If I only knew her from work, I'd have to pull her in for a talk about her attitude. It's so unlike her." Maddie thought for a moment. "Do you have any idea what she meant when she said she can't trust anything?"

Lyn shifted on the daybed so she could face Maddie with her legs crossed, a position interpreted by Puddles as an invitation to climb into her lap. "Not for certain, but the last time I was at her mom's house, she had boxes out and was packing things away," Lyn said as she automatically began stroking the silky coat of the cat who was now purring loudly. "She said she wanted to de-clutter the house, but the only things I saw in the boxes were photos. Every single one. Even the one of her and Nan."

"I wondered if it might be something like this," Maddie said thoughtfully.

"Like what?"

"I think maybe Leisa is feeling like everyone she was closest to has left her. It's almost as if she's trying to push the rest of us away, and, I have to admit, she's doing a really good job of it. The only one she hasn't distanced herself from is Mariela. I think she feels as alone as that little girl right now."

Lyn thought about this for a moment. "You know, the ironic thing is that if she were any of our other friends, we'd ask Nan to talk to her."

Maddie nodded. "You're right." A few seconds passed, then she exclaimed, "Oh, shit!"

"Madeline Oxendine," Lyn scolded. "You know better than to use language like that. Your mama would tan your hide."

Maddie stared at her, wide-eyed. "Today is Leisa's birthday."

"Oh, shit," said Lyn.

Leisa groaned a little as she eased herself onto the couch in the family room and propped her legs up on the ottoman. She patted the sofa, and Bronwyn hopped up and curled up next to her.

"I don't know why in the world I thought a gym membership was a good thirty-fifth birthday present," she said to Bron as she leaned over for the wine glass sitting on the end table. She sat in the dark, the family room lit only by the strobing blue glow of the television as she flipped disinterestedly through the channels. "I've had way too much to drink tonight," she muttered as she took another sip.

The telephone rang. She let the machine pick up, listening to Rose's recorded voice. Then she heard Nan's voice saying, "Leisa? Are you there?" After a few seconds with no response, she heard a click, and continued flipping through channels.

About five minutes later, the phone rang again. This time Nan said, "I know you're there. Jo said you left their house over half an hour ago." She paused. "Please pick up."

Reluctantly, Leisa picked up the handset from the end table. "I'm here," she said.

"Hi."

When Leisa remained silent, Nan said, "I wanted to be sure you got the package I left."

Leisa glanced at the otherwise bare mantelpiece where a framed watercolor of a beach scene leaned against the wall. "Lyn painted it from that photo you took last summer at Corolla," Nan said.

For a long time, there was only the sound of their breathing.

"Are you all right?" Nan asked at last.

"It's..." The wine was muddling Leisa's thoughts. "It's just a very odd feeling, knowing that there's no one left who has any memories, any connection to your beginnings."

"You've still got Jo Ann and Bruce," Nan reminded her gently.

"I know, but we didn't move back to Baltimore until I was three. It's just not the same. I can't ask them why -" She stopped and was silent again.

"Why what?" Nan probed.

"Nothing."

"Can I come over?"

"I don't think that's a good idea," Leisa replied. Her words were a little slurred.

"How much have you had to drink?"

"That's why it's not a good idea." Leisa pressed her wine glass to her forehead. "Sometimes," she whispered, "sometimes I wonder if she remembers this day..."

———

Nan's last client of the day, Ellen Cavendish, wrapped up her final thoughts as her session drew to a close. Ellen was also a psychologist, doing group therapy at the regional women's correctional facility. She came to Nan regularly "or they'll drive me crazy," she joked. Despite her jokes, the psychological and emotional issues the imprisoned women were dealing with - abuse, rape, addiction - were enough to throw anyone into a depression if they took it all in.

"Nan," Ellen said after confirming her appointment for the following week, "please understand that I'm speaking as a friend and colleague. I don't know what's going on with you the last couple of weeks, but I can tell something's not right. I don't know if you see anyone, but if not, you may want to." She picked up her purse and gave Nan's shoulder a squeeze on her way to the door.

Nan gathered up her laptop and a few files, plus the day's mail. She drove home, or rather, to her house. "It doesn't feel much like a home anymore," she'd admitted to Maddie. When she opened the front door, the interior of the house was dark despite the bright spring sunshine outside and she realized she'd neglected to open the blinds again. She forced herself to open all the blinds and saw the pillow and blanket on the couch where she'd slept last night - *and how many other nights?* There, spread across the coffee table were the photo albums. In a masochistic fit of nostalgia, she'd spent the previous evening crying her way through their old photo albums - remembering earlier days when things were good and they were happy. Sighing, she went into the kitchen to find something to eat.

Sitting at the table a few minutes later while the microwave zapped a frozen meal, she sorted through her office mail. Mixed in with the bills and insurance payments was a large manila envelope with Bill Chisholm's return address. The microwave beeped and she transferred the steaming plastic bowl to the table where she pried the flap of Chisholm's envelope loose and tipped out the contents. Staring up at her from an 8 x 10 school photo was a dark-haired teenage boy who looked just like her. Todd had written a letter also, explaining that the photo was last year's when he was a sophomore because he didn't have any hair now.

She wasn't sure how long she sat there staring at the photo. Her untouched chicken fajita had grown cold when she reached for the phone. "Hey, can I come over?"

"Oh, my gosh," said Maddie and Lyn in unison a few minutes later when she showed them the photo and letter.

"I know," Nan said miserably. "It's not that I thought Chisholm was lying before, or that I thought he had the wrong person, but it didn't feel real. Not like this."

"That's why he did it," Maddie observed wryly. "You'd have to be dead not to have a visceral reaction to this." She set an extra place at the table as Lyn put large bowls of rice and stir-fried vegetables on the table.

"Has this changed your mind about meeting him?" Lyn asked.

"Probably," Nan admitted. "I don't know how I could say no after that."

"Will you have them come up here?" Maddie asked as she poured water into three glasses.

"No," Nan answered emphatically. "No. I want neutral territory. They live in Savannah, so I was thinking of suggesting Raleigh."

Maddie looked up in surprise. "Does he know that that's where he was born?"

Despite the fact that Maddie and Nan had "practiced" being ready for months, Maddie was groggy as she groped for the phone ringing in the dark. "Hey." She squinted at her bedside clock and saw that it said three-ten.

"I'm not sure what labor feels like, but I think I'm in it," came Nan's voice.

"Has your water broken yet?" Maddie asked, wide awake now.

"I don't know."

"What do you mean you don't know?"

"I mean I don't know," Nan said crossly. "I've never done this before. I think I might have peed myself. How am I supposed to know?"

"I've never done this before, either. This is supposed to be one of the benefits of being a lesbian, remember? But from everything the books say, I think you'll know when your water breaks," Maddie pointed out reasonably.

"Then it hasn't."

"It better not happen in my car," grumbled Maddie. "I'll be right there."

Maddie stayed with Nan through thirty hours of labor, thirty hours during which Nan's most enduring memory – "besides the endless pain," she would have added – was Maddie's Afro, lit from behind by the ceiling lights. "It looked like a halo," Nan remembered always.

Nan refused an epidural until it was too late.

"Why didn't you talk me out of it?" Nan demanded as she gasped in pain, squeezing Maddie's hand until Maddie winced in pain, too.

"You never listen," Maddie answered through clenched teeth.

When the baby finally came, Maddie went to where he was being wiped down and wrapped in a blanket. Awestruck, she held him, her eyes shining with tears. Nan shook her head when the nurse asked if she wanted to hold him. The staff had been made aware of Nan's situation. Maddie held the baby a few minutes longer, then handed him back to the nurse. She went to Nan and held her tightly while she sobbed.

———

"Does he know that that's where he was born?"

"At nine fifty-two on August thirty-first," Nan murmured as she absentmindedly poked a water chestnut with her fork. "I don't know." Her expression suddenly shifted as she remembered her conversation with Leisa and understanding dawned. "That's what she meant."

Chapter 11

"DO YOU REALLY THINK that was a coincidence? If you could re-live that moment, and do things differently, how do you think things would change?"

Those used to be some of Leisa's favorite topics of conjecture. "Just imagine the possibilities of all the alternate realities for every choice we could make. It's mind-boggling," she would say.

"Yes, it is," Nan would usually agree. "My mind is completely boggled by the stupid choices people make. Whether they realize it or not, they create most of their 'coincidences' by where they choose to be or who they choose to hang out with, and then blame the universe for the fallout. They never see their own choices as the source of their misery."

"You're such a skeptic," Leisa would laugh. "I absolutely believe that chance encounters really do happen, and that they change people's lives."

"Which kind was this?" she wondered a few days after joining her gym.

She had finished running on a treadmill and was going through the weight circuit when she heard, "Leisa? Is that really you?"

Leisa turned around to see Sarah standing there. Sarah "I'm getting married, but I still want you" Atherton. Or whatever the hell her name was now.

"Hi," Leisa said lamely. "Do you belong here?"

"No," Sarah laughed. "I work here. I'm one of the personal trainers." Leisa self-consciously pulled her stomach in a little as Sarah looked her up and down.

"You look great," Sarah said admiringly.

"Thanks," Leisa mumbled, cussing herself as she felt the blood rush to her cheeks.

Sarah glanced over to her client who was done with one machine and waiting by the next.

"Gotta go," she said, flashing a big smile. "We should catch up."

"Yeah. We should do that."

"Yeah, we should do that?" Leisa berated herself as she turned to her next machine.

"What were you thinking?" She started yanking on the handles. *"You should have told her to go f – Don't!"* She stopped herself. *"Don't do this. She's just someone you haven't seen in a long time."*

The next machine positioned her so she could see Sarah reflected in the mirror. Damn, she looked good. She was lean and muscular and didn't mind showing it off. She looked up suddenly and caught Leisa looking. She flashed that smile again. For the remainder of her workout, Leisa tried not to look in Sarah's direction and she managed to get out of there with no further conversation.

When Leisa got home from the gym that night, all thoughts of Sarah were driven from her mind by an envelope from the New York State Health Department. Inside was a letter of consent authorizing them to give out her identifying information. That could only mean that someone biologically connected to her had registered also.

"If you sign this, there is no turning back." In her head, Leisa could clearly hear Nan's voice warning her. It would have been so comforting to be able to talk to Nan about this. Leisa actually picked up the telephone, her finger poised to punch the numbers, but she put it back down.

"So, what went wrong with your relationships?" Leisa had asked Nan when they were in the early stages of getting to know one another.

Nan settled back into the corner of the sofa, tucking her legs under her.

"I guess I was always flattered if someone really attractive was interested in me, and I kept thinking if they were willing to settle for someone like me they must be ready to get serious –"

"Wait a minute," Leisa interrupted. "What do you mean, 'settle for someone like me'?"

Nan stared hard at her knees. "You know what I mean. Beautiful women aren't attracted to intellectual geeks like me."

"Okay," said Leisa, holding up both hands to make Nan stop. "First, I'm not even going to comment on how you just insulted me."

"What? No, I didn't –"

"Second," Leisa interrupted again, "we need to have a serious talk about your self-esteem issues." She cocked her head. "Why don't you see yourself as beautiful?"

Nan picked at an imaginary piece of something on her pants. "Believe me, in my family, I'm not. And I was reminded of it frequently."

"I've seen photos of your family. You look just like them." Leisa paused. "Sometimes I wonder what that would be like," she mused.

"What?"

"To look like other people. To look like you're part of a family."

Leisa focused on Nan again, reaching out to take Nan's hand in hers. "You are beautiful," she insisted gently. "And intelligent." She scooted closer. "And funny in a sarcastic kind of way." Closer still. "And did I mention that you're beautiful?"

She pulled Nan to her for a kiss. She savored the softness of Nan's mouth as she responded to the pressure of Leisa's lips. After a long while, Leisa pulled away and said, "I want you to know I am not settling for you. I deserve better than what I've had and so do you."

"I can't," she said now to Bron. "I can't just call her when I need something." Bron answered by rolling on her back for a tummy rub. Just then the telephone rang.

"Hi." It was Nan.

"You must be a mind reader. I was just thinking about calling you."

"You were?" Nan asked cautiously.

"Don't sound so worried," Leisa said guiltily. "I just wanted to talk to you."

"Really?"

"There are... things we need to talk about."

"Yes," agreed Nan. "I was calling to see if you could come over for dinner tomorrow evening?"

Leisa thought for a couple of seconds. "That sounds nice. What can I bring?"

"Bron?" Nan asked hopefully. "I miss her." She paused awkwardly. "I miss both of you."

Leisa emerged from the toilet stall, wiping her mouth with a wad of tissue. She went to the sink and rinsed her mouth and face. She raised her eyes to her reflection in the mirror. "Who the hell are you?" she whispered to herself. The face staring back seemed to her to be the face of a stranger, one she wasn't sure she wanted to know.

She was startled by Maddie's entrance into the restroom.

"Hi," Leisa said as she quickly began washing her hands.

"Hi," Maddie returned. She went into a stall. "Nan said you went over for dinner a couple of nights ago. How was it?"

"It was... okay."

"Just okay? From what Nan said, it sounded as if you two had a good talk."

"We did." How could she explain that by the time she got back to her mother's house that night, it wasn't Nan she was angry with, it was herself.

Nan's face had lit up with delight when she answered the door. "You don't have to ring the bell, you know," she said as she squatted down to hug Bronwyn. "This is your house, too."

"I know," Leisa said awkwardly, "but..." She looked around at the familiar foyer, trimmed in the original oak that she and Nan had painstakingly refinished.

When Bron calmed down enough to let Nan up, Leisa extended a hand to pull her to her feet.

"Thanks," Nan smiled, holding onto Leisa's hand a few extra seconds.

"Dinner smells wonderful," Leisa said, noticing as she passed the dining room that Nan had set the table with a tablecloth and candles. "I brought a bottle of the merlot you liked at the wine tasting we went to last Christmas."

"How about pouring then? I think everything is about ready," Nan said.

Leisa retrieved the corkscrew from the drawer where it always was. This was so weird. Her furniture, her dishes, her house... but not. Leisa poured two glasses of wine while Nan put a bowl of chicken and rice on the floor for Bronwyn and then dished out huge servings of pot roast with potatoes and carrots. There was a basket of warm, fresh rolls already on the table.

"This is delicious," Leisa commented as she took her first bite.

"You always were easy to impress," Nan smiled. "Remember the first meal I made for you?"

Leisa grinned. "Grilled cheese sandwiches and tomato soup," she recalled.

"That's what you said you wanted."

"I love simple food," Leisa shrugged.

They ate for a few minutes in silence.

"How are you doing?" Nan asked. "You didn't seem like you were in a really good place on your birthday."

"Oh, that." Leisa said sheepishly. "Yeah, well, I guess I was just having a night of feeling sorry for myself. Fueled by this," she added, swirling her wine.

"It sounded like a little more than that," Nan probed gently. "I didn't realize what you meant at the time, but it sounded like you were wondering if your birth mother ever thinks about the day you were born?"

Leisa's cheeks burned with her embarrassment at the memory of that pathetic whimper.

Nan knew her well enough to read her thoughts. "There's nothing wrong with wondering about that connection." She hesitated before adding, "I don't know about anyone else, but I always remember that day, the exact time..."

Leisa looked at her, searching Nan's face – a face that was as familiar as ever, but different as she opened up about this topic for the first time. "Was it hard?"

Nan's eyes were hard, flinty. "It was the hardest thing I've ever done in my life." For several seconds, Nan held Leisa's gaze, then she asked, "Would you like to see what he looks like?"

Leisa blinked. "Yes, I would."

Nan got up and returned a moment later with Todd's photo and letter. Leisa stared transfixed at his image. She was reminded again that for them, life was now defined as "before Williamsburg" and "after Williamsburg" and nothing would ever be the same. "It was the start of the monsoon," Nan was to say much later when they looked back and realized that that overheard conversation, that unintended revelation had become the thing that knocked their shaky relationship off its crumbling foundation.

"You know," Leisa said wistfully, "over these past few weeks, I've wondered what life would have been like, what our life together would have been like if you'd raised him. Our son."

"I've wondered that, too," Nan admitted. "Paths not taken."

"Are you going to meet him?"

Nan brushed back the loose strands of hair hanging along her cheek. "I wasn't going to when Chisholm first contacted me, but now..." she glanced at Todd's letter. "I'm not sure when, with his treatment schedule, and he wants to stay caught up in school as much as he can. He and his parents will drive up from Georgia and we'll meet in Raleigh."

She looked over at Leisa. "What about you? It sounds as if you've been thinking a lot about your birth mother. Have you considered trying to find her?"

Leisa took another bite of roast before replying, "I think I may have already found her."

"Really?" Nan asked, sitting back in surprise.

"In New York, if both parties register and indicate they want to exchange information, the state will do it. I registered a couple of weeks ago and I think someone else has registered also."

"Wow." Nan was at a loss for words. "I'm just surprised, since you never seemed like you had any desire to find her before. What did Jo Ann and Bruce say?"

Leisa took a long time chewing and swallowing before replying, "I haven't told them." Nan stopped as she reached for her wine glass. "I'm not sure how they would feel about it," Leisa said, staring at her plate. "Especially Jo. I don't want her to feel like I'm trying to replace Mom."

Nan sat back and looked at her fork as she twirled it in her fingers. "So," she began in a cautious tone, "you've avoided telling your aunt and uncle about this because you're not sure what their reaction might be and you don't want to hurt them."

Leisa froze as she caught the full weight of Nan's implication.

"I'm going to get dessert," Nan said as she rose from the table.

Leisa followed a couple of minutes later, bringing dinner dishes in and rinsing them for the dishwasher.

"What triggered this sudden desire to search for her?" Nan asked, her back to Leisa as she set out coffee cups and began cutting a large carrot cake.

"I guess it was the note mostly."

Nan turned to her. "What note?"

"I forgot. That was one of the things we never got to talk about." She accepted a cup of coffee and a plate from Nan, and returned to the dining room. "In Mom's papers I found my adoption folder. There was a handwritten note from my biological mother. Apparently, when I was born, she changed her mind about giving me up and kept me for six weeks before deciding to go ahead with the adoption."

Nan stared at her. "Your parents never told you any of this?"

Leisa shrugged. "Jo said that was part of what they wanted to explain when I started asking questions, and I never did."

Nan watched Leisa's face intently. "So, you lose your mother, and find out that she kept a secret from you your whole life, then find out that I've kept a secret from you, too." She leaned her elbows on the table. "That's a lot to deal with."

"Don't!" Leisa said angrily. "Don't treat me like one of your clients."

Patiently, Nan said, "I'm not treating you like one of my clients. I'm treating you like someone I love, someone I know I've hurt; only now I'm finding out that I'm not the only one who hurt you."

Leisa pushed away from the table and called Bron. Nan hurried after her. At the door, she caught Leisa by the arm, and said, "Whatever you're going through, I'm here for you. I love you, and I am not giving up on us."

Unable to say anything in reply, Leisa broke loose from Nan's grasp and bent to snap the leash to Bronwyn's collar. She hurried down the steps with Bronwyn, fighting the urge to run, wishing she could run from the person she'd become. A person guilty of exactly the same kind of lie of omission Nan had committed, by not telling Jo Ann and Bruce about the adoption registration. *And guilty of not telling Nan about Sarah tonight*, she reminded herself. No matter how hard she tried to convince herself that she hadn't said anything because it was meaningless, part of her knew better. Realizing she was capable of lying about this, she wondered what else she was capable of.

———◆———

"Well, that explains a lot," Maddie said later that night when Nan had told her and Lyn about the evening. "No wonder she's been so angry, pushing everyone away."

"Keep a close eye on her," Nan pleaded. "She's standing on quicksand right now, and I don't think she knows it. It's going to pull her in at some point."

94

"Maybe that will be a good thing," Lyn said. "It might force her to realize she needs to reach out to you."

"I just hope it's me she reaches for."

Chapter 12

LEISA'S TELEPHONE BUZZED. LOOKING at the blinking light, she could see it was Sadie from the front office.

"Yes?"

"Maddie needs to see you as soon as you can get up here," Sadie announced.

"What's up?"

"You'll see." Sadie loved knowing things others didn't yet.

When Leisa got upstairs, Sadie said, "Maddie wants you to sit and wait until he leaves."

"Until who leaves?" Leisa asked, her curiosity piqued now.

Sadie raised her penciled eyebrows. "You'll see," she repeated mysteriously.

Puzzled, Leisa took a seat in one of the chairs along the wall. Within a few minutes, Maddie's door opened and she escorted a man out. He was small in stature, dark-complected. Maddie towered over him.

"When can I take her?" he was asking.

"I'm not exactly certain, Mr. Gonzalez," Maddie responded. "I'm sure you understand that there are several legal steps we need to follow before Mariela can be released to your custody." Leisa nearly fell off her chair as she heard Maddie add, "I'm sure Mariela will be very happy to learn she has an uncle."

Leisa tried to observe him surreptitiously as he left. Maddie went to the window behind Sadie's desk to watch him descend the front steps. After a few seconds, she turned to Leisa and said, "Come on into the office."

Maddie shut the door behind them. Leisa imagined Sadie's chagrin at not being able to eavesdrop.

"Mariela's uncle?" Leisa asked incredulously.

"So he claims," Maddie said, picking up her pad of notes from her conversation with him.

Leisa was relieved to hear the skeptical tone of Maddie's voice. She leaned forward and started to move a water glass sitting on Maddie's desk.

"Don't touch that!"

Maddie leaned forward, and used a tissue to carefully pick the glass up and move it to the bookshelf behind her desk.

"What are you doing?" Leisa asked in confusion.

"I thought it would be a good idea to ask the police to run his prints," Maddie explained.

"What is going on?"

"I don't trust this guy. He shows up out of nowhere, claiming to be Florida Gonzalez' brother. He supposedly just returned from Mexico to find his sister dead and his niece here with us."

Leisa leaned her elbows on the desk. "Mariela has never mentioned any other family."

"I know," Maddie nodded. "And Florida's police record didn't indicate any family in the States."

"Who do you think he is then?" Leisa asked.

Maddie shrugged. "Pimp? Dealer? Those are my guesses. What I do know is that he's not asking for Mariela because he has paternal feelings for her. He wants something from her. I just don't know what it could be."

Leisa looked alarmed. "Surely, no one would order her handed over to him?"

Maddie's eyes glinted angrily. "Not if I can help it."

———◆———

"It happens to all of us, if we're there long enough," Maddie had said to Lyn when she first saw the connection between Leisa and Mariela. "We fall in love," she said wistfully, and Lyn knew Maddie was thinking of Tobias.

Tobias Baker was the youngest child of Mathias and Loretta Baker, of whom the caseworker from Social Services had said, "I swear those two were related before they got married and bred." Tobias was different from all the other Bakers. Where his elder siblings had all been dim-witted and had missed more school than they attended, Tobias was intelligent, and lived for a kind word or a hug. Despite his smelly clothes and unkempt straw-colored hair, when Tobias's grubby face broke into a smile, he could charm anyone.

He was pulled out of the home briefly a few times, but was always returned to his parents who angrily insisted they would school him at home, "the Lord's way." Always, he managed to talk his mother into letting him return to school where, despite his obvious disadvantages at home, he quickly made up ground from his lapses in getting any real education. He finally came to Maddie and St. Joseph's when it was discovered that he had suffered a broken arm, most likely at the hands of his father, although it could never be proven. Toby's elbow was permanently crooked because the fracture had never been properly set. The bond between Tobias and Maddie was instant and deep. It was Maddie's first year as director, and "I'm trying so hard not to show any favoritism," she told Lyn, "but I love that little boy."

Tobias had been at St. Joseph's for about three months when he was once again ordered to be returned to his parents' custody despite overwhelming evidence from social workers, teachers and neighbors that the Bakers were abusive and that Tobias would be in grave danger.

"I promise to be good," he cried as he clung to Maddie.

"Oh, honey, you're not being punished. You didn't do anything wrong," Maddie murmured as she knelt and held him tightly, choking

99

on her own tears. "The judge said you should be back with your mom and dad. But I'll come see you soon, okay?" The social worker had to pull him loose. "I promise," Maddie said through the car window as he was driven away.

But the very night Tobias got home, his mother locked the two of them in his room and poured gasoline around the bed. Mr. Baker told authorities later that Loretta had only said that no one would ever take Tobias from her again. All anyone could do was watch as the house burnt to the ground.

Maddie channeled her grief into a campaign to have that judge removed from the bench. She personally went door to door with a petition; she got churches and civic organizations involved with more petitions and protests in front of the courthouse; she got Baltimore news stations to air Tobias's story.

"He has no idea what he has unleashed," Lyn said.

In the end, the judge was promoted to a federal appeals court. "I don't care," Maddie swore, "as long as the bastard can never hurt another child."

"Not if I can help it," Maddie repeated, more to herself than to Leisa.

"Good," Leisa sighed in relief. It had already crossed her mind in a wild, fleeting thought that she would take Mariela and flee before she would let that man have her.

As if she could read Leisa's mind, Maddie narrowed her eyes and said, "I promise. I won't let anything happen to her. Oh, and we got the burial service for Mariela's mother scheduled for the Saturday before Easter."

"Oh no," Leisa groaned as she sifted through the mail, and held up a hand-addressed envelope from an Eleanor Miller in Ithaca, New York. "Not today."

She deposited the mail on the kitchen counter and let Bron out the back door where the little dog promptly chased all the birds out of her yard. Leisa went back to the kitchen and picked up the envelope. She was supposed to have dinner with Jo and Bruce tonight, and was planning on telling them about the adoption registry. After her dinner with Nan, she realized she couldn't keep this from them any longer, but it suddenly seemed more complicated if this letter turned out to be from her biological mother. Her heart was beating rapidly as she pried open the flap. Taking a deep breath, she removed the contents. A photo fell from the folded paper within. She picked it up and stared at it for a moment before reading,

Dear Margaret Marie,

I know that's not your name now, but it's what you've always been to me. I was so excited to receive your address and other information. You probably have many questions to ask me. I can't help but wonder what you look like now and what you've become. You might be interested to know that you have a half-brother named Donald. He is 28. I am divorced now. I work as an administrative assistant to a dean at our university here.

I am enclosing a photo of Donny and me. Please send me a reply and a photo of yourself when you can.

Leisa picked up the photo again. Eleanor was a moderately attractive woman who looked as if she was in her late fifties, plump with blondish hair and gray-green eyes behind large eyeglasses. Donny was pudgy, dark-haired and pale. Leisa didn't feel any connection to him at all, but she stared at Eleanor's image, for the first time in her life seeing someone she looked like.

She suddenly felt nauseous and rushed to the bathroom where she threw up. This was the third time she'd vomited in the last few days.

"I must be coming down with something," she muttered as she rinsed her face and mouth with cold water.

She ate a few saltines, trying to settle her stomach before facing her aunt and uncle. Jo Ann and Bruce had always been there for her, a second set of parents. She'd always been able to talk to them, even when she couldn't talk to her own parents.

———◆———

"You've got to be honest with your father," Bruce had advised her at age seventeen when she confided that she wanted to quit the job her dad had obtained for her with one of his long-time customers. It was a sales job and she hated it.

"But Dad helped me get this job," she fretted. "I don't want to make him look bad."

"As long as you handle it professionally, it will be okay," Bruce said as he planed a board for a table he was making. "You give Mr. Thompson at least two weeks' notice so he has time to look for someone else, and you do your best work until you're done." He grinned at her. "There's nothing that can't be dealt with if you're honest about it."

———◆———

Sitting at the kitchen table now, she cradled her forehead on her arms, trying to calm her stomach. When it was time to leave, she called Bronwyn and leashed her for the walk to the Gallagher house. All the trees were leafing out, casting deeper shadows in between the lit patches of pavement under the streetlamps. At the end of their block, Leisa turned left toward her aunt and uncle's house, but there was sudden tension on the leash as Bron tried to go the other way, toward Nan.

"No, we're not going there tonight," she said as Bron looked at her from the far end of the taut leash. "C'mon," she cajoled with a firmer tug on the leather. Bron sat down, a tactic she had learned as a puppy when she was ready for a rest or wanted to sniff something a bit longer. For a small dog, she was amazingly strong, with a low center of gravity that made her hard to move. She was also amazingly stubborn.

"It's a good thing she's adorable," Nan used to laugh when Leisa would get red in the face trying to train Bronwyn who was quietly training them. Or not so quietly. Like when they thought hanging a sleigh bell on the back door would be a good way for her to let them know when she needed to go out. Soon, she was ringing the bell every fifteen minutes.

"Well, we learned very quickly how to respond to that stimulus, didn't we?" Nan observed ruefully as she untied the bell.

Now, Leisa stared at Bron who stared back, still not moving.

"We don't have time for this, you stubborn beast," Leisa grumbled as she picked Bron up and carried her in the direction they needed to go. After about fifty yards, she set the dog down. "Now let's go."

Bronwyn gave up and trotted toward Jo Ann and Bruce's house like this was her plan all along. When they got to the house, Leisa knocked and opened the door.

"In the kitchen," Jo called.

Bron trotted in to say hello, and Leisa followed.

"Oh, it seems like ages since we've seen you," Jo Ann said as she hugged Leisa tightly. She held her at arms' length and searched her face. "Are you feeling all right? You look pale."

"To tell you the truth, I'm not feeling very good," Leisa admitted. "So don't be offended if I don't eat much."

At the table, she took tiny helpings and, bracing herself, began telling her aunt and uncle about registering to find her biological mother. She tried to gauge their reaction as she talked.

"Did they say how long it might be before you hear back?" Jo asked.

"Well," Leisa said, "I've already heard back."

"You've heard from her already?" Bruce asked in surprise.

Leisa nodded. "I guess she was already registered, and all they needed was for me to register also."

Jo Ann tried not to look worried. "It sounds like she really wanted to find you."

Leisa looked from one of them to the other. "You're okay with this?"

"Of course we are," Bruce assured her, laying a large hand on her shoulder as she slumped with relief.

"Were you afraid to tell us about this?" Jo asked.

"Kind of," Leisa admitted. "I just didn't want to hurt you."

"We've been prepared for this for thirty-five years, honey," Jo Ann reminded her. "The only thing that would hurt us is losing you."

Leisa smiled in relief. "That will never happen."

Chapter 13

LEISA GROANED AS SHE used the armrests on her desk chair to gently lower herself to the seat. Her legs were so sore from yesterday's workout that she could barely walk. It had been her first time back at the gym since her dinner with Nan. Partly because she'd been busy. Partly because she felt guilty about not telling Nan about Sarah. When she got there, she glanced around to see if Sarah was in the weight room with a client. She breathed a sigh of relief when she didn't see her.

"Hey."

Leisa stiffened and turned to see Sarah coming out from behind the staff desk.

"Hi." Leisa forced a smile.

"I was starting to think you weren't going to come back," Sarah said teasingly. Leisa wasn't sure if she was only imagining the taunt in Sarah's eyes.

"I've been busy at work."

"What are you doing these days?" Sarah asked as she handed Leisa a towel and herded her toward the weight room.

"I'm a social worker at a home for orphaned and abandoned kids."

"Really?" Sarah paused in the midst of pulling on a pair of weightlifting gloves. Leisa tried not to let her eyes drift down to the muscles she could see rippling in Sarah's arms.

Leisa felt a grim satisfaction at the fact that she was doing something more worthwhile to society than working in a gym, until she remembered that Sarah was probably making a lot more money than she was. She realized Sarah was leading her toward a squat rack.

"Don't you have a client?" she asked hopefully.

"No," Sarah smiled. "I'm done for the evening and I was going to work out anyway, so how about working out with me?"

Unable to quickly think of a reason why not, Leisa allowed Sarah to take her through a lower body routine that soon had her legs trembling.

"I love this workout," Sarah growled as she finished her last couple of repetitions on the knee extension machine. "This is better than sex!"

Leisa scoffed as she dropped onto an empty bench. "You definitely need better sex," she retorted before she realized what she was saying. She could feel the flush creeping up her neck to her cheeks.

Sarah got off the machine and leaned close. "You're right," she whispered conspiratorially. "But I remember when it used to be incredible."

Leisa leaned down to re-tie her shoe, waiting for Sarah to move away. "I don't think my legs will take any more tonight," she said to the floor.

"How about going to grab something to eat?" Sarah suggested.

"I don't think –" Leisa protested.

"Oh, come on. You should eat right away after that workout, and I'd like to catch up with you," Sarah insisted. "You're not afraid to have dinner with me, are you?"

A few minutes later, Leisa found herself seated across from Sarah in a dark corner of a tavern near the gym. Sarah talked freely about her marriage and divorce, seemingly oblivious to the fact that the marriage had coincided with her painful breakup with Leisa. Or maybe not so painful for her, Leisa realized.

"And what about you? What about this?" Sarah asked, reaching out to take Leisa's left hand, twirling the ring there, her eyes scanning Leisa's face curiously.

"Me?" Leisa stalled, uncomfortably aware of the other people sitting nearby. She sat back and pulled her hand from Sarah's. She swirled her ice water in the glass so that the ice clinked rhythmically, filling the brief silence as she tried to figure out how to answer. "I'm with someone. Ten years," she added, forcing herself to smile and look up.

"A woman?"

"Of course," Leisa answered sharply. Suddenly furious, she bit off the scathing reply that leapt to her lips.

"For years, you've fantasized about having the opportunity to tell her what a hypocrite she was for loving women, and only marrying for social approval," Leisa would say to herself later, "and when you had the chance, you couldn't do it. You are such a goddamned coward."

Leisa felt confused, off-balance. She didn't understand where all these volatile emotions were coming from. All the garbage with Sarah was years in the past. Why did it suddenly feel so raw?

"But... she's not working out with you?" Sarah pressed, leaning forward with her elbows resting on the table. Leisa tried not to stare at the cleavage showing above her sports bra.

"She works evenings." Leisa glanced at her watch. "I really need to get going."

Sarah accompanied Leisa to her car in the dimly lit parking lot. Leisa unlocked her door and turned to find Sarah standing very close.

"Does she ever tell you how beautiful you are?" Sarah asked softly. When Leisa didn't answer, Sarah brushed her fingers over Leisa's bare arm. She smiled a little as Leisa shivered, but didn't pull away.

Leisa felt hypnotized, powerless as she looked into Sarah's eyes, like a bird hypnotized by a snake. Sarah drew closer and kissed her.

———◆———

Sitting at her desk, Leisa closed her eyes, remembering the wetness, the softness of that kiss, the slightly salty taste of Sarah's mouth, the heat of her body as she pressed Leisa against the car, the way her body had responded to the touch of Sarah's hands....

"Stop!" she whispered angrily to herself. She grabbed her open file drawer and slammed it shut.

"Whoa," Maddie said from behind her, making Leisa jump. "What was that about?"

Leisa's face burned. "Nothing," she muttered, turning back to her desk.

"Okay," Maddie said, clearly unconvinced. She held out a series of police mug shots. "Meet Pedro Alarcon."

Leisa stared at the images of the man who had been in Maddie's office a few days ago. "He really does have a record?"

"Yup. Drugs mostly. He's been investigated for more than one murder, all women, probably the ones he was pimping, but the police could never find any others who would testify. Too scared. So he got off."

Leisa looked up. "You don't think he killed Mariela's mother, do you?"

Maddie shrugged. "I don't think so. She definitely died of an overdose. But what if the heroin wasn't hers? What if she took some she was supposed to deliver to someone else? I don't know what he wants with Mariela, but whatever it is, it can't be good."

———

Leisa heard a car horn beep. "You stay here," she said to Bronwyn as she backed out the front door, locking it behind her. She ran to Jo Ann and Bruce's car.

"Ready?" Bruce asked as she got into the back seat and buckled up.

Within twenty minutes, they were pulling into the parking lot at St. Joseph's. She led the way into the old school gymnasium where chairs had been set up facing a table draped with a colorful woven cloth.

Maddie had insisted that any child who wished to attend could come to the funeral for Mariela's mother.

"We shelter children from death so that they're afraid of it. Most of these kids have seen the ugly, violent side of death. With this funeral, there won't be a body, nothing to scare them. Linus will make it beautiful."

Father Linus Chappa was a young Franciscan priest who volunteered part-time at the Home.

"He cannot be a priest. He looks like he's sixteen," Leisa had muttered to Maddie the first time she saw him.

"I know." Maddie smiled broadly, watching Linus as he crouched at the foosball table in his jeans and t-shirt with his shaggy blond hair and long sideburns. "But the kids love him."

The love affair was mutual. Linus loved the kids, too. He had described Mariela's heart-breaking situation to his superior, Father Ignatius, who cautioned, "Do not assume this girl is innocent, simply because she is young. She has undoubtedly seen, and possibly experienced, more than you and I combined."

Linus did make the funeral beautiful. He wore colorful, joyful vestments. Mariela had made new decorations for the paint can - spring flowers strung together in a chain draped around the can. Linus talked about family.

"All of us are born to some family, somewhere," he began. "Sometimes we get to stay with them, sometimes we don't. I was one of the ones who didn't get to stay with my family. I was raised by foster parents."

Most of the children looked at one another in surprise and sat up to listen more attentively.

"You knew?" Leisa whispered to Maddie. Maddie smiled.

"I was actually raised by lots of foster parents," Father Linus continued. "I made things tough for them. I was angry. I didn't want them to like me. They weren't my family. But what I didn't understand then, was that we all have the chance to make another family - the family we choose. I thought if I loved new people, became part of a new family, it would mean I didn't love my original family anymore. But it doesn't work that way. God made us so we can love more and more people, and it never takes away from the love we had for the people who came before. It never gets used up."

Linus had all the kids' attention now.

"No matter what kind of family you come from, sometimes people have to go away. Maybe it's their job, like the army. Maybe they went to prison. Maybe they died, like Mariela's mama. When that happens, the thing to do is remember the good things about them, remember the things you loved, and let your other family – your new family – help you through it. And some day, even if we have to wait until we get to heaven, we will see them again. And since tomorrow is Easter, this is a perfect time to remember that God is greater even than death, that this world is not the end for us."

After the service, a small group drove to the cemetery. Mariela rode in the back seat of Bruce's car with Leisa, the paint can held securely on her lap. When they got there, Bruce opened the trunk as Maddie, Lyn and Linus pulled up beside them.

Bruce pulled two large wreaths of flowers out of the trunk.

"What are those for?" Mariela asked.

Bruce squatted down so that he was at eye-level with Mariela. "People often bring flowers for the graves of people they loved, on holidays or birthdays. We thought you might like to have a wreath for your mother's ashes, especially since tomorrow is Easter."

Mariela thought about this. "Why do you have two?"

Bruce glanced up at Leisa. "We thought you might like to lay a wreath on your parents' graves, also."

Startled, Leisa accepted the second wreath. "Thank you."

Maddie and Lyn led the way to a mausoleum in the center of the cemetery. There, a small vault awaited Florida Gonzalez' ashes. Leisa didn't find out until long after that Maddie and Lyn had paid for the vault themselves. A man affiliated with the cemetery was waiting for them. He let Mariela place the paint can in the small opening. Linus sprinkled the can with holy water and said a prayer, and then the man sealed the vault with a bronze door engraved with Florida's name. The wreath was hung on a small hook on the door, so that Florida's name was encircled by flowers.

Mariela beamed and turned to Leisa. "It's your turn."

She shyly took Jo Ann's hand as the group began wending its way through the headstones toward Rose and Daniel's graves. Leisa became aware of movement off to her right. When she glanced over, she saw a man who looked familiar pausing to look at a headstone. Puzzled, she tried to place him. Suddenly, it came to her. Pedro Alarcon. She turned to say something to Maddie as they walked around a massive grave marker for a family named Boone, but what she saw then drove Alarcon from her mind. She stopped so abruptly that Mariela bumped into her.

Nan was just laying a large bouquet of flowers against Rose's side of the shared headstone.

Leisa whirled and glared at Maddie and Jo Ann. Jo held up her free hand and said, "We had nothing to do with this." Maddie nodded in agreement.

Nan spotted them and waited uncertainly as Leisa approached.

"What are you doing here?" Leisa asked in puzzlement.

Nan looked back toward the brightly colored flowers leaning against the polished granite. "Your mom was always so good to me," Nan explained. "She was more a mother to me than my own. I just –"

"You've been here before?" Leisa interrupted, spying a dried, wilted bouquet in Nan's hand.

Nan shrugged. "A few times."

Leisa stood there, bewildered. She herself hadn't been here since the funeral. As the silence stretched awkwardly, Jo Ann said, "Mariela, this is our good friend, Nan."

Nan tore her gaze from Leisa and turned toward Jo, then blinked down at Mariela.

"Hello," Mariela said softly.

"Hello," Nan returned.

Maddie introduced Nan to Linus who shook her hand. They gathered around. Linus sprinkled the grave with holy water and said a blessing over Rose and Daniel's graves. Leisa realized she was still holding the wreath. She stepped forward and laid it propped against the middle of the headstone. When she remained kneeling there, Mariela came nearer and put her small hand on Leisa's shoulder.

"Don't be sad," she said. "Remember what Father Linus said? We'll see them again."

As Leisa patted Mariela's hand and got to her feet, she heard Jo Ann say, "Nan, we're all going back to our house for dinner. Won't you join us?"

"Are you sure this wasn't pre-arranged?" Leisa hissed at Maddie as they walked back to the cars.

"Completely accidental," Maddie swore.

Maybe, but Jo wasn't going to waste the opportunity. She made sure that Nan was seated next to Leisa at dinner, with Mariela on Leisa's other side.

"Mariela?" Jo prompted once everyone was at the table. "Would you like to say grace?"

Mariela looked up at Leisa who smiled and nodded encouragingly. Everyone clasped hands as Mariela prayed, "Dear God, thank you for this good food. Thank you for my mama's beautiful funeral. Thank you for my new family. Amen."

Leisa was so acutely focused on the touch of Nan's hand in hers that she didn't really hear Mariela's words at first. When she glanced around the table, she saw everyone covertly dabbing at their eyes and clearing their throats. Slowly, she relinquished Nan's hand to accept the ham platter being passed her way.

———◆———

"Did I see you talking to Mariela?" Lyn asked Nan later that evening back at their house.

"For a while," Nan admitted. "She seems like a sweet little girl, but who is she? I mean, why all the fuss at the cemetery?"

Maddie explained about Mariela's past, and asked, "Didn't Leisa ever talk to you about her?"

"I think she tried to," Nan recalled as she began to put the pieces together. "But she never got the chance." She saw Maddie and Lyn glance at one another. "What?"

"Um," Maddie began hesitantly, "from some of the things Leisa has said, I think she has thought about possibly trying to adopt Mariela."

Nan stared at both of them for several seconds. "Oh."

"She knows now is not the right time," Maddie hastened to add, "but... I think you should know she's been thinking about it."

"Speaking of which, kind of," Lyn interjected when Nan continued to gaze mutely at them, "have you written to Todd?"

"We weren't speaking of that," Nan said testily.

"Yes, well, that's kind of the point. We never really do speak of that, do we?" Lyn pointed out with gentle sarcasm.

Chapter 14

LEISA WOKE IN A sweat. Lying in the dark, she continued to feel the throbbing between her legs. That dream had felt so real. What had begun as Nan making love to her had morphed into Sarah humping her madly while Nan looked on with unspeakable hurt in her eyes. Leisa threw her arms over her face, expelling a frustrated breath. When it became clear that she was not going to be able to go back to sleep, she kicked the covers off angrily and stomped into the bathroom. Bronwyn opened one eye just enough to give her a reproachful look. The clock said four-thirty. The gym opened at five.

After hurriedly washing her face and brushing her teeth, she pulled on workout clothes and a baseball cap.

"Don't see her again," Lyn had said.

The day after the kiss, Leisa had gone over to Lyn and Maddie's after work, knowing that Maddie had a late meeting. She found Lyn in the studio. To her relief, Lyn was done painting for the day and was at the sink washing her brushes. "Do you have a minute?" she asked tentatively.

"Sure," Lyn said, her hair tied into a loose bunch at the nape of her neck. "What's up?"

Leisa cracked her knuckles nervously. "There was a woman – before Nan – my lover in college," she stammered. "It ended badly." She began pacing. "She got married. I moved on. But... I ran into her. She works at the gym I joined."

Lyn stood very still, running her fingers back and forth over the bristles of the brush in her hand.

"She's divorced now. We had dinner together last night." Leisa stopped pacing and turned to face Lyn. "I haven't told Nan."

Lyn's eyes narrowed a bit as she regarded Leisa. "What else happened last night?"

Leisa's cheeks burned a splotchy red. "We kissed."

Lyn leaned against the sink, crossing her arms. "Why are you telling me this? Are you asking for absolution? Because if you are, you came to the wrong place," she said coolly.

Leisa's face went from red to a chalky white. She looked as if she might pass out. Lyn's expression softened as she guided Leisa to the daybed.

"Are you still in love with –?"

"Sarah."

"Sarah. Are you still in love with her?" Lyn asked.

Leisa shook her head. "No. I guess part of me has always wondered, you know, what if?"

Lyn scraped flecks of paint off her fingernails as she considered. "Look, I can understand never getting over an old lover. Especially your first lover. I can understand falling out of love with someone you've been with for years. It happens." She looked up at Leisa. "I don't understand cheating on someone who still loves you. If that's what you're contemplating, I can't be part of that. I won't do that to Nan."

"I wouldn't, either," Leisa said hastily. "I won't."

"Then why are you kissing Sarah?"

Leisa averted her gaze, unable to respond.

"Don't see her again."

"It's not that simple."

"It is if you want it to be," Lyn insisted firmly.

———◆———

"It is if you want it to be," Leisa repeated to herself as she drove in the darkness to the gym. She had contemplated simply quitting and joining another gym elsewhere, but she felt as if the specter of Sarah's presence would continue to haunt her if she just ran away. When Sarah had trapped her against the car - "when I let her trap me," Leisa reminded herself - she had suddenly felt powerless. It was like being back in college all over again, back when she tortured herself, wondering and waiting to see if Sarah would come back to her. And the longer she went without telling Nan about Sarah, the more it felt as if she were cheating - "or at least thinking about it," said a sly voice in her head.

Angrily, she pounded her fist on the steering wheel, which only succeeded in making her hand hurt.

"When did this happen?" she wanted to scream. "When did I become the one who needs to ask forgiveness, who needs to earn Nan's trust again?" She sat in the gym's parking lot, and pressed her forehead against the steering wheel. Nan. The feel of Nan's hand holding hers last Saturday when they were all at Jo Ann and Bruce's for dinner, the look in Nan's eyes when she was talking with Mariela and glanced up to see Leisa watching them. Nan was what she wanted, but she couldn't remember... couldn't remember how to tell her that; couldn't remember what it used to be like to spontaneously throw her arms around Nan and tell her how much she loved her, or what it felt like to be held safe in Nan's loving arms.

But that wasn't all she couldn't remember anymore. She couldn't remember her mother's scent unless she went into her bedroom and sniffed her perfume bottle. She couldn't remember the sound of her father's voice telling her the story about the baby store - she could remember the words, but not his voice... She was losing memories when memories were all she had left.

She put the car in gear and squealed out of the parking lot. Back at the house, she began packing a suitcase and got on the Internet to print out driving directions to Ithaca.

———

Nan hurried along the cobbled street near Fell's Point. The April sun was surprisingly warm as it reflected off the cobbled and brick surfaces. She was supposed to meet Lyn and Maddie for dinner at Jimmy's and then go to the gallery for a new exhibit. She'd been held up by a couple of telephone calls she had to return before the weekend, and now was running late. She got to the restaurant and saw them already seated at a table.

"Hi," she said as she dropped into an empty chair.

"Long week?" Maddie asked.

Nan released a pent-up breath. "Interminable. How was yours?"

"Not too bad. No catastrophes. That's always cause for celebration," Maddie replied, raising her iced tea in a toast.

Nan turned to Lyn. "How about you?"

"I've had a great week. Got a few new pieces on exhibit at the gallery, but Pat Moran's work is being showcased this month."

Their server came to take their orders. After she left, Nan said, "I don't suppose Leisa is coming tonight?"

Maddie shook her head. "I don't think Leisa's in town. She called me early this morning and asked for the day off. Said she was going to New York for the weekend."

Nan frowned. "You're kidding."

"No, why?"

"The only reason I can think of for her to go to New York is to meet her biological mother," Nan explained.

"What?" Lyn and Maddie asked in unison.

Nan relayed what Leisa had told her about the registration process. "The last we spoke about it, she hadn't heard back from anyone and hadn't told Jo Ann and Bruce yet."

Lyn leaned forward and rested her chin on her hand. "What is going on with you two? Are you talking? Is there any sign of getting back together? I mean, it's been what... four, five weeks?"

Nan wound her straw wrapper around her finger as she said, "I don't know. It's weird. It's not like our time together is angry or hurtful. Easter weekend was the best it's been for a long time. The way she looked at me a couple of times... but she hasn't said anything about coming home, and I haven't wanted to push."

Maddie leaned forward, too. "Why haven't you wanted to push? This whole thing has been strangely civil."

Nan brushed back the strand of hair tickling her cheek. "I know. I'm... I'm just afraid that I've got to be ready to give her an ultimatum if I decide to push, and I'm not there yet." She glanced back up at both of them. "What do I do if I force her to make a decision and she says no?"

"Are you ready to just be friends with her and let the relationship go?" Lyn asked.

"No! Absolutely not," Nan said emphatically. She sat back, her hands gripping the table. "Has she said that's what she wants?"

"Not at all," Lyn replied, laying a reassuring hand on her arm. "That was just me wondering, that's all."

Their food arrived and they ate quickly to get to the gallery on time. As always, there was a nice turnout of patrons and several of the artist-members of the gallery co-op. As Nan wandered through the exhibit looking at the various pieces, she rounded a corner and nearly ran into a woman coming from the opposite direction.

"Nan!" said the woman as Nan mumbled an apology without really looking at her.

Nan glanced up and said, "Shelly. Hi. I'm sorry. I didn't realize it was you."

"Oh my God!" said Shelly with a tinkling laugh. "How long has it been?"

"Um, I'm not sure," Nan said, biting her tongue to keep from adding, "but not long enough."

Shelly batted her eyelashes at Nan and ran a hand up and down her arm. "I've missed you."

"Too bad you didn't miss me while you were cheating on me," but Nan didn't say that, either. "Um..."

If Shelly noticed that Nan hadn't returned the sentiment, she ignored it. "How are you?" she asked.

"Fine," Nan said guardedly, pulling away.

"I was so sorry to hear about you and Leisa," Shelly said. Her voice and facial expression were sympathetic, but the glint of curiosity in her eyes suggested otherwise.

"You know, it's the weirdest thing," Nan said in puzzlement the second time she had run into an old girlfriend after she and Leisa had moved in together. "Women who left me high and dry suddenly seem all interested now that I'm with you."

"Of course they are," Leisa said with a smug expression. "They know what they were stupid enough to let go of, and now they know I have it."

"It?" Nan asked, eyebrows arched.

"Well," Leisa grinned coyly, wrapping her arms around Nan's neck. "You know what I mean. That magic you have – in your lips... and your tongue... and your hands," she added, punctuating each named body part with a kiss.

Nan laughed. "If it's magic, it's only magic since it found you."

"I was so sorry to hear about you and Leisa."

Nan frowned a little. "Where did you hear that?"

Shelly covered her mouth with her hand. "Oh, my God, I'm sorry. I thought you knew word was out. You know how fast it travels. And then, the thing with Leisa and her trainer –"

Even Shelly had the grace to look genuinely distraught at having let that slip. "I've got to go. Bye," she said hurriedly as she continued on her way.

Nan found an empty bench along one wall and sat heavily. Lyn saw her and hurried over.

"Are you all right?" Lyn asked. "Was that Shelly?"

Nan nodded, still not saying anything.

"What did she say?" Lyn asked angrily, sitting beside Nan on the bench. "You look awful."

Nan looked up at her. "She knew about Leisa and me, but she also said something about Leisa and her trainer. What the -" She saw the abrupt change in Lyn's expression. "Oh, please..."

Lyn couldn't meet the tortured look in Nan's eyes. "It's not what you think." She glanced quickly around. "Give me a minute to tell Maddie we're going."

Lyn was back in a moment and guided Nan outside. She took her by the arm and steered her toward the waterfront. "Maddie will meet us down here."

"What do you know?" Nan forced herself to ask at last when Lyn didn't say any more.

Lyn sighed. "A couple of days ago, Leisa came to me. Apparently an old lover from college is working as a trainer at the gym she joined. Someone named -"

"Sarah," Nan interjected.

Lyn looked over at her. "Yes. Leisa told me she had a hard time getting over her."

Nan nodded. "She did. It wasn't completely over when we met. Sarah was married by then, but wanted Leisa back on the side. That was one of the reasons it took us so long to get together; Leisa had to sort all of this out." A stony expression settled over her face as she braced for what she didn't want to hear. "What happened?"

"Not much," Lyn said, trying to reassure Nan. "They had dinner, they kissed. Leisa swears she has no intention of letting it go any further. I was pretty pissed at her. I hope I didn't scare her away from talking to me again, but I pretty much told her I would have no part of covering if she was cheating on you."

Nan stood watching the reflections of the street lamps on the water, fighting the nauseous feeling in her gut. "I thought I would never have to feel this way again." She shoved her hands into her pockets. "Maybe I should face reality and reconsider what I told you earlier about not being ready to let the relationship go."

Lyn wrapped an arm around Nan's shoulders. "Don't. Not yet. I would tell you if I thought it was hopeless, and I don't think it is. Leisa is confused right now. I don't know what all is going on in her head, but don't give up."

Chapter 15

LEISA PULLED UP IN front of a small Cape Cod in the southeast out-skirts of Ithaca. She double-checked the address written on the printed Internet directions lying on the passenger seat. It took her a moment to locate the house numbers hidden in the midst of the ivy crawling up the concrete steps and scrolled cast-iron pillars of the front portico. This was it. She saw a face appear briefly in a window as she climbed out of her car.

Her heart was pounding as she stood there and looked around. The yard looked a little unkempt, but she supposed winter lasted so long up here that maybe April was still a little early to do any spring cleanup. As she went up the walk, she couldn't help but notice that the house badly needed painting, and there was debris overhanging all the gutters along the front of the house. There were three over-grown flowerbeds planted around the yard, each anchored by a different statue: one of the Virgin Mary, one of Jesus and one of St. Francis.

She tried to curb the growing sense that she was making a mistake, and fought the urge to run back to her car and leave.

"This will be wonderful if she turns out to be someone nice, someone you like," Jo Ann had said when Leisa asked them to watch Bronwyn for the weekend, "but what will you do if she isn't?"

"And at the risk of sounding like a lawyer," Bruce interjected before Leisa could respond, "you just inherited a lot of property and money. I don't know if you've told her about your mother's death, but my advice would be to get to know her much better before you divulge too much."

Leisa looked at both of them fondly. "I really don't know what I'd do without you two," she said. "And I have thought of these things." She shrugged. "There's just no way to know until I meet her."

Just as she raised her hand to rap on the front door, it opened and Leisa found herself, for the first time in her life that she could remember, looking into a face that looked like hers. She and Eleanor Miller stared at one another for several seconds.

"Oh, heavens," Eleanor said at last, her eyes – the same gray-green eyes as Leisa – filling with tears. "You look just as I imagined you would." She unclasped her hands and held them out tentatively. "Could I... could I give you a hug?"

Leisa smiled her assent, and found her own eyes tearing up as she remembered that the last time she was held by these arms, she'd been six weeks old.

"Come in, come in," Eleanor said at last, letting Leisa go and stepping back to let her in. Leisa looked around as she entered the living room. She felt immediately that she had stepped back in time to the 1980s. All the furniture was overstuffed chenille in faded shades of mauve and teal. There were frilly floral-patterned curtains hanging from scrolled wooden cornices. She saw a crucifix and a framed photo of Pope John Paul II hanging on the wall. The end tables held cross-stitched Bible verses in various-sized frames.

"You made good time," Eleanor was saying. "I was so surprised to hear from you."

"I hope it was all right that I decided to come with so little notice," Leisa said apologetically. "I made a reservation at a nearby motel."

"Oh, nonsense. You didn't need to do that," Eleanor insisted as she led Leisa into the kitchen. "Would you like something to drink?"

"A glass of water would be great, thanks," Leisa said, noticing that nearly the entire front of the refrigerator was covered with photos of Donald.

"Please, sit down," Eleanor said as she handed Leisa her glass and cleared away some of the accumulated mail cluttering the surface of the kitchen table.

"Well, I've always imagined this moment, and now I don't know what to say," Eleanor said with a nervous laugh as she sat also.

Leisa smiled. "I know. I've imagined this conversation so many times..."

"Tell me about yourself. Where did you grow up? Where did you go to school?"

Remembering Bruce's advice, Leisa told her in rather vague terms about Rose and Daniel, about growing up in Baltimore and going to the University of Maryland, and about her work at St. Joseph's. As she spoke, she covertly eyed more of the mail on the table and saw that much of it was in the form of various Catholic magazines and newsletters. She had come to this meeting intending to be absolutely open and honest about her relationship with Nan, but now she found that resolve wavering. She decided to try and learn more about Eleanor.

"Tell me more about yourself," she suggested.

"Oh, well..." Eleanor seemed embarrassed. "Well, after I told him - my boyfriend, your father - about, you know, being pregnant, well... he left. I was just out of business college, and couldn't go home like... like that. I found a home run by nuns who took in girls like me, and they arranged the adoption. I thought it would be easy," she said, her eyes growing moist again. "But you were so beautiful. I almost changed my mind," she added with a watery smile.

"I know," Leisa said softly. "My parents kept your note."

Eleanor raised a hand to her mouth, her eyes blinking rapidly. "I always hoped you wouldn't hate me," she said tremulously.

"No," Leisa insisted, leaning toward Eleanor. Instinctively, she started to reach out to Eleanor, but pulled her hand back to clasp her water glass. "I had a wonderful childhood. You made the right decision. For both of us."

Eleanor's tears spilled over. She reached for a tissue. "Thank you."

"So," she said, dabbing at her cheeks, "what do your parents think about you coming up here?"

"Um... well," Leisa stammered awkwardly, picturing Bruce shaking his head, "they've both passed away."

"Oh, I'm so sorry," Eleanor said sincerely. "You're all alone now?"

"No," said Leisa quickly. "I have... I have an aunt and uncle I'm very close to." Inside, she cringed at her cowardice in not telling her about Nan.

They sat in an awkward silence broken unexpectedly by the sound of heavy feet coming down the stairs. Eleanor quickly shoved her tissue in her pocket and stood as Donald entered the kitchen. "Donny, this is Leisa," she said, somewhat apprehensively.

Leisa and Donald appraised one another. She supposed he must look like his father, because she couldn't see any of Eleanor in him. Like in his photos, he was taller than his mother, grossly overweight with a grayish pallor to his skin. He obviously saw her resemblance to their mother as he gazed at her curiously. She was startled to see what looked like a flash of resentment in his eyes as she stood to shake his hand. He gave her a flaccid handshake in return and turned to his mother. "When's dinner going to be ready?" he asked.

"Oh, heavens," Eleanor said. "I've been so busy, I forgot about dinner. It won't be but a few minutes, honey."

Donald frowned in irritation as he turned to go back upstairs. "Call me when it's ready."

Eleanor bustled about the kitchen, pulling things from cupboards and the refrigerator as she explained, "Donny is very intelligent, a genius, really. But he's always been ill. Diabetes. He went to RIT for a year, but the strain was too much for him."

"So what does he do now?" Leisa asked.

"Oh, well, he does things on the computer," Eleanor explained vaguely. "He has friends all over the world."

"So if he doesn't work, how come he can't clean up the yard and the gutters?" but Leisa decided not to ask it aloud, sensing that Eleanor would make excuses for him no matter what. Instead, she offered to set the table.

"Oh, thank you," Eleanor said from the stove where she was pan-frying chicken and putting frozen homefries in the microwave.

Within a short while, dinner was ready. Eleanor went to the stairs to call Donald. Leisa re-filled her water glass and went to what she supposed was her place at the table where Donald was already seated.

Eleanor carried two large platters of chicken and potatoes to the table.

"Drink?" Donald asked in exasperation.

"Oh, heavens, I forgot," Eleanor apologized again as Leisa bit back the retort that sprang to her tongue. Eleanor returned a moment later with a two-liter bottle of soda and poured Donald a large glassful.

Leisa couldn't help herself. "I thought you were diabetic?"

"I am," Donald answered curtly, talking through a mouth filled with potato.

"Donny hates all that diabetic food," Eleanor said as if she were sharing a confidence. "I don't have the heart to make him eat it."

Forcing herself to be quiet, Leisa ate her own meal, wishing there were a green bean or broccoli tree somewhere to be found. She asked Eleanor more questions, hoping to learn more of her extended family, but was disappointed to learn that Eleanor had only a father with whom she was not close, as she didn't get along with his shrewish third wife, and a brother who lived alone in Schenectady whom she hadn't spoken to in years. "It's just Donnie and me," she said affectionately, reaching a hand out to his arm. He impatiently pulled from her grasp. Throughout dinner, Donald didn't say a word as he refilled his plate, and then got up to leave the table as soon as he had finished eating.

"Don't you want to stay and visit?" Eleanor asked, clearly embarrassed.

Donald paused for a moment. "Later," he said, giving his mother a meaningful look before continuing upstairs.

"He's always been shy," Eleanor smiled.

"Yes, I can see that," Leisa said with not-so-subtle sarcasm as she picked up both her own plate and his and carried them into the kitchen.

Leisa insisted on helping with the dishes and was washing the frying pan at the sink when Eleanor went back to the dining room to gather the platters. She thought she heard Donald's footsteps come back down the stairs. She turned off the faucet and in the sudden silence in the kitchen, she heard his carrying whisper, "Have you asked her?"

"Not yet," Eleanor whispered back.

"What are you waiting for?" he hissed angrily before going back upstairs.

Leisa turned the water back on and busied herself with her scrubbing as Eleanor covered the leftovers in plastic wrap and put them in the refrigerator.

"I should probably be going," Leisa said as she put the last pan in the dish drainer.

"Oh, no, not yet," Eleanor said quickly. "We still have so much to talk about," she said with a nervous glance toward the dining room.

———◆———

Nan sat in the dark, trying to calm the panic that had threatened to overwhelm her since her conversation with Lyn at the waterfront. All through the estrangement with Leisa, it had never occurred to her that Leisa might not come home, that she might end up with someone else. Looking around at the shadowy silhouettes of the living room furniture, the house suddenly felt like a mausoleum, empty and lifeless. Up until now, she'd told herself this was just temporary, "just until I can re-gain Leisa's trust," but now... now nothing seemed certain.

She got up and restlessly wandered the house. She hadn't slept more than an hour or two all weekend and the thought of facing clients tomorrow was not an appealing one. She went to the den and looked at her Monday schedule, considering cancelling the day, but "what would you do if you don't go to work?" she asked herself.

The telephone rang.

"I'm fine," she said as she picked up.

Maddie laughed. She'd already called four or five times over the weekend. "Glad to hear it. We wondered if you wanted to come over for some dinner."

Nan sighed. "I don't think so. I'm not very good company right now."

"You think we don't know that?" Maddie said. "But you still have to eat, and not that frozen microwave junk you always do when you're on your own."

Nan smirked. "You know me too well."

"Come on. We've got plenty," said Maddie.

Before Nan could think of an objection, Lyn called out in the background, "If you don't get over here, we're bringing dinner to you."

"Hear that?" Maddie asked.

"All right," Nan grumbled. "I'll be there in a minute."

Despite her foul mood, she smiled as she grabbed her car keys.

"Hey," Lyn said, opening the door to greet her a few minutes later. She pulled Nan into a hug and held her tightly for a few seconds. "Get in here."

Nan could hear Maddie's voice in the next room. "No, it's not okay. You're giving me no notice and it's unprofessional." Maddie pressed her fingers to her forehead as she listened to whoever was on the other end.

Nan frowned as she noticed Lyn biting her lip.

"All right. Back at work on Wednesday." Maddie hung up and stood glaring at the phone.

"Who was that?" Nan asked, though she thought she knew.

Maddie glanced up at her. "Leisa. She's still in New York. Wants to stay a couple extra days."

"What for?"

Maddie shook her head. "I'm not sure, but I don't have a good feeling about this."

Leisa used her sleeve to wipe the sweat out of her eyes as she stood to stretch her aching back. She looked around with some satisfaction at the cleaned-out flowerbeds, the raked and mowed lawn and the clean gutters. She glanced up and saw, again, Donald's pale face watching from an upstairs window. This time, she didn't bother hiding her disgust as she muttered, "Thanks for offering to come down and help, you worthless lump of shit."

"Oh, no," Eleanor had protested when Leisa first offered to stay a few extra days and help out with some of the yard chores, but she hadn't put up much of an argument when Leisa insisted. Eleanor herself had come out to help on Sunday, but on Monday, while Eleanor was at work, Leisa had continued alone while Donald stayed up in his room, emerging only to get food from the kitchen and take it back upstairs.

"I guess it's just us for dinner tonight," Eleanor said with an embarrassed laugh Monday evening as she came downstairs. "I'll just take Donnie a tray. He's busy with some project on his computer."

"I'll bet he is," but Leisa didn't say the words aloud.

Leisa had the table set for the two of them by the time Eleanor returned.

"I almost didn't recognize the house when I got home tonight," Eleanor said as she dished out two bowls of stew from the crockpot and carried them to the table. "You got so much done."

"It wouldn't be hard if someone would just keep up with it," Leisa couldn't help saying.

If Eleanor got the point, she ignored it. "I might have to keep you around," she said with a little laugh.

Leisa glanced at her but Eleanor was buttering a piece of bread. Leisa looked back down at her bowl and said, "What's the job market like for social workers around here?"

It was Eleanor's turn to look up in surprise. "I don't know, but we could make some inquiries. Is that something you would think about?"

Leisa shrugged. "I don't know," she said with a nervous laugh. "Just thinking out loud."

"What about your aunt and uncle?"

"Well, it's not that far away," Leisa said. "It's doable for weekends or holidays." She speared a chunk of beef and said, "How would you feel about... you know, if I were to move up here?"

"Oh, heavens," said Eleanor, her eyes shining. "I was hoping, maybe, you would want to do this."

Leisa met her eyes. "You were?"

Eleanor blinked at her. "I have something I've wanted to show you." She got up from the table and went to the living room where Leisa could hear a cupboard door opening and some things being moved about. Eleanor returned a moment later with a small book. She slid it across the table to Leisa. Curiously, Leisa opened the book to find herself staring at a tiny pair of inky footprints. Printed in below them was:

Margaret Marie
Born March 28, 1975 at 2:47 a.m.
Weight: 6 lb 12 oz
Length: 19 inches

Transfixed, Leisa flipped the pages of the small keepsake book to find faded photos of a newborn baby girl, so blond she seemed to be bald.

"I kept these, tucked away all these years," Eleanor said softly. "I didn't know if I would ever have the chance to show them to you. I never imagined we'd ever really meet and get to know each other."

Forgetting her earlier caution, Leisa reached across the table and took Eleanor's hand. Eleanor opened her mouth as if she were going to say something and then seemed to change her mind.

"What is it?" Leisa asked.

Eleanor looked at Leisa shyly. "I did have something I wanted to ask you."

"You can ask me anything."

Nan finished an appointment with a client and turned to her computer to document the session. She glanced at her cell phone and saw that she had missed a call from Leisa. She pressed her hand to her mouth as she stared at the screen, debating what to do. After a long while, she picked the phone up and called Leisa back.

"Nan?"

The silence stretched on for several seconds before Nan spoke. "I'm here."

"Are you in between clients?"

"Yes. Where are you?" Nan asked, carefully controlling her voice.

"In the car on the way back from Ithaca," Leisa sighed. "Probably a mistake. One of many lately," she mumbled.

"What?"

"Nothing."

"So, you met her," Nan said.

"Yes."

"And?"

"She's actually very nice," Leisa said.

"I can hear the 'but'," Nan said.

"But she has a son about seven years younger than I am. He is a monster, and she completely dotes on him. It's kind of sickening to watch, because he treats her like dirt. He doesn't lift a finger around there, and she waits on him hand and foot because he's diabetic."

"So what kept you longer than just the weekend?"

"Well, I wanted to spend more time with her," Leisa said. "I helped clean things up around the house and yard, because I know he won't do it."

Nan was again silent for several seconds. "Do you feel like meeting her was the right thing to do?"

"I don't know. I guess. But they definitely had a plan," Leisa said.

"What do you mean?"

"They want me to be tested to see if I could donate a kidney to him."

"They want what?" Nan asked in disbelief.

"He's on the verge of kidney failure," Leisa explained. "Apparently, there's something weird about his blood type or antigens or something, and they haven't been able to find a suitable donor." She was quiet for a moment. "That's probably the only reason she registered to find me."

"I doubt that," Nan said. Something about the vulnerability in Leisa's voice prompted her to offer comfort even as part of her brain questioned why she was being so understanding. "I'm sure she wanted to meet you even if there were also other reasons. What did you say?"

"I didn't say anything," Leisa said. "I didn't know what to say."

"What are you thinking now?"

Leisa was quiet again as she thought. "I'm not sure how I could say no."

"Simple," Nan said curtly. "You just say no."

"You know what I mean. If he has to go on dialysis or dies because he doesn't get a kidney, how am I going to live with myself?"

"I guess."

Nan could hear Leisa's turn signal and the rumble of a truck in the background. "Thanks for being there," Leisa said. "There isn't anyone else I could really talk to about this."

"Not even Sarah?"

Nan's eyes squeezed shut as she heard Leisa's sharp intake of breath. She hadn't meant for that to come bursting out like it did. "I'm sorry," she murmured. "That was..." Her voice cracked.

She covered the phone with her hand, trying to muffle the sounds of her crying.

"Who -?" Leisa began. "Never mind. It doesn't matter how you found out. I should have told you right away when I ran into her." There was a pause. "Are you all right?"

Nan couldn't answer right away. They sat silently, listening to one another's breathing as long seconds ticked by.

"Nan?" Leisa prompted hesitantly.

"No, I'm not all right," Nan managed to say in a strangled voice. "How do you expect me to be? I've tried to be patient, giving you time to work through what you need to work through, thinking that's all you're doing. And then I find out you're... you're... with Sarah of all people for God's sake!" Nan shoved her fist against her teeth to stop herself before she said something she really regretted.

"I need to get off the phone," she whispered, feeling more tears coming.

"Please –" Leisa began, but her voice was cut off when Nan hung up.

———

"It's amazing how cruel people can be," Nan had observed often. She was appalled at the things people said to one another – the hurtful, cutting comments. "Just the lack of common courtesy, and then they wonder why there's no respect in the relationship." Trying not to sound judgmental, she would usually point out to her clients, especially in couples' counseling, that it was not healthy for a relationship when typical arguments included terms of endearment such as "Fuck you" or "Go to hell".

But Nan knew from first-hand experience how harmful it could be to someone's self-esteem when they heard things like that on a daily basis. "It's so easy to start believing you deserve to be spoken to like that," she had admitted in shame to Maddie more than once, and more than once, Maddie had said to her, "You need to get out of this relationship."

That had been one of the most wonderful things about meeting Leisa. "She's kind," Nan said in wonder to Maddie. "She's polite. She says 'please' and 'thank you' for everything. She makes me feel good about myself. I can't see her ever saying anything nasty or mean."

Maddie smiled knowingly. "I told you meeting her would be a good thing."

———

Nan cradled her head in her hands. She and Leisa had never had an actual fight. No shouting. No walking out the door. No silent treatment. Any arguments had been discussed and worked out until they had made up. Up until Williamsburg. Now everything felt different between them. *Hanging up is not a constructive way to handle anything,* she reminded herself as the telephone rang again. "I'm sorry I did that," she said before Leisa could say anything. "We'll talk when you get back. I do not want to do this over the phone."

"I'll be back tonight," Leisa said.

"I'll be waiting."

Chapter 16

"I DON'T BELIEVE IN 'happily ever after'," Nan said as they strolled.

It was about a year after she and Leisa had met. They'd gone to Provincetown for a long fall weekend, flying up to Boston and taking the ferry over.

Leisa tilted her head. "What, you don't believe people can stay together their whole lives?"

Nan shook her head. "Not happily, and not faithfully. Not both at the same time. I'm sure there are exceptions, but I think they are exceptions."

They stopped at the marina, watching the brightly painted boats bobbing on the water.

"You are such a cynic," Leisa laughed.

"Occupational hazard," Nan replied dryly. "Why aren't you more of a cynic? Sarah wasn't faithful to you. None of my lovers were faithful to me. My father may be faithful to my mother – I don't really want to know – but he isn't happy."

"What about Lyn and Maddie?" Leisa challenged. "What about my parents and my aunt and uncle? I don't know for certain they've all been faithful, but I'd be willing to bet they have. And they all truly love one another."

Nan didn't respond.

"Listen," Leisa said as she took Nan's hand. "We're going to be one of the exceptions. I will never cheat on you," she promised. "And to prove I mean what I'm saying, I want to shop for rings while we're here."

Leisa clenched her jaw as she remembered that conversation. She rubbed her thumb on the ring on her left hand. It had taken years for Nan to stop questioning if Leisa was tiring of being with her, if she was still happy.

"I keep expecting you to say, 'I've had enough'," Nan had said over and over.

And Leisa had happily replied over and over, "Not yet."

When she finally got back to Baltimore Tuesday evening, she avoided driving by Jo Ann and Bruce's house. She had called them to say she'd be in late and would be by the next evening to get Bronwyn. She didn't want to get waylaid by their questions about what Eleanor was like. Not now. She pulled up behind Nan's Mini and sat there for a few minutes, not sure what she would say. She remembered when her heart used to quicken at getting home to Nan, not this painful thudding in her chest. At last, she got out and knocked on the front door.

Nan opened the door after a moment, and stood back silently to let her in. She followed Nan to the kitchen.

"Are you hungry?" Nan asked. "Do you want something to drink?"

"Uh, sure," Leisa replied. "A Coke?"

She sat at the kitchen table as Nan went to the refrigerator.

"Glass?"

"Yes, please." She waited while Nan brought her a glass with ice and took the seat opposite.

"I'm not sure where to start," Leisa said when Nan just sat there looking at her. She fumbled with the tab, and poured her Coke into

138

the glass. She took a nervous drink before the foam settled and snorted what felt like half the contents up her nose.

Nan folded her hands. "When did you first see Sarah?"

Leisa thought. "Shortly after my birthday. I went to the gym and she was there."

Nan nodded. "But you didn't know she worked there when you joined?"

"No, I didn't."

Nan nodded again, her mouth tight. "Why didn't you tell me?"

Leisa fidgeted, wiping the frost off her glass with a fingertip. "I'm not sure," she said lamely. "I... I meant to, but..."

Nan's intertwined fingers tightened almost imperceptibly as she asked, "Was it because part of you was already thinking you might not be coming back?"

"No!"

"Then you were thinking you'd be coming home?" Nan prompted, her voice betraying none of the anxiety she felt inside as she pushed Leisa for an answer for the first time.

"I... I wasn't..." Leisa stumbled. Her mind flashed back to the morning she'd left for Ithaca, the morning of that damned dream, and all the things she felt but couldn't say out loud.

Nan looked at her and said very quietly, "I know I've been far from perfect lately, but you know me well enough to know there is a line I will not cross. You're getting dangerously close to it."

Leisa sat there helplessly, still unable to voice all the emotions churning within her.

Steeling herself, Nan said, "You have some decisions to make."

———◆———

"Come in, come in," said Jo Ann Wednesday evening, impatiently pulling Leisa inside.

Bronwyn loudly scolded Leisa for being gone so long as she wriggled and wagged her stump of a tail.

Jo led the way to the family room where Bron jumped up into Leisa's lap on the couch, nestling into the crook of her neck.

"So, honey," said Jo Ann, sitting on the edge of her chair while Bruce lowered his newspaper and looked at her over the tops of his glasses. "Tell us all about her. What was she like?"

"Well, she was really nice," Leisa said. "She never married my father. He took off when he found out she was pregnant so I don't know anything about him. She did marry later, but is divorced now. I told you she has a son." Leisa paused, not sure how much detail to offer about Donald. "He's okay. Kind of lazy."

"Does she have other family?" Jo asked.

"Nobody she's close to. And no one who knows about me," Leisa said, stroking Bronwyn who snuffled contentedly in her arms.

"Do you plan to see her again?" Bruce asked, watching Leisa with narrowed eyes.

Leisa could feel her cheeks get hot. "Well, yes. He, Donald, is diabetic and is close to being in kidney failure. They asked me if I would be tested to see if I'm compatible to donate a kidney."

She'd been prepared for some resistance to the idea of donating a kidney. She was not prepared for Jo Ann's anger.

"They just met you!" Jo declared. "And this is the first thing they ask you? To give up a kidney? You don't even know what kind of people they are."

Bruce, who had continued to watch Leisa closely, laid a calming hand on Jo's arm. "It doesn't matter what kind of people they are. We know what kind of person our niece is." But he turned back to Leisa and said, "Did they ask for anything else?"

"No... well," Leisa squirmed. "They didn't ask, but she, Eleanor, did say that Donald doesn't have any insurance and she's not sure how she's going to pay for this."

"You didn't offer?" Jo Ann asked immediately.

"No," Leisa hastened to say. "I'm not offering any money. I only said I'd be tested. And if I'm compatible, the donor isn't supposed to have any financial obligation."

"Oh, honey." Jo Ann blinked as her eyes filled with tears. "Is this the only reason they looked for you?"

Leisa didn't answer. She couldn't admit to her aunt that she had wondered the same thing. She remembered the baby book, kept squirreled away all these years. *It has to be more than that,* she said to herself.

———————

Maddie peered over the top of Leisa's cubicle. "Hey. Medical tests go okay?"

Leisa immediately locked her computer monitor and turned around. "Yeah. It looks like I'm a match."

"Really?" Maddie came around into the cubicle and sat down. "Are you going to donate?"

Secretly, Leisa had hoped against hope that she wouldn't be a match, so the decision would be taken from her hands, but "I feel like I don't really have a choice," she admitted now.

"You don't owe them anything," Maddie pointed out.

"I know but…" Leisa had tried to imagine the guilt of getting a letter from Eleanor one day telling her that Donald had died of kidney failure when she could have done something to save him. "I don't think I could live with myself if I didn't."

Maddie nodded, glancing at the dark computer screen. "Anything else you want to talk about?"

Leisa felt the telltale flush in her cheeks but said, "No. Nothing else."

Maddie nodded again. "Okay." She got to her feet. "By the way, have you seen Mariela lately?"

With another pang of guilt, Leisa realized she hadn't spent any time with Mariela since Easter weekend. "No, why?"

Maddie shrugged. "She was asking about you. Said she hadn't seen you in a while."

"I'm sorry," said Leisa. "I've been so busy with getting to New York and all this medical stuff. I'll go talk to her today."

"Okay. I'll let you get back to whatever you were doing, then," Maddie said as she left.

Leisa turned back to her computer and brought the screen up to a job posting for a social work position with Ithaca social services.

She printed off the application and put it in her bag. Then she went looking for Mariela.

Outside on the playground, Leisa spied Mariela sitting on one of the swings, barely moving. Leisa wondered if she knew how to swing and made a mental note to teach her. No one else was swinging. Even after all this time, Mariela often preferred to be alone.

"Hi," she said, taking the empty swing next to Mariela.

Mariela didn't respond and didn't smile.

"What's the matter?" Leisa asked.

Mariela looked at her sternly.

"Mariela?" Leisa prompted.

"Where have you been?" Mariela asked. "You haven't been to see me for a long time."

"I know," said Leisa. "I'm sorry. I had to go out of town for a few days, and then I got busy when I got back here." Mariela stared at her stonily. "But, you're right. It's not a good excuse. I should have come to find you when I got back."

She reached over and gave Mariela a little push and then pushed off herself.

"Are you going away?" Mariela asked.

"What?" Leisa dragged her feet in the dirt and stopped the swing. "Why would you ask me that?"

"You're different," Mariela replied. "Something is wrong. Like with my mama."

Leisa frowned. "What do you mean?"

Mariela twisted on the swing to face Leisa. "I could tell when my mama was going away. She got different. Now you're different."

"They're like abused dogs," Maddie had said to the staff more times than Leisa could count. "The things they pick up on - body language, off-hand comments, your eye contact - they have learned how to read the people around them like you wouldn't believe. Sometimes their lives have depended on it. They pick up on signals we don't know we're giving. Often when they've been acting up, we eventually realize it's in response to something we didn't even know we were doing."

"You don't look the same," Mariela said.

Leisa tilted her head, puzzled. "You mean my appearance has changed?"

Mariela's brow furrowed as she struggled to express herself. "Yes... but you don't look the same," she repeated. She got off the swing and stood in front of Leisa and placed her hands on either side of Leisa's face. "You don't look at me the same. You're different."

Leisa took Mariela's hands in hers. "I guess I am different. I've... I've had some problems I have to figure out. But that doesn't change how I feel about you," she insisted.

"You said you wouldn't leave."

Leisa thought for a long moment, trying to remember. "What do you mean?"

"The night you came to get me, you told me, 'Go to sleep. I won't leave you.'" She stared hard into Leisa's eyes. "Are you going away?"

Leisa looked down at Mariela's hands in hers. "I may have to go see someone who is sick," Leisa said. "And I might be gone for a while. But I'll be back."

"You promise?"

Leisa pulled Mariela to her and held her tightly. "I promise."

A short while later, Leisa sat at her desk, her hands covering her face.

I won't leave you.

When she was little, maybe six or seven, she'd gone through a period where she had nightmares almost every night which would wake her, sobbing and terrified. She could never remember any details, only the sensation of something ominous waiting for her in her sleep. Rose and Daniel would hurry in, holding her and murmuring reassuringly that nothing could hurt her while they were there. Usually, Rose would send Daniel back to bed and she would lie down next to Leisa. "It's all right," she would croon. "Go to sleep. I won't leave you."

"But you did," Leisa cried into her hands. "You both left me."

Chapter 17

NAN PULLED UP AT the house and was surprised to see Maddie's Explorer parked on the curb. Maddie got up from where she was sitting on the porch steps as Nan got out of her car.

"What's wrong?" Nan asked.

"We need to talk," Maddie said, following Nan inside.

Nan dropped her briefcase on the couch.

"Not your bed any longer, I see," Maddie commented as she took one of the chairs.

"No. I'm sleeping upstairs again," Nan said cautiously. "But I'm beginning to think these chairs are cursed. This is where Leisa was waiting for me after Williamsburg," she added at Maddie's questioning look.

"Well, I hate to add to that tradition, but..."

Nan's mouth tightened as she waited for what could only be bad news.

Maddie hesitated. "My mother would slap me silly for carrying tales, but I really feel like you ought to know. I saw a job posting on Leisa's computer. For Ithaca, New York."

Nan sat impassively at this news.

"What?" Maddie prodded.

"We talked when she got back from New York. I confronted her about Sarah," Nan said in a strangled voice. "I told her she had some decisions to make."

Maddie sat there, miserable in her inability to shield Nan from this. "I'm sorry."

Nan gave a small nod. "Me, too."

———

Leisa was sitting at the kitchen table, filling out the job application.

"Why are you doing this?" asked an annoying voice inside her head.

She gave her head a tiny shake. She couldn't answer that question. She felt almost as if she was moving through some kind of weird dream - one where her actions didn't really make sense, but she couldn't seem to stop what was happening. She couldn't honestly say that she wanted to move to New York. It was more like a path had opened before her that she couldn't make herself turn away from.

"When are you going to tell Nan and Jo and Bruce about this?" asked that voice.

"There's nothing to tell yet," she whispered irritably. "I'm only filling out the application."

She paused. That was how this whole thing had started. "I'm only registering" and then, "I'm only replying to their request for release of information" and then, "I'm only going to meet her."

She stared at the forms before her. Where was it going to stop? She couldn't see that far.

The unexpected opening of the front door startled her. Jo Ann stormed into the kitchen as Leisa jumped up from the table. She quickly flipped the application upside down.

"A knock might have been nice," Leisa said coolly.

"Why? Something to hide?" Jo asked.

"What are you talking about?" Leisa asked, cursing as she felt her cheeks redden.

Jo Ann stood with her hands on her hips, looking so much like Rose that it took Leisa aback for a moment.

"Sit down," Jo said, and it wasn't a request.

Leisa sat back down, neatening the table by pulling the newspaper over top of the application and stacking everything in a pile.

Jo folded her hands and looked at Leisa. "Do you have something to tell me?"

"I don't know -"

"Let me simplify this. I understand you're applying for a job in Ithaca," Jo Ann said bluntly.

Leisa's mouth fell open. "How -"

"How did I find out?" Jo finished for her. "Obviously not from my niece. Nan told me."

"Nan?" Leisa repeated, feeling as if she was missing some vital pieces of this conversation. "How did she find out?"

Jo Ann sat back, staring hard at Leisa. "So it's true," she said.

At realizing she'd fallen into her aunt's trap, Leisa's expression took on a mulish expression, the same one she had so often had as a child - "she knows she's wrong, and she knows she's been caught, but she is too stubborn to admit it!" Rose used to complain to Jo in frustration.

Jo took a deep breath and leaned forward, folding her hands in an attitude of calm. "How she found out, we can discuss later," she said. "I stopped by to bring her some cookies and -" She held up her hand to silence Leisa who had opened her mouth again. "I've been bringing her food ever since you moved out. I knew she wouldn't cook for herself and I've wanted to see how she was doing."

"You're my aunt! Why are you checking on her?" Leisa knew how childish it sounded as she said it, and judging by the bemused expression on Jo's face, she felt like she had just gone back in time to about age ten. "What else did she tell you?"

"What else should she have told me?" Jo asked, her eyes narrowed.

"Nothing."

"You are the one who brought Nan into this family," Jo pointed out. "We love her almost as much as we love you."

"Probably more lately," Leisa almost blurted.

"Just because you split up with her, doesn't mean she's going to disappear from our lives," Jo was saying.

It took a moment for her words to register with Leisa. "Wait, what? Who said anything about splitting up?"

Jo's eyes flashed angrily. "What do you think is going to happen if you continue with this?" She reached for the pile of paper on the table, and pulled out the application forms from the bottom. "You can't stay married to someone while you move off to a different state with a different family." Jo was breathing heavily, but there was a wounded look on her face. "You'll never lose Bruce and me, honey, but you're going to lose Nan if you don't wake up."

The telephone rang. With an exasperated sigh, Leisa got up to answer it.

"Donny's in the hospital," came Eleanor's voice. "He's in kidney failure."

"Oh." Leisa glanced back at Jo who was still sitting at the table.

"The doctors said they got the results and you're a match," Eleanor was saying.

Leisa turned to look out the kitchen window. "Yes."

There was a tense silence.

"Will you do it?" Eleanor asked. "Will you come?"

Leisa squeezed her eyes shut. She'd known this moment was coming. "Yes. I'll donate," she heard herself say.

She could hear Eleanor laughing and crying at the same time.

"Oh, thank you. Thank you so much." Eleanor said. "When can you get here?"

"I'll need to make arrangements for time off at my job, but I'll try to get there later this week," Leisa said.

"Okay. I'll let them know at the hospital," Eleanor said. "You have no idea what this means to me."

"I'll see you in a few days."

When Leisa turned around to hang up the phone, Jo Ann was gone.

"Hold still now."

Leisa lay in the CT tube, trying not to move as tears leaked from her eyes. The staff at the transplant center in Syracuse had been guiding her from one test to another in preparation for the surgery, which was scheduled for the next day.

As she lay there, she tried not to think about the fact that she had left Baltimore without saying anything to Nan or Jo or Bruce. Only Maddie. "I'll be back at work in a week," she'd said.

"That sounds kind of soon," Maddie said. "Don't push it."

"My incision will be small, they said. I should be able to at least do deskwork in a week," Leisa insisted.

When the CT was done and the plinth slid out of the tube, the tech noticed her red eyes. "It's okay," he said kindly, mistaking the reason for the tears. "It's not a bad surgery." Leisa nodded, too embarrassed to correct him. After the last of the tests was done, she was escorted to her hospital room where she was stunned to find Nan and Jo Ann sitting there, waiting for her.

"What are you doing here?"

"You didn't think we'd let you do this alone, did you?" Jo chided her.

"Considering what an asshole I've been, yeah, I did." But Leisa couldn't bring herself to say it. She glanced at Nan and saw that her eyes looked puffy and bruised. "Thanks," she said instead. It was all she could manage.

Jo, seeming to sense what Leisa couldn't say, came to her and folded her in a hug. "Of course we were going to be here with you. Bruce wanted to come, too, but he decided to stay home with Bronwyn."

Leisa nodded, choking back the new tears that sprang to her eyes. "Come on," she said, turning away to wipe her eyes. "I want to introduce you."

"To them?" Jo asked dubiously.

"Yes," Leisa laughed, taking her by the hand. "To them."

They walked down the hall and passed a bulletin board where there were pinned dozens of photos of successful transplant recipients with their families, many posing with their donors as well.

"You'll be up here in a few days?" Jo asked.

"I guess," Leisa said.

Eleanor, as expected, was in Donald's room, waiting on him. "Oh, thank you so much for doing this," she gushed when Leisa knocked and entered. She came over to wring Leisa's hand gratefully. Despite her continued dislike of Donald, Leisa couldn't help but feel a small burst of warmth inside for Eleanor.

"I want to introduce you to my Aunt Jo Ann and my partner, Nan," she said, pulling them in.

Eleanor and Donald looked at each other. "You mean, like a business partner?" Eleanor asked innocently.

Holding back a laugh, Leisa said, "No. I mean my life partner. Nan is my spouse." She met Nan's eyes for the briefest moment, afraid of what she might see in them, but there was only love. "And doubt," she realized.

A shadow settled over Donald's pasty features. "You're a... a..." He couldn't quite bring himself to say the word.

"Yes," said Leisa with a sweet smile. "You're going to have a lesbian kidney inside you. See you tomorrow. Sleep tight."

"Your kidney might be the most manly thing about him," Jo muttered under her breath as they left the room.

———

Nan paced the waiting room while Eleanor and Jo sat restlessly flipping the pages of magazines. After several hours, the surgeon's assistant came to tell them that everything had gone perfectly. Leisa's kidney had been removed through a small laparoscopic incision, and Donald's body seemed to be accepting it without any early signs of rejection. Jo and Nan couldn't help but sympathize with Eleanor's tears of relief. She really had no one but Donald as she had told them repeatedly during the long hours together in the waiting room. Anxiously, they waited until Leisa and Donald were transferred to their rooms. Donald's was an isolation room, not because he was contagious, but to prevent anyone bringing in any germs that might compromise his immune system. For at least a few days, Eleanor would be wearing a gown and mask while she sat with him.

When Leisa woke, Jo and Nan were sitting on either side of her bed. "We're here," Nan murmured. Leisa smiled and went back to sleep. When she woke again, she was more alert.

"Everything went fine, they said," Jo told her as she raised the head of Leisa's bed, plumping the pillows behind her.

"How do you feel?" Nan asked.

Leisa winced a little as she shifted in bed. She placed a hand on her right side. "A little sore," she admitted. "Should be a pound or two lighter."

"Up already?" asked her nurse in surprise when she came in with a dinner tray. "Think you could eat something?"

"Maybe a little," Leisa replied. After a few bites, she pushed her tray away. "Could you help me into the bathroom?" she asked Nan. "They're pumping me with enough fluid to float a boat."

Nan wheeled the IV pole and held Leisa's elbow as she guided her toward the bathroom.

"Oh, for Pete's sake," Leisa grumbled when she saw the toilet was outfitted with a plastic container for measuring her urine.

"Well," Nan chuckled as she stood by. "How else are they supposed to know if your remaining kidney is doing its job?"

Leisa's voice echoed inside the tiled confines of the bathroom. "I just never thought pee could be such a big deal."

———

Donald was doing so well that they removed him from isolation precautions after two days. Leisa was off her own IV, and would probably be discharged the next day. Eleanor had been in to see her only one time, the day after the surgery.

"Leisa's doing just fine, thank you for asking," Jo Ann said quite pointedly after listening to Eleanor talk for several minutes about Donald without asking once about how Leisa was doing.

Eleanor had the grace to blush. "Oh, of course. I just can't thank you enough for all you've done."

"No, you can't," Nan said coolly. "I think you should remember that."

"I just can't believe them," Jo huffed indignantly after Eleanor had left.

Leisa tried to shrug it off, saying nonchalantly, "It doesn't matter," but she couldn't look them in the eye as she said it.

The morning Leisa was to be discharged, she dressed in her own clothes and went to say good-bye to the Millers while Nan and Jo were checking out of their hotel. As she passed the bulletin board, she paused and looked, remembering that no one had taken their photo. But there, pinned in the middle of the board was a photo of Donald with Eleanor hugging him happily. Leisa stood there looking at Eleanor beaming at her from the photo. She had to reach out and brace herself against the wall as the floor shifted under her.

"Are you all right?" A nurse came rushing over to check on her.

"I'm fine," Leisa said. "Just a little dizzy." She glanced again at the photo. "I'm back to normal now."

As she approached Donald's room, she smelled a peculiar aroma. She knocked and entered the room to see Eleanor hurriedly crushing a paper bag and pushing it into the trash can by the bed while Donald very obviously finished chewing something and swallowed.

Leisa's eyes became icy. "You missed some ketchup," she said, tossing a napkin to him. "I hope the hamburger and fries were good."

His face transformed into something ugly as he stared at her defiantly. "It was."

"He was just so hungry, you know," Eleanor said quickly. "The diet they have him on is so awful." When Leisa continued to stare at Donald, Eleanor continued in a slightly panicky voice, "It's just a little hamburger. You won't say anything, will you?"

Leisa turned her cold stare to Eleanor. "No," she said quietly. "I won't say anything. I won't say anything to them. I won't say anything more to you, either."

"What are you going to do, take back your kidney?" Donald sneered.

Turning her gaze back to him, Leisa said disdainfully, "I didn't give it for you. Or for you," she added, looking again at Eleanor.

When they exchanged puzzled glances, she laughed derisively. "I wouldn't expect you to understand."

She turned toward the door. "But when you ruin this kidney, you're on your own. Don't call me."

Fuming, she went back to her room. When Nan and Jo arrived a few minutes later, Nan took one look at her face and asked, "What's wrong?"

"Nothing," Leisa said flatly. "Let's get out of here."

Chapter 18

"WE'VE BEEN DYING TO hear all about it," Lyn said as Maddie led Nan into the kitchen. She went to the stove and stirred a boiling pot of fettuccini. "What were they like?"

"When did you get back?" Maddie asked.

Nan looked from one to the other. "Day before yesterday and I need a glass of wine before we jump into this."

Maddie obliged with a big glass of cabernet. "Here. Talk."

Nan slid onto a stool at the island and took a big sip of her wine. Closing her eyes, she let the wine warm her as it went down. "Could have used some of this in the hospital."

"That bad?" Maddie said.

Nan rolled her eyes. "They're awful. Well... he's awful, the half-brother, and the mother lets him get away with it. I'm honestly not sure how Leisa stands them." She paused, swirling her wine around and around. "She wouldn't have before."

Maddie was watching Nan closely. "How is she?"

Nan's lips compressed. "I'm not sure. I'm glad Jo and I were there for her because they sure weren't. I'm not sure how to describe it. It's almost like she's begging or hoping for their approval. It's kind of

155

hard to watch."

"Did you talk?" Lyn asked, pouring the fettuccini into a colander.

Nan shook her head. "It wasn't the right time. Jo tried to talk me into driving back with her, but that much time alone in a car together... I don't know where she's at with everything and I just didn't want to get into it when she's still recovering. I haven't seen her since we got back."

"The operation went well, though, right?" Maddie asked.

"Yeah. As far as that part, it went very well."

Lyn dished pasta out into three plates and poured Alfredo sauce over top. They carried their plates to the table.

"She hasn't said anything about the job up there?" Maddie asked.

"Nope. Jo said she just clammed up when she confronted her about it. I'm not sure if she's figured out that it was you who told me," Nan said.

Lyn reached for a piece of bread. "Why haven't you gone over?"

"I told her she had some decisions to make," Nan said. "It's up to her now." She took a bite, chewing as she thought. "She did introduce me as her partner."

Lyn and Maddie looked at one another. "That's a good thing, then, isn't it?" Lyn said.

"I hope so."

———

Leisa exhaled impatiently as she clicked through television channels. "How can we have three hundred channels and still have nothing worth watching?" she grumbled. She pushed painfully to her feet, grimacing as she grabbed her side. *For such a small incision, it still hurts like hell.* She went into the kitchen and opened the refrigerator. After staring at the contents for a minute, she closed the frig door and called Bronwyn out into the back yard. She sat at the picnic table watching Bron run around, inspecting every corner of the yard. She pulled her cell phone out of her pocket and glanced at the screen. Nothing. No calls from Eleanor - "not that I expected any," she reminded herself sulkily, remembering the photo - but no calls from Nan, either.

She'd been home for three days - almost as long as the longest car ride of her life. *At least it felt that way.*

"I don't know how you thought you were going to drive yourself home," Jo Ann had said as Leisa squirmed in the passenger seat, trying to get comfortable.

"I didn't think I would have to drive home the day I got out of the hospital." But Leisa didn't say it. Didn't even like to think it. She felt so stupid, thinking that Eleanor had been ready to accept her as a daughter. She turned to look out the window so Jo wouldn't see the sudden tears that had sprung to her eyes.

Since getting back to Baltimore, Jo had come by each day to bring her food and check on her - "you really should come stay with us," she fretted - but there had been no contact from Nan. "She's waiting for you," Leisa reminded herself. She knew, too, that Nan had left it to her where they went from here.

"You have some decisions to make," Nan had told her.

Only, Leisa didn't seem capable of making any decisions at the moment. "How did it come to this?" she fumed. Every time she tried to think back, to trace the chronology of the events that had led them to this point, it seemed her brain jumped from Williamsburg to now, "but that can't be right." There was Eleanor and Sarah and - "Damn!"

Restlessly, she got up and called Bron back inside, wandering from room to room, but there was nothing to straighten, nothing that needed doing. She was too sore anyhow. She sat down and tried to read, but gave up after a few minutes, tossing the book aside and getting to her feet again. Bron raised her head hopefully.

"Want to go for a walk?" Leisa asked, thinking that some fresh air and a little exercise would do her good.

Bron jumped up at the 'w' word and danced around as Leisa tried to clip the leash to her collar.

"Stand still, you silly little beast," Leisa laughed. "Ready?"

Gingerly, Leisa descended the porch steps and headed along the sidewalk toward Herring Run Park. Distracted by the splashes of sunlight filtering through the leaves, she tried to breathe deeply, but it hurt.

Suddenly, Bronwyn yanked the leash out of her hand and raced down the street, heading toward Nan. Leisa yelled and sprinted after her, ignoring the pain in her side. Bronwyn rounded the next corner and disappeared from sight. Before Leisa could get to the corner, she heard the screech of car brakes and a heart-wrenching yelp of pain.

Rounding the corner, she saw a car stopped diagonally in the street and Bronwyn's limp form on the asphalt. An elderly woman was getting out of the car. She looked up as Leisa ran to the scene.

"Oh, Leisa," said the woman, her hands fluttering anxiously. Leisa glanced up at her and realized she was a neighbor. "I'm so sorry. She just came out of nowhere. I couldn't stop in time."

"I know, Mrs. Samuels," Leisa said. "She got away from me." She knelt beside Bronwyn, and could see that she was still alive, panting rapidly.

"Oh dear, oh dear," cried Mrs. Samuels helplessly as Leisa bent over Bronwyn. "I'll go get Nan," she said, trotting down the street as fast as she could.

Fighting the lump rising in her throat, Leisa ran her hands over Bronwyn's head, soothing her. She could feel how cold the little dog's ears were already. Bron's frightened brown eyes stayed focused on her as she leaned close and whispered, "Hang on. You'll be okay. Hang on, you hear me?"

She kept murmuring, saying whatever came to her for what felt like long minutes, as she stroked Bronwyn's face, trying to keep her calm. Trying to keep herself calm.

She glanced up the street toward the house, but could see no sign yet of Nan. "Oh, please hurry," she prayed. Looking back down at Bronwyn, she realized she was no longer breathing.

"Oh, no," she whispered as her eyes filled with tears. "No, no, no, no." She picked up the still-warm body, cradling it to her and rocking. She heard footsteps running toward her, but couldn't see anything clearly through her tears. Then Nan was there, kneeling beside her, wrapping her arms around both Leisa and Bronwyn.

"Come on," Nan murmured through her own tears. "Let's take her home."

She said something to the distraught Mrs. Samuels and then helped Leisa to her feet, and together they walked back to their house. There, they laid Bronwyn on her bed near the fireplace. She looked like she was sleeping.

"It's all... my fault," Leisa managed to say in between her sobs as she collapsed on the floor in front of the couch and pulled her knees to her chest.

Not sure how her touch would be received, Nan tentatively wrapped her arm around Leisa's shoulders. "It was an accident," she said as Leisa let herself be pulled close. Nan held her tightly as they cried together for a long time.

Nan's tears slowed after a while, but Leisa's sobs seemed unending, now they had been released. The living room darkened and time crept by, and still Nan held her as she seemed unable to stop crying.

"I'm so sorry," Leisa gasped during a lull.

"I'm sorry, too," Nan said, caressing Leisa's face with her other hand. "I'm sorry I wasn't honest with you from the beginning. I'm sorry I haven't held you and touched you and loved you the way I should have. I'm sorry I ever made you doubt how much I love you." She felt she couldn't hold Leisa tightly enough or find words strong enough to make her know all the things she was trying to say.

It was late when Leisa's tears finally seemed to slow.

"Are you hungry?"

"No," Leisa sniffed as she sat up.

Apprehensively, Nan said, "Please stay here tonight."

In the dark living room, lit only by the streetlights outside, Nan couldn't read Leisa's eyes, but she could see her nod.

"Why don't you go upstairs?" Nan suggested glancing over to the dog bed where Bronwyn's still body lay. "I'll be up in a minute."

Leisa's eyes filled with tears again as she gave Bron one final caress before going upstairs. Nan swaddled Bronwyn in one of the towels reserved for her baths, and carried her down to the basement, tears falling again down her own cheeks as she laid the small bundle on a workbench for the night.

When she got upstairs, Leisa was undressing and getting into bed. "I'll just be a minute," Nan said as she went into the bathroom. When she emerged, she could hear Leisa crying again as if her heart were breaking.

"What is it?" she asked softly, spooning in behind Leisa and wrapping an arm around her.

Leisa couldn't answer. She wasn't sure she even knew the answer. This upwelling of despair felt tangible and malevolent, as if it were a shadowy force threatening to pull her into its grasp and keep her there forever. But it was also familiar, something that only now did she realize had been stalking her for months, always just out of sight, but there, waiting. And it was all tied up with the things she couldn't remember anymore, as if this... this thing was blocking all memory, all ability to feel anything happy. Until today, she had evaded its grasp, but now, she had no words to describe the terrible, aching aloneness she was feeling, an isolation and sorrow that went beyond Bronwyn's death, beyond even her parents' deaths.

"I'm here," Nan whispered, sensing some of what Leisa couldn't say. "I've got you, and I promise I will not leave you."

———

"So, how is she?" Maddie asked a couple of evenings later as she and Nan did the dishes while Leisa and Lyn walked through the backyard to Bronwyn's grave, marked by a chunky white stone.

Nan watched through the kitchen window as Lyn wrapped her arm around Leisa's shoulders. "I'm not sure," she said pensively. "We're talking, but... there's something different about her now." Nan looked up at Maddie who was drying a skillet. "It's almost like she's not all here with me, like part of her has gone away."

"Maybe it has," Maddie mused. "She's lost so much that she loved, maybe part of her has died, too." She put the skillet away. "Has she heard from the bio mom?"

"No," Nan said darkly. "Nothing. After everything she did for them, they haven't called to see how she is or say thank-you or anything."

"You know, that's something else I've wondered," Maddie said as she hung her dishtowel on the rack. "What does that do to your head, to expect this cathartic meeting with your biological mother, only to find she basically wants to use her genetic mistake to take care of her real child?"

"You know, that's exactly the phrase Leisa used," Nan murmured.

They had spent that night wrapped in each other's arms when Leisa was finally able to sleep. She didn't say anything when they awoke. She went down to the basement while Nan cancelled her day. Wordlessly, they buried Bronwyn in the backyard. Nan cried again as they dug the grave then placed the small body, still shrouded in a towel, in the hole, but Leisa's supply of tears seemed to have been exhausted at last. They went back inside and made breakfast. Leisa pushed her plate away after a few bites, and sat with her coffee cup cradled in her hands.

"I'm not really sure what I expected," she began when she finally spoke.

Nan waited. Knowing how Leisa's mind worked, she knew she would understand in a moment what Leisa was talking about.

"She doesn't know me. She didn't raise me. He's the one she loves, the one she has memories of watching grow up, no matter how big an ass he is now. The real child," she added wistfully.

Nan reached for her hand, and was surprised when Leisa took it. "You know better than that," Nan said. "You were the real child for your parents."

Leisa's gaze focused on some far off memory and Nan saw a smile tug at the corner of her mouth.

———◆———

"Rose! Where are you?"

Rose looked up in surprise at the sound of Leisa's voice calling from the foyer after school one afternoon. "I'm upstairs," she responded. "And may I ask," she added as Leisa came noisily up the steps, "since when do you address your mother by her first name?"

"I'm not really your daughter, and you're not really my mother," Leisa announced as she dropped her backpack on the floor.

Rose paused as she pulled a t-shirt from the laundry she was folding. "Where did you get that idea?"

Leisa flopped across the bed next to the pile of clean laundry. "Randy Butler said so. He said if I'm adopted, then we're not a real family. He said you're not really a mother if you never had a baby, and I'm not your daughter."

Leisa's voice was casual, but Rose knew better. She'd learned long ago that Leisa's mind worked in ways that continually surprised her. She also knew how softhearted Leisa was, no matter how tough she pretended to be. She lay down on the bed next to Leisa, propping herself up on one elbow. "And what makes Randy Butler such an expert?" she asked, running her free hand through Leisa's silky blond hair.

"Well, he's older," Leisa shrugged.

"How old?"

"Third grade."

Rose suppressed a chuckle. "I see. And since you're only in second grade, he knows more?"

Leisa shrugged again, not looking directly at Rose.

"I want you to listen to me carefully," Rose said. "Having a baby does not make someone a mother or father. Raising a child, being there with her every day, taking care of her even when she's sick or has a scary dream, loving her no matter what..." She paused and turned Leisa's face to her. "No matter what," she repeated. "That's what makes a mother or father." She looked into Leisa's serious eyes. "Do you understand that?"

Whatever Leisa read in Rose's eyes must have satisfied her. "Yes," she said with relief.

"So," Rose said, sitting up, "what do you call me?" She gathered an armful of folded laundry.

Leisa grinned wickedly. "Rose?" she teased.

Rose dumped all the laundry on top of her, grabbing Leisa and tickling her until she squealed with laughter. "Stop, Mom!"

"That's more like it."

"Yes, I know better."

Leisa's eyes were focused on their intertwined hands, but Nan wondered what she was really seeing.

"You don't have to deal with this alone," Nan said softly, afraid of pushing Leisa away just as she seemed to be drawing near again.

Leisa's gaze shifted to Nan's, searching her face. "Would it be okay if I came home?"

Chapter 19

"THE REAL DAMAGE FROM monsoon does not come in the first rains and winds," said the little Indonesian woman. She was the matriarch of the family that ran an Indonesian restaurant where Nan and Maddie used to go when they were in school. She could have been fifty or ninety - it was impossible to tell as her bright black eyes peered from a face wizened and wrinkled by a hard life. "The real damage come later, after the winds and rains have battered you and weakened you and you think you cannot hold on any longer. Then the waves and flooding come and try to sweep you away completely."

Nan remembered those eyes gleaming like onyx, staring intently into her own. Had the old woman been telling her future? she wondered as she drove home. Leisa was finally home, life was slowly getting back to some semblance of normal, and just as it had seemed the worst was over... Bill Chisholm had called earlier that day. "Todd has had a relapse," his message on the voice mail said. "He's back in the hospital. If there is any way for you to come now, you probably should."

"How do I tell her I have to leave again her very first week back home?" Nan muttered worriedly as she drove home. She had been hypervigilant, watching for any signs of another emotional breakdown, trying not to let Leisa see her worrying. Leisa still seemed fragile and emotionally distant, often staring off into space for long periods of time, gone somewhere Nan couldn't follow. Yet, she craved touch. She willingly let Nan hold her, and frequently rested an arm or leg where she could stay in contact with Nan, as if making sure she was nearby, but she hadn't indicated she was ready for anything more. Nan guiltily wondered if, after her prior refusals of Leisa's attempts to be intimate, Leisa would be brave enough to initiate anything even if she was ready to make love.

Nan was the first one to arrive home. She paused on the threshold. Over the past several weeks, she'd gotten used to coming home to an empty house, but coming home now, knowing Bronwyn wouldn't be there ever again was still hard. She went to the office and began looking on the Internet for flights to Savannah.

"I'm back here," she called out when she heard Leisa come in the door. She did a double take when Leisa came into the den, still caught off-guard by how haggard Leisa looked. She wasn't the only one to notice.

"I'm not trying to pry," Jo Ann had said to Nan a couple of days earlier, "but she doesn't look good. She's lost I don't know how much weight; she's got dark circles under her eyes. She looks like she's aged twenty years in the last couple of weeks."

Nan weighed her words carefully, trying to reassure Jo Ann without saying too much. "I can't tell you she's really okay," she began. "I'm not sure I even understand everything she's dealing with, but I think she's working through it. And I think coming home was an important step in that process."

"What's up?" Leisa asked now, glancing at the display on the computer monitor.

Nan sighed. "I just heard from Chisholm. Todd is worse. He's back in the hospital. He said I should come now if I can." She stood to face Leisa. "I hate to leave you so soon, but..."

"Oh, Nan," Leisa said, taking her hand. "Of course you should go. I... I wanted to go with you when you went to meet him."

"Really?"

"Yes," Leisa said, laying her hand tenderly on Nan's cheek. "He's part of you. And that makes him part of me. I just don't know how Maddie will feel about me asking for more time off work right now."

Nan looked intently into her eyes. "I love you very much."

Leisa's throat tightened suddenly. She saw the truth of Nan's words in her eyes, and felt that monster stir within her as if it sensed a threat to the hold it still had on her emotions and her memories, roaring in her ears as it felt its grip loosening... "I love you, too," she was able to say over the noise in her head.

Nan looked away, blinking rapidly. "You haven't said that since... since before Williamsburg," she said, her voice cracking a bit.

Leisa pulled Nan to her for a kiss. Tender and gentle at first, her lips parted and the kiss became more assertive. Nan still felt hesitant, and pulled away. "I want you so much," she said softly, "but I want to be sure you're ready for this."

Leisa's eyes were cloudy, unfocused. "I need you," she managed to say, though she seemed to have a hard time speaking. She reached for Nan's hand and pressed it to her breast where Nan could feel the nipple hardening. "I need you," she repeated.

Needing no further encouragement, Nan pulled Leisa's shirt and bra off and laid her back on the couch. They made love, exploring each other's bodies as if doing this for the first time. The ache that had filled both of them exploded in seismic orgasms as their bodies found release denied for months. When they were physically spent, they lay together on the couch, their discarded clothing on the floor.

"I didn't think you were ready for that," Nan said, still breathing heavily, tracing her fingertips over Leisa's ear as Leisa's head rested on her shoulder.

"I didn't either," Leisa admitted, stroking a hand along Nan's ribs. "I haven't felt much of anything for so long..."

"How are you?" Nan asked softly, broaching this subject directly for the first time.

Leisa didn't answer immediately. "Better. Not good... but better."

She was quiet for a while, and then said, "I've never felt like that before. I've never experienced such hopelessness, such absolute despair." Nan held her a little more tightly. "I think I understand better what some of your clients must feel. If I felt like that for very long, I'm not sure it would be worth... I can understand how someone can get to the point of thinking they just want it to stop."

Nan closed her eyes at this admission. "Please," she whispered, "please don't ever - do you need to talk to someone? Someone professionally? I could -"

"No." Leisa lifted her head so she could look into Nan's eyes. "No. I don't need anyone else." She spoke deliberately, trying to make Nan understand. "I don't hurt as badly as I did. It is getting better. It will be better," she added softly as she laid her head back down on Nan's shoulder.

"Yes, you can have the time off for this," Maddie said when Leisa explained about Todd. "I'd go if you weren't. I don't want her doing this by herself. But you have to talk to Mariela before you go."

Mariela had learned so much so quickly that the decision had been made to enroll her in kindergarten for the last grading period of the year. Leisa had taken time that first morning to walk her to school, taking her into the office to introduce her to the school secretary. Mariela gave Leisa one last hug around the waist and went to meet her new classmates. She'd been thrilled to be in school at last and had instantly charmed her teacher, but recently, "she won't go to school," the staff had reported. At first, she'd come down with various ailments - "I have a cold" or "my tummy hurts". The staff, not knowing what was really wrong, had let her stay at the Home where she was content to do her schoolwork, but "now, she's not pretending to be sick. She just refuses to go," they said.

With a pang, Leisa remembered she'd received those reports a couple of weeks ago and had planned to talk to Mariela, but it was all mixed up with everything that had been happening with Eleanor and the surgery and then Bron....

"She won't tell anyone what's wrong," Maddie said in frustration now. "Maybe she'll tell you."

Leisa found Mariela in the classroom where she had once found her practicing her writing. She ran to give Leisa a hug.

"I told you I'd be back," Leisa smiled. She sat down at the next desk and looked at the arithmetic Mariela was working on. "Wow, those are big numbers."

Mariela glowed at the praise.

"I thought you liked school," Leisa prodded.

Mariela's face fell and she lowered her face, letting her hair swing forward. Leisa reached out to brush it back.

"What's going on?"

Mariela only shrugged.

"Has someone been picking on you? The other kids? Don't you like your teacher?" To each of these questions, Mariela would not respond beyond more shrugs. "Can't you tell me why you don't want to go?"

Mariela shook her head.

"Why not?"

"I'm afraid," Mariela whispered.

"Oh." Leisa rubbed Mariela's back. "Tell you what. Miss Maddie has arranged a trip to the zoo later this week. I have to go away again for a few days, but when I get back, I want to hear all about the zoo. And then I will go with you to school."

Mariela looked up. "You will?"

Leisa nodded. "I will. Together, we can tackle whatever it is that's scaring you, okay?"

Mariela thought about this for a moment and then nodded.

———◆———

Nan and Leisa's connecting flight from Atlanta brought them to a warm, slightly humid evening in Savannah. They picked up their rental car and drove straight to their hotel.

"Are you sure you don't want to go to the hospital this evening?" Leisa asked.

Nan shook her head. "I'd rather rest this evening, and go tomorrow."

Leisa knew that Nan wouldn't get much rest, but let it drop. Nan did call the Taylors' house and leave a message that she was in town, and would be at the hospital the next morning by ten.

Nan was quiet all through dinner. Leisa didn't push for conversation. She let Nan have the remote when they got back to the hotel. Nan flipped absent-mindedly through channels until Leisa was regretting her decision.

"I won't know what to say to him," Nan said so softly that Leisa needed a few seconds to register that she had spoken. She reached over for Nan's hand.

"He probably feels the same way. I didn't know what I would say," Leisa told her. "You could let him guide the conversation. He may have lots of questions. Maybe he just wants to get to know you a bit. Relax and see where it goes."

But Nan looked anything but relaxed as they entered the hospital the next morning. Todd was on the oncology ward on the fifth floor. As they neared his room, Nan reached for Leisa's hand and leaned against the wall. She looked like she might pass out.

"I don't think I can do this."

Leisa squeezed her hand reassuringly. "Yes, you can. I'll wait out here."

"No, you won't," Nan insisted as she took a deep breath and knocked softly on the door.

Mr. and Mrs. Taylor were there, sitting in chairs on either side of Todd's bed. They both stood as Nan and Leisa entered. Mrs. Taylor was small-boned and very pretty, in contrast to Mr. Taylor who was a large, burly man who looked like he had been a football player in earlier days. Todd was lying in bed, bald and very thin with dark circles around his eyes, made even more prominent by the oxygen mask covering the lower half of his face.

"Hello, Todd," Nan said nervously as she entered. "I'm Nan Mathison."

She shook hands with Mr. and Mrs. Taylor, and introduced Leisa.

Todd pulled his oxygen mask off. Even with the changes his illness had wrought, his resemblance to Nan was unmistakable. Leisa saw Mrs. Taylor's hand fly, trembling, to her mouth. Todd raised the head of his bed so he could sit up straighter. He stared at Nan as if he were seeing a vision.

"I've wanted to meet you for so long," he said, his eyes hungrily searching her face.

Nan gave a wan smile. "Mr. Chisholm is very persistent." She moved a little closer to the bed. "How are you doing?"

Mr. Taylor answered for him, saying, "He's doing fine. Gonna be up and around in no time, aren't you, boy?"

Leisa looked at him pityingly as he tried so valiantly to deny what was right in front of him.

"Yeah, Dad," Todd said, giving the required response as he smiled at his father. But he turned immediately back to Nan who pulled a chair up closer to the bed. "So," he said shyly, "what do you do?"

"I'm a psychologist," Nan responded.

"How... how old are you?" Todd asked uncertainly. "If you don't mind me asking," he added apologetically.

Nan smiled. "I was in college when you were born."

Todd nodded. "What about my –" he glanced quickly at his father, and faltered. "I mean, what about the guy who got you pregnant?"

Nan looked down at her hands, frowning. "He was someone I knew in college, but... he didn't even know about you." She looked back up at him. "I really can't tell you anything about him."

Todd nodded, thinking. His mouth opened and closed a few times as he vacillated about what to ask next.

"You can ask me anything," Nan prompted gently.

"Why did you give me up?" he blurted.

Nan looked into those eyes so like her own. "I was supposed to start grad school in a few months; I wasn't married or attached to anyone. It just seemed crazy to think about keeping a baby." She paused. "The truth is," she admitted after a moment, "all these

171

years, I've thought of you as a mistake, as something that never should have happened, but," she glanced at his parents, Mr. Taylor's arm wrapped protectively around his wife, "now, I think everything happens for a reason. I wasn't ready to raise you, but I can see that you have been a gift to your parents. So, my mistake turned into something good, after all. I think the hardest part for anyone who gives up a baby is wondering if they made the right decision. Now, I know I did."

———

Nan and Leisa stayed in Savannah for three days. They visited Todd a couple of times a day at the hospital, but he tired quickly, so they kept their visits brief. He turned out to have Nan's wicked sense of humor. When he finally figured out that they were lesbians, he said, "No wonder you thought I was a mistake!" - but he did wait until his parents weren't around to have that conversation.

Leisa watched Nan slowly evolve from stoic resignation at having to meet him to genuinely enjoying talking to him. As she sat there watching them argue about the Ravens' and Falcons' chances in the upcoming football season, she couldn't help but compare this reunion with her own with Eleanor. Todd, who'd always wondered, always felt he'd been given away, was getting to know a woman who really liked him for himself, while she, who'd been content just to know her parents had chosen her, who had never felt abandoned before, felt more abandoned after meeting her biological mother.

"What?" Nan asked one evening as they walked back to their hotel from the hospital.

"You're different with him than I thought you'd be," Leisa said.

Nan thought for a moment. "It's not as bad as I expected," she conceded. "He's a nice kid." She glanced over at Leisa. "Don't."

"Don't what?" Leisa asked.

Nan reached for her hand and held it. "Don't keep wishing and wondering about how things might have been."

"How do you know I am?" Leisa challenged. Nan just looked at her sideways until Leisa laughed a little. "Okay, I am."

"I know you are. I can see it in your eyes when you look at him," Nan said gently. "But you of all people, you who loves to think about alternate realities for every choice we make, should know that if I had decided to keep him, chances are very good that I wouldn't have gone to grad school, wouldn't have stayed near Maddie and would never have met you." She brought Leisa's hand to her lips and kissed it. "Things unfold more or less the way they're meant to."

She smiled as she heard Leisa mutter, "In this reality."

———

Leisa watched Nan and Todd say good-bye, both pretending for Mrs. and Mr. Taylor's sake that they would see each other again, making tentative plans to get together again later that summer, when Todd was strong enough to travel. Nan managed not to cry until they were alone in the elevator. Leisa wrapped her arms around her, oblivious to the other people who got on and off the elevator. As they exited on the ground floor, Nan wiped her eyes on her sleeve. Her cell phone beeped, indicating a text. She checked it, and started laughing and crying at the same time. She held it out so Leisa could read it.

It was from Todd. "How many kids get to have two extra moms?"

———

They were packed and carrying their suitcases down to the rental car when Leisa's phone rang. She stopped in the lobby to dig it out of her pocket. "It's Maddie."

"Hey, when are you guys due back?"

"This evening," Leisa said. "Our plane gets in at seven-forty. Jo and Bruce are supposed to pick us up."

"Tell them we'll pick you up," Maddie said.

"Why? What's wrong?" Leisa asked. Nan leaned near so she could hear.

"It's Mariela. She's missing."

Chapter 20

"THE KIDS WENT ON their field trip to the zoo this morning,"
Maddie reminded Leisa over the phone as she and Nan waïted impa‑
tiently for their plane to board. "The chaperones don't know what
happened. She was with them one minute then gone the next. They
put out an alert and searched the entire zoo, but there was no sign of
her."

Leisa listened to this as she paced. She pressed her other hand to
her eyes, and suddenly froze. "Alarcon."

"What?"

"I never told you," Leisa groaned. "At the cemetery, the day we
buried the ashes, I saw someone I couldn't place at first. Then I real‑
ized it was Alarcon. I forgot all about it until now."

"He was shadowing us?" Maddie asked incredulously.

"He must have been."

Leisa suddenly gasped. "That's why she's been afraid to go to
school! She must have seen him hanging around there, too. You have
to let the police know he's the one who has her," Leisa insisted anx‑
iously.

Nan sat helplessly beside Leisa on a tense, nearly silent flight back to Baltimore, knowing there was nothing she could do or say to comfort her or to ease the guilt she felt. It was a feeling Nan knew from personal experience.

"How is this your fault?" Maddie had asked Nan several years ago when one of her clients had committed suicide. "You can't be responsible for this. You couldn't have known."

"That's just it," Nan tried to explain. "It wasn't anything he said, or threatened to do. It's just that I ran into him downtown, coming out of a pawnshop that specializes in selling guns. I thought it was an odd place for him to be, and I meant to follow-up at our next session, but he cancelled and before I could call him to re-schedule, he had shot himself. If I had taken the time to put the pieces together, if I had made more of an effort and followed up... but I didn't and now he's dead."

"I can't believe I forgot to tell Maddie about him," Leisa kept muttering.

"The police at least know where to start looking now," Nan tried to reassure her. "That's more than they had before."

It was almost eight p.m. when they landed at BWI. Maddie and Lyn were waiting for them. Lyn was driving their Explorer and Maddie was listening to someone on her cell phone as Nan and Leisa slid into the back seat. "All right," Maddie was saying. "Let me know if you find anything."

She turned around in her seat as she hung up. "Nothing yet."

"But they know about Alarcon?" Leisa asked anxiously.

Maddie nodded. "They do. They don't have a current address on him." Seeing the look on Leisa's face, she hastened to add, "But they've circulated his photo and Mariela's to all their patrols and the local news stations. They'll find him."

"What are we going to do?" Leisa asked.

Maddie glanced quickly at Nan before saying emphatically, "'We' are not going to do anything. We're going to let the police handle this."

Nan reached for Leisa's hand. "Maddie's right. Let's go home and wait."

Lyn drove them to their house where she made a pot of decaf, lacing each cup liberally with a couple of shots of Kahlua. "This will help you relax and get some sleep tonight," she said soothingly as Leisa paced anxiously.

"I don't think I'll be able to sleep until she's safe," Leisa fretted. "Why didn't I listen more carefully to her? She had a reason for not wanting to leave St. Joseph's. She knew he was out there. She knew how dangerous he was."

"I'm more at fault than you are," Maddie said miserably. "We all missed it."

———

A few hours later, Nan called Maddie and Lyn in a panic. "She's gone. I woke up, and she wasn't here. I found a note that said she had to try and find Mariela. She said she'd call later. She's not answering her cell. Where would she even start?" Nan asked in bewilderment.

Maddie thought for a minute. "The only place I can think of is the building where Mariela and her mother were living. I'd have to look it up in her file." She mumbled something to Lyn that Nan couldn't make out. "We'll be by to get you in a few minutes."

Together, the three of them drove to St. Joseph's. There, lying open on Leisa's desk was Mariela's file. Maddie quickly found the original police report and wrote the address down.

"This is crazy," Lyn muttered a short while later as they drove into a very bad section of downtown Baltimore. "Shouldn't we call the police?"

"Probably," Maddie admitted, "but if Alarcon is here with Mariela, any sign of the police will make him take off." She drove slowly, reading the street signs while Nan scanned the alleys for any signs of movement.

"Here's Leisa's car. This is it," Maddie said, parking behind the Sentra in front of a run-down brick building that stood five stories high. She pulled a flashlight out of the glove compartment.

They got out of the vehicle, quietly closing the doors. "We're a bunch of lesbians, for crying out loud. Why didn't we at least bring baseball bats?" Lyn asked nervously.

"Because we don't play softball?" Nan reminded her.

"Let's look around the outside first," Maddie suggested. "See if we see any sign of Leisa or Mariela."

Staying close together, the three of them walked down the alley that ran along one side of the building. There were several overflowing dumpsters and the equally strong odors of rotting trash and stale urine.

"This is disgusting," Nan whispered.

"This is what Mariela came from," Maddie replied, also whispering.

They all jumped at a rustling in the shadows near one of the dumpsters. Maddie aimed her flashlight in the direction of the sound. A homeless man sat up, peering at them with bleary eyes as he tried to shade his eyes from the harsh beam of light. Reaching into her pocket, Maddie pulled out a couple of bills and crouched near the man, lowering her flashlight.

"Have you seen a little Latina girl around here today?" she asked in a low voice.

The man squinted at her, then at the money in her hand. "There's lots a them Mexicans lives here," he said.

"This little girl used to live here, but hasn't for a while. She may have come back here today, maybe with a Latino man." She dangled the money, but didn't offer it to him yet.

The man wiped a grimy hand across his eyes. "I seen 'em. I think she ran away from him, 'cause he was cussing in Mexican, lookin' for her." He chuckled. "He didn't find her, though. That little chica knows how to hide."

"Thanks," Maddie said, holding the money out to him. As he reached for it, she yanked it out of reach again. "Is there a back way into this building?"

Scowling, he jerked his head to the left. "There's a door to the basement down there. It's s'posed to be locked, but the lock is broken."

Maddie gave him the money and got to her feet. "Ready?" she asked, leading the way to the door the man had indicated.

Spying a broken pallet leaning against the wall, Nan tore a piece of two-by-four loose and, thus armed, followed Maddie and Lyn inside.

———

"Where is it?"

Leisa glared up at Pedro Alarcon who was pacing agitatedly, his hand spasmodically gripping and releasing the butt of the revolver tucked in the waist of his pants. She worked her jaw back and forth, trying to tell if it was broken. She could feel her lips swelling and taste the blood inside her mouth.

Alarcon was the only man Florida Gonzalez had been truly afraid of. Most other men were stupid, especially if she could get them drunk or hard. Then they only thought of one thing. Occasionally, one of them might hit her if he was a mean drunk, or couldn't get off, but mostly, they were easy to manipulate. Not Alarcon.

He was never drunk or stoned. Florida had never seen him with one of the girls. He was always in control, and he was dangerous. One night, she had watched in horror as he slit the throat of one of the other girls, slowly, as if he was enjoying it. Calmly, he looked up at her as he wiped the bloody blade on the woman's dress and Florida knew that he would do the same to her if she said a word. She warned Mariela, "Never let him see you. Hide when he's here." Now she would have said to Leisa, "Be careful what you say."

"I asked you a question, bitch," he said, standing over her as she sat on the floor of the empty apartment. He drew the revolver and aimed it at her.

She had no idea what he was talking about, but whatever it was, he wanted it badly. She didn't think he was likely to shoot. She decided to stall. "Where's Mariela?" she countered.

It was apparently the wrong question, as he responded by kicking at her viciously, catching her in the right flank. Gasping in pain, she tried to catch her breath, grateful she didn't have a kidney on that side anymore because she was certain it would no longer function if she did.

"I know she told you where it is!" he shouted, sounding desperate. "Why else would you be here?"

Blinking rapidly, trying to clear her vision, Leisa managed to croak, "I don't know what you're talking about."

Mariela saw all of this while peering through a tiny crack in the door of her hiding place. A couple of years ago, she had discovered a sliding panel at the back of one of the closets in their apartment. It opened to reveal a kind of dumb waiter that was originally intended for moving tools and maintenance supplies from one floor to another. If there were clothes or boxes in the closet, it was nearly undetectable. When Mariela found it, it hadn't been used in decades, but the well-greased pulleys were still operational. She discovered how to manipulate the pulley system to take her all the way down to the basement. This was how she got in and out of the building most of the time, especially when her mother had men in the apartment. She had remained silently crouching in the cramped space for the past several hours, since she'd managed to get away from the man who took her from the zoo.

She knew what he wanted. Her mama had given it to her the day before she died, saying, "Take this, Mariela, and give it to the *policía*. They will know what to do with it."

Mariela had taken the bundle, but was too afraid to go to the police. The police had taken her mama away before, and she knew they would do the same with her. She had hidden the bundle on the top of the moving carriage instead. When she returned to the apartment late that night, her mama was still and wouldn't wake. She was like that sometimes. But this time she didn't wake up the next day or the day after that. Then the police did find her, and then Leisa came.

Silently, Mariela slid open the access panel above her, and cautiously reached up, feeling for the bundle. It was still where she'd left it. She was just about to pull it down, when she heard the sound of the basement door being opened four stories below her, as even quiet sounds were magnified if you were inside the shaft.

"Mariela?"

Startled, Mariela heard her name being whispered from below.

"Mariela, it's Miss Maddie. If you're here, let me help you."

Mariela quickly peeked through the crack again. Leisa was on her side on the floor, and Mariela could hear the pacing footsteps of the man. She knew he could hurt Leisa because he used to hurt her mama. Carefully, she began pulling the ropes that moved the box down. She hoped the box would still move silently like it did before.

When she got to the basement, she slid open the door that closed off her carriage. There, she saw the beam of the flashlight, but couldn't tell who was behind it. She knew better than to show herself if she wasn't sure who was there.

"What floor did Mariela and her mother live on?" a voice whispered.

"I think the apartment number was 4C," another voice whispered.

"I'm here," Mariela said softly, scaring all three of the women.

The flashlight beam whipped through the darkness, illuminating her as she stood outside the dumb waiter. Maddie rushed over to her and dropped to her knees, hugging Mariela to her.

"Oh, honey, are you all right?" Maddie asked.

Mariela nodded. "He has Miss Leisa. She's hurt."

Maddie released her and held her at arm's length. "Where?"

"Upstairs," Mariela replied.

Maddie thought quickly. "Lyn, you need to go call the police. Lock yourself in the car until they come, and then bring them up to the fourth floor." She looked at the dumb waiter. "Does this open directly into your apartment? Is that where Leisa is?"

Mariela nodded. "It's my secret place. He has her up there."

"I'll never fit in there," Maddie muttered.

"I'll go," Nan offered. "You go up the stairs. Maybe if we surprise him from two sides, we can get the upper hand before he hurts Leisa." She was trying not to picture what might be happening upstairs.

"All right," Maddie agreed. She watched for a few seconds as Nan squeezed into the carriage with Mariela. "Be careful."

Mariela was the only person who could recall later precisely what happened. When the dumb waiter got up to her old apartment, she and Nan peered through the crack at the edge of the door. The only thing they could see were Leisa's legs all askew. She seemed to be lying on her side. They could see no sign of Alarcon.

Nan knew they had to have gotten up to the fourth floor faster than Maddie could by the stairs. Just as she decided to wait a couple more minutes to give Maddie time to get up there, Alarcon stepped into view, a knife in his hand.

"If you don't know where it is, *puta*, then you are of no use to me," he said menacingly.

Without thinking, Nan slid the door open and ran at Alarcon. He saw movement behind him, but before he could react, Nan hit him on the side of the head with her two-by-four, dropping him senseless to the floor.

Mariela scrambled after her, running to Leisa who was conscious, but clutching her side, blood running from her mouth.

Leisa looked up at Nan who dropped her two-by-four, breathing hard and looking stunned by what she had just done. She rushed to Leisa's side and helped her sit up.

"Are you all right?" she demanded. "What did he do to you?"

"I'm okay," Leisa reassured her. "Just a little bruised."

Then several things happened simultaneously - Mariela's eyes widened as she screamed and pointed; Nan turned her head just in time to see Alarcon moving; without thinking, she threw herself across Leisa and Mariela; behind him, Maddie burst through the door. Alarcon was raising the handgun and fired two quick shots as Maddie tackled him from behind, planting her knee on his neck and mashing his face painfully into the floor. She grabbed the two-by-four and bashed his forearm as he fired a third shot. The snap of the bones was masked by his howl of pain.

A couple of seconds later, three police officers ran into the apartment, closely followed by Lyn.

"What the f-?" one of the officers began upon surveying the scene.

He was stopped mid-word by a jab in the ribs from the female officer next to him.

"Leisa?" said the third officer as he recognized her still sitting with her back to the wall, a bullet hole in the plaster not a foot from her head.

"Matt," she smiled, although her swollen, bloody lips made that an effort.

Matt Wellby scanned the bizarre scene before him. His eyes lit on Mariela. "Isn't -" he pointed. "Isn't that the little girl you came down for last winter?" he asked in complete bewilderment.

"Ma'am?" the female officer interrupted, looking at Nan who was swaying where she sat.

"Nan!" Leisa cried, reaching for her as she slumped to the floor, a growing patch of crimson spreading across her back.

Chapter 21

"WHAT WERE YOU PLAYING AT?"

No one voiced that question aloud, but Leisa knew they must have been thinking it, because she was.

Impatiently, she had shrugged off the paramedics who tried to examine her in the apartment. "I'm fine," she repeated emphatically, insisting they take care of Nan.

It didn't matter that the police finally had enough evidence to charge Pedro Alarcon with various crimes, aided by Mariela when she produced a paper-wrapped bundle that contained thousands of dollars and a large plastic bag of heroin.

It didn't matter that Leisa was injured, her still-healing abdomen bruised and bleeding internally where she'd been kicked. She refused to stay in her hospital room once Nan was out of surgery, insisting on sitting by her bed in the ICU to receive her own transfusion.

"What were you playing at?"

That wasn't how the police worded it, but that was the implication as they gathered data for their report, and the entire story fell into place.

She'd known it was foolish, to say the least, to wander into that part of town at that hour of the night, to think she had any chance of finding Mariela on her own, but "I couldn't sit and do nothing while Mariela was in danger," she would have explained, except then she would have had to add, "because it was all my fault." Only now, because of her, Nan was the one in danger.

Mariela sensed Leisa's anguish and felt she was to blame.

"None of this is your fault," Maddie said, trying to make Mariela understand. "You were very smart and very brave to be able to get away from him and stay safe." She and Lyn took Mariela back to St. Joseph's as the ambulance pulled away with Nan and Leisa inside.

The bullet had bored through Nan's right lung, piercing one of the pulmonary arteries, and it had taken hours of careful surgery to repair the delicate tissue. She'd lost a tremendous amount of blood, and looked very pale and fragile as she lay there, not really unconscious, but medicated into a heavy stupor with a chest tube and vacuum pump in place.

Leisa reached through the bedside rails and held Nan's hand. "Please, don't leave me," she whispered, trying to quell the fear of that shadow, that presence she knew was looming there, waiting to pull her back into its grasp.

———

"What's the bravest thing you've ever done?" Leisa had asked as she stood on a ladder, carefully running her paintbrush along the ceiling's edge, cutting in so Nan could roll paint onto the walls of the living room.

Nan shook her head. "I will never understand how your mind works," she said somewhat absently as she concentrated on not hitting the ceiling with her roller. "It bounces along like a tumbleweed, and random thoughts pop out of your mouth. I never know what's going to come out."

Leisa laughed. "Stop stalling and answer. What's the bravest thing you've ever done?"

"Buying this house with you," Nan answered.

Leisa paused long enough to look down at her ruefully. "Be serious."

"I am being serious," Nan replied, risking a quick glance up at her. "This is scary shit. I'm tied to you legally now." She shook her head. "I never thought I'd be doing this in my lifetime."

Leisa came down off the ladder and wrapped her paintbrush arm around Nan's neck, kissing her.

Nan pulled back and looked askance at the paintbrush. "If you get that in my hair, you are going to get this roller someplace you don't want it," she warned.

"Are you sorry?" Leisa asked.

"Sorry about threatening you with this roller?"

"No, silly," Leisa said with a grin. "Sorry about buying this house with me?"

Nan wrapped her free arm around Leisa's waist and drew her close, kissing her again. "No. I'm not sorry."

"So what's the bravest thing you've ever done?" Leisa asked insistently.

"You are like a dog with a bone," Nan sighed in resignation. "Nothing," she shrugged. She thought about Marcus and never standing up to her mother in his defense, and she thought about giving up her baby to strangers because she didn't want to be saddled with the responsibility, and she shook her head. "I've never done anything brave in my life," she said flatly.

———◆———

Leisa recalled that conversation as she sat there, and thought about all the things she knew now that she hadn't known then, all the times Nan had sacrificed herself for others.

"You are the bravest person I know," she whispered.

"No," Nan mumbled groggily. "I was just the closest target."

"You're awake!" Leisa stood, clutching her own side in pain as she leaned over the bed rails to kiss Nan's forehead.

"I think that's the only place that doesn't hurt," Nan grimaced as she tried to sit up a little higher in bed.

"I don't think you should move yet," Leisa said worriedly.

"Oh, I think you're right," Nan agreed, sinking back into the same depression in the mattress. She looked up at Leisa. "How are you?"

"I'm fine," Leisa said, brushing Nan's hair back off her forehead. "I'm so sorry. I shouldn't have gone down there."

Nan squeezed Leisa's other hand, still clasped in hers. "You had to go."

"I couldn't bear the thought of losing someone else, but then I almost lost you," Leisa said, her eyes filling suddenly.

"You almost got yourself killed," Nan reminded her.

"You saved our lives, Mariela's and mine."

Nan laughed a little and immediately winced. "I don't know who that was, but it wasn't me."

"Oh, yes it was," Leisa said. "You can't fool me anymore. I've seen you without your mask on and I know who you are." She kissed Nan's hand tenderly. "You're my hero."

"There you are," said Jo Ann when she found Leisa sitting in the family room, staring out the window.

Jo and Bruce had insisted that Leisa come home with them when she was discharged from the hospital, and told Nan they expected her, too, whenever her doctor released her. Jo drove her over to visit Nan briefly each day, but reminded Leisa that she was still supposed to be resting.

"I keep forgetting to ask if you've ever heard from the people in New York," Jo Ann said casually as she sat at the other end of the couch. She rarely called them by name, and never, Leisa noted, referred to them as her biological mother or brother.

Leisa looked at her aunt. She hadn't told anyone about that last day in the hospital in Syracuse. "I don't really expect to hear from them," she said vaguely, turning back to the window.

"What is it, honey?" Jo Ann asked. "You've been so quiet."

Leisa didn't answer for long seconds. "I've made such a mess of things." She blinked hard, not wanting Jo to see her crying. "They didn't..." She pressed her fingers to her eyes, ashamed to admit, even to herself, how much she had wanted them, wanted Eleanor, to want her.

"They got what they wanted and didn't need you anymore?" Jo Ann guessed astutely.

"I know I sound horrible," Jo had confessed to Nan back when they were still waiting for the results of the bloodwork, "but I hope she isn't a match. I know I shouldn't deny the poor boy a kidney –"

"He's not a boy," Nan interrupted. "He's a twenty-eight-year-old man who sponges off his mother and does absolutely nothing to keep himself healthy. And I know exactly what you mean," she sighed.

"I'm worried about Leisa," Jo said. "I don't really understand what she thinks she's going to find with these people, but I'm afraid she's going to get hurt."

Nan looked at Jo and nodded. "I know. It's like... like she's lost. Like she's searching for – I don't know what. I'm not sure even she knows what she's searching for, but I agree with you," she said darkly. "I don't think she's going to find it with them."

Jo Ann reached out now and squeezed Leisa's knee. "Was it so important to be part of that family?"

"No, it's just..." Leisa wiped her eyes impatiently. "I don't know why it mattered so much. I am such an idiot."

"You're not an idiot," Jo said reassuringly. "But you have a family here that loves you."

Leisa couldn't meet her aunt's eye. "I've messed things up so badly," she said again, turning back to the window. "How do I fix that? How do we go back to the way we were before?"

"Life is never the same after monsoon," the old Indonesian woman would have told her. "All the things you know, wiped away like they were never there. You start over, build new. Try to make stronger than before so next monsoon cannot wash it away."

The day Nan was discharged, Maddie and Lyn picked her up from the hospital and took her to the Gallaghers' house. Leisa heard them come in and rushed to the foyer to throw her arms around Nan. Almost immediately she let go.

"Did I hurt you?" she asked anxiously.

"No," Nan smiled. "That's the best medicine I've had. Well, almost the best," she added, stepping aside.

There, standing between Lyn and Maddie, was Mariela. Mutely, Leisa knelt down and hugged her.

"Mariela has been very worried about both of you and insisted on seeing for herself that you're all right," Maddie said.

Leisa pulled back so she could look at Mariela. "We're fine," said with a questioning glance at Nan who nodded her agreement. "How are you?"

"I'm okay," Mariela shrugged.

"When you and Nan feel up to it," said Maddie, "we thought it might be nice if all of us took a trip to the zoo since the last one didn't go as planned."

"That sounds like fun," Nan said to Leisa's astonishment.

"If you expect to eat tonight, I need help in the kitchen," Jo Ann announced. "Except for you," she said sternly to Nan. "You sit and rest."

"I've done nothing but rest," Nan complained.

"All right," Jo conceded. "I do have a job for you."

A few minutes later, Jo Ann had Nan and Mariela seated at the dining room table with a bowl of icing for the chocolate cake while everyone else helped Jo in the kitchen. Leisa stood at the island where she could watch them as she made a salad.

"I've had some bad dreams about what happened," Nan said as she spread a big gob of icing.

"You have?" Mariela looked at her with wide eyes as she knelt on her chair to reach the cake.

"Mmm hmm, and then I can't go back to sleep."

Several seconds passed as they both concentrated on the cake. "Me, too," Mariela admitted finally.

Nan scraped some more icing out of the bowl. "Have you said anything to Miss Maddie or anyone else?" she asked.

Mariela shook her head.

"It's normal to be scared after what we went through," said Nan.

"It is?" Mariela asked doubtfully. "I bet Miss Leisa isn't scared."

"I'll bet she is," Nan whispered loudly enough for Leisa to hear.

"Are you?" Mariela asked, looking over at Leisa with her spatula suspended in mid-air.

Leisa nodded. "I have bad dreams, too. But when I wake up, I remember that he's in jail and the people I love are safe."

Mariela resumed icing the cake, frowning and biting her lower lip. "What people?" she asked after a while.

"What do you mean?" Leisa asked as she sliced cucumbers.

"You said, 'the people I love'," said Mariela very softly.

Leisa and Nan's eyes locked. Leisa put her knife down and came to the table. Kneeling between Nan and Mariela, she put an arm around each of them. "You and Maddie and Nan, of course. I love you all," she said.

"I love you, too," Mariela said happily, wrapping her arms around Leisa's neck.

Trying not to laugh, Nan gently pried the icing-covered spatula from Leisa's hair just before Mariela turned around and hugged her as well.

"Oh, for goodness' sake," Jo Ann burst out from the kitchen where she, Lyn and Maddie were all drying their eyes. "We're never going to eat if you keep this up."

Chapter 22

"OH, MY GOSH, IT feels so good to be back in our own home," Nan sighed contentedly as she eased herself down on their bed.

Leisa had gone back to work over the past week, but Nan was still very easily tired and had not yet resumed scheduling clients. "I think I'm going to refer a lot of these people on to other therapists," she'd said, looking over her client list. "I'm going to lighten my load."

"I think that is an excellent idea," Maddie said when she heard.

"I know," Leisa agreed now, stretching out beside her. "Jo Ann and Bruce were wonderful, but I am so glad to be home." She rolled over and nestled her head on Nan's shoulder. "I've been thinking... it's time to sell Mom's house."

"Really?" Nan rested her cheek against Leisa's head. "Are you sure you're ready to do that?"

Leisa was quiet for a moment. "It feels like the right thing to do."

"You know I'll help any way I can," Nan said.

Leisa gave her a gentle squeeze. "Thanks, but you're going to be exhausted going back to work. I'll ask Jo to help me get things packed up and I'll contact a real estate agent."

They lay there silently for several minutes, before Leisa propped up on her elbow, looking down at Nan. "There's something else I have to do," she said seriously. "But I want to make sure you're okay with it."

"What is it?"

Leisa took a deep breath before responding. "I need to see Sarah again. I need to tell her I don't want to have anything more to do with her. If I just leave it the way it is now, if I never go back there –"

"I understand," Nan said. "And I think you're right. This will continue to hang over you, over us, if you don't get some resolution."

Leisa flopped back to the mattress in relief. "Thank you for understanding. I don't think I can do it this week. I'm so far behind at work, but I'll get over there soon." She glanced over at Nan. "How about something to eat? Jo sent us home with enough food to get us through next winter."

———

Leisa worked feverishly for the next few days, trying to get current on her case files, making and returning telephone calls and e-mails. Her work was inconveniently interrupted by her mind's frequent wanderings to her hypothetical conversation with Sarah. This was not something she was looking forward to, but she'd known ever since she ran away to Ithaca that this was inevitable.

On Thursday, she felt like she could finally breathe at work, and called Nan at lunchtime. "I'm going to go by the gym after work today," she said.

"All right. I'll see you when you get home," Nan replied.

Leisa felt a little foolish as she blurted, "I love you," before Nan could hang up.

She thought she could hear Nan smile. "I know."

She couldn't remember what kind of car Sarah drove, but she scanned the cars in the gym parking lot anyway. Realizing Sarah might be with a client and she would have to wait to talk to her, Leisa entered the gym. She'd thought about bringing clothes and actually working out, but "No," she'd said to herself. "It puts you too much in Sarah's realm and you need to be in control for a change." Sarah was with a client in the free weight area; Leisa saw her reflected in one of the mirrors. She took a seat in the lobby, waiting and trying not to fidget. When the client's session was over, Sarah came to the staff desk and smiled when she saw Leisa.

"Hi," she said, coming over to Leisa and sitting beside her, a little too closely. "Where've you been? I haven't seen you since..." She let her voice trail off suggestively, eyebrows raised a little.

In an instant, all of Leisa's nervousness disappeared. "I've been out of town, but I realized it probably looks like I've been avoiding you and I wanted to clear that up."

Sarah's expression shifted as she picked up on the cool tone of Leisa's voice. She looked around quickly, checking to see who might be within hearing distance. "Why don't we go –"

"No," Leisa cut her off, not bothering to lower her voice. "I don't need to go anywhere with you. I just want to tell you very clearly, so that there is no misunderstanding, that I don't want to be touched by you, or kissed by you, or fucked by you ever again." She stood. "I'm not changing gyms, and when I come in here, I expect you to behave appropriately, staff to client."

She almost whooped out loud as she walked to her car. It was so liberating to feel for the first time since she'd met her that she wasn't under Sarah's control. "Fifteen years it's taken you, but you finally did it," she crowed as she started her engine.

She was still feeling jubilant as she pulled up in front of the house, noting a strange car parked in front of Nan's on the curb. Nan met her in the foyer as she entered.

"Hi," she said nervously before Leisa could say anything. "We have a surprise visitor."

Puzzled, Leisa looked past her as a tall, thin figure entered the foyer. It took her a few seconds to recognize Todd. "Oh, my."

—◆—

Todd, it turned out, had arrived without warning mid-afternoon. "We've almost got dinner ready," Nan said, leading Leisa into the kitchen with a warning look that Leisa understood to mean, "Don't ask questions, I'll explain later."

Leisa poured drinks for everyone while Todd finished setting the table and Nan got the hamburgers off the grill. When they were all seated at the table, Leisa said, "Todd, you look good, much better than the last time we saw you."

"Yeah," he responded with a half-smile. "Another miracle."

"So this has happened before?" Nan asked. "You've responded to treatment?"

Todd nodded morosely. "For a few months, maybe a year, then it always comes back, worse than before."

Leisa watched him and couldn't help feeling sorry for him, his still-bald head making his eyes seem very large. "Do your parents –" She stopped abruptly, remembering she wasn't supposed to ask questions.

"He's going to call them after dinner," Nan said pointedly.

Todd grinned sheepishly. "I know I shouldn't have left like that..."

"No, you shouldn't have," Nan agreed. "They must be worried sick. But we will talk about that later."

Todd ate ravenously, downing three hamburgers, a large helping of green beans and a whole bag of potato chips. Apparently his appetite was coming back faster than his hair. He talked about his drive up north – he'd left Savannah yesterday afternoon and driven through the night. "It was so cool," he said, his eyes bright. "Just me and some loud music and the windows down. I've never been anywhere by myself."

When he was done eating, Nan asked him to go call his parents while she and Leisa cleaned the kitchen. "And be sure to tell them this was not my idea," Nan called after him, "or they'll think I'm trying to steal you back." He grinned again as he disappeared into the living room.

"Did you have any idea?" Leisa whispered.

"None," Nan whispered back. "He called me when he got to D.C."

"What's going on?"

Nan shook her head. "I have a guess, but he hasn't said yet." She turned at the sound of Todd entering the kitchen.

"It's my mom," he said, holding out the phone. "Would you talk to her?"

Leisa saw Nan's jaw clench, but she took the phone. "Hello, Mrs. Taylor... No, I didn't know anything about this," she said with a stern glance at Todd who refused to look abashed. "Please... look, he's here and safe now. Let him rest tonight and he'll call you again tomorrow... all right... good-bye."

"And now," she said as she handed Todd's cell phone back to him, "we are going to talk."

"Could I have a beer?" Todd asked hopefully.

"Absolutely not!"

Leisa choked back a laugh as Nan pointed to the refrigerator and said, "You can have another Coke."

"I'll go upstairs –" Leisa started.

"No!" blurted out Nan and Todd simultaneously.

"Okay..." Leisa said, realizing she was going to be some kind of referee. "Let's go to the living room."

Todd's long, skinny legs folded almost double as he sat on the couch.

"Now," began Nan. "What happened?"

Todd's expression became serious for the first time. "It's more like, 'what didn't happen'," he said. "What never happens." He played with the tab on his soda can. "My parents... especially my dad, they just won't talk about it."

"About your leukemia?" Nan prodded gently.

Todd nodded. "He pretends like I have something I could get better from if I just tried harder," he said in frustration. "Every time it goes into remission, he talks like it's gone and life is normal and now I can go out for football." Todd's jaw worked back and forth a few times before he added quietly, "Sometimes I just wish it was over."

"That part must be really hard, the ups and downs of getting better only to get sick again," Nan said.

197

Todd nodded again, keeping his eyes focused on his soda can. "The first few times, you believe them; you believe you can get better, but..." He swallowed hard. "Not any more. It's just a waiting game."

They all sat in silence for a long moment before Leisa tentatively said, "You know, I can kind of understand where your dad is coming from, though. If you were... if you were our son, I wouldn't be able to stand the thought of letting you go, and talking like it's not going to happen would push it back, make it not so real."

Todd glanced at her and shrugged his understanding of what she'd said. "Maybe. I never thought of it like that."

"But it also means you haven't had anyone you could talk to about what it's like to face death," Nan said, as Leisa winced a little at her direct approach to such a horrible topic, but Todd's expression brightened.

"Yes!" he said with the relief of one who has been released from an evil spell compelling him to be silent. He leaned forward, bony elbows resting on bonier knees, and began talking. It seemed a dam had been broken as he began talking, finally able to express all the things he hadn't been able to talk about to anyone else. He wasn't emotional or morbid, but facing the possibility, the probability, of death had been his reality for nearly half of his life.

Nan and Leisa listened attentively. Nan asked questions every now and then, but mostly she listened.

"There have been times," Todd was saying, "usually at night, when I'm laying there, and..." He stopped, clearly embarrassed.

"Go on," Leisa said softly.

"It's like, I can feel someone there in the room with me," he said as if he was afraid they would think he was crazy. "Like that movie."

"*City of Angels*," said Nan.

"Yes!" His eyes lit up. "Like one of them is there, and if I was ready, I could just go and they'd take me... wherever." His face burned a deep crimson. "You probably think I'm nuts," he said with a half-laugh.

"I don't think that's crazy at all," Nan said. Leisa shook her head in agreement.

"Really?" Todd asked, looking at them for any sign that they were laughing at him.

"Not at all," said Nan. "I absolutely believe we go on from here, that the people who loved us will be waiting for us."

"But you haven't been ready to let go yet," Leisa observed.

Todd shrugged a little.

"So maybe you still have things you're supposed to do here," she suggested. "Maybe your job here isn't done."

———

Daniel pushed himself up from his chair, grimacing in pain and grabbing for his walker. Leisa rushed over to him. "Dad," she said, wrapping an arm around him, "what do you need? Let me get it for you." She could feel all of his ribs. He was down to about a hundred twenty pounds after several months of chemo and radiation. Despite the treatments, his prostate cancer had metastasized to his spine and pelvis, becoming much more painful.

"I'm fine, little girl," he said. "Got to keep moving. Where's your mother?"

"I think she's at the computer," Leisa said.

Daniel's expression darkened. "Come with me," he said, leading the way slowly up the stairs to the office where Rose was searching the Internet.

"Hi, honey," she said, glancing up.

"Rose –"

"I've been finding all kinds of information..."

"Rose –"

"...on holistic treatments and other types of chemo we can ask about..."

"Rose!" Daniel said more forcefully.

Rose froze at the computer. Behind her, Daniel shuffled to a chair and lowered himself to it. Leisa knelt beside him, holding his hand, her heart pounding.

"Rose," he said again, more gently this time. "We have to talk."

She sat stiffly and silently, staring at the computer monitor.

"I can't," Daniel said simply. "I can't go through any more. It's time."

Leisa closed her eyes as tears sprang to them. She hadn't wanted to cry in front of her father, but she couldn't help it.

Over at the computer, Rose's shoulders shook as she cried silently.

"I want to enjoy the days I have left with my girls," Daniel said affectionately.

As far as Leisa knew, her mother did all her crying that afternoon. She was sure she must have cried more, but Leisa never saw it. They called hospice when Daniel couldn't easily get out of bed anymore, and within three weeks of that conversation, he was gone. He died peacefully, at home, with his family around him. "Don't be afraid," he said to Leisa the day before he died. "It's not hard if you're ready."

———◆———

"You're still here for some reason, Todd," Leisa said, though talking was hard as she remembered that afternoon with her parents. "As much as you trust that there's someone waiting for you when it's time, you need to trust that they haven't taken you because there's something you haven't completed yet."

———◆———

Todd's father wanted to fly up to Baltimore immediately on Friday to drive back to Georgia with him. Nan convinced him to give Todd a couple of days. "He's dealing with a lot, and it would probably do him some good to have some time away from... from doctors and hospitals," she quickly amended. "You can call anytime you want, and I promise we'll call you if he gets sick."

Leisa went to work on Friday, Nan's last scheduled day home before returning to work the following week.

"You sure you'll be okay?" Leisa asked.

Nan sighed in resignation. "I have to admit, it's not how I planned to spend my last day at home, but we'll be fine." With a touch of wry humor, she added, "I feel like this is a warm-up for my clients."

Todd slept in late and had two huge bowls of cereal for breakfast.

"How about a walk?" she suggested when he was done. "I could use some exercise."

"I don't want to tell him what happened with the shooting," Nan had insisted. "He's got enough drama in his life. We'll just say I've been sick if he asks."

She led the way now to the park, passing houses where azaleas and dogwoods and redbud were just coming into bloom. Todd looked around at everything with interest. "These already bloomed down in Georgia," he observed.

"I remember," Nan said. "Savannah's beautiful."

"Yeah."

"What are your plans for the summer?" she asked as they walked.

Todd rolled his eyes. "There's a family reunion in June," he said dully.

Nan looked up at him curiously. "You don't want to go?"

He shook his head. "Both sides of the family are the same, but this is my mom's side. There's tons of them."

"So what's the problem?" Nan asked.

Todd bent down to pick up a stick and began peeling the bark off as he walked. "I don't fit in."

"What do you mean?"

He walked a few more steps before saying, "Well, the cancer thing for one. No one ever knows what to say to me. They never ask me where I'll be going to college or anything about the future."

"Does that make you feel like they've already written you off?" Nan probed.

Todd looked down at her and smiled. "You're the only one who says the things everyone is thinking, but won't say out loud."

Nan laughed. "Lots of practice trying to figure people out. You do know that they just don't want to remind you of what you might not have. Death is an awkward topic of conversation. It's hard trying to know what's okay to say and what's not. Especially with a young person."

"I know," he admitted, snapping the stick in his hands. "Plus... I'm the only one who's adopted," he added as if it didn't matter.

"Is that a problem for the relatives? I mean, your parents obviously are proud of you and love you very much," she reminded him.

"Yeah, but, we're in the South. I swear, every time we get together with any relatives, someone makes some comment about 'blood being thicker than water' or 'family is everything'. And all the comments about how much the grandkids look like this person or that person..." He released an exasperated breath.

Nan thought about the things Leisa had said to her over the years. "And you don't look like anyone. Don't you feel like family?"

Todd looked skyward as he struggled to explain. "It's not me. It's like... every time someone says something about family, they look at me real quick like they're afraid they said something that would offend me, so it's more like they don't think of me as family."

Nan laughed and said, "Believe me, even when you're born into a family, you can feel like you aren't part of it." She proceeded to tell him a little about her family.

"Wow," Todd said after listening. "Your family is more screwed up than mine."

"You know, it's really weird talking to you about this, because, technically, I suppose they're your family, too, except they don't know anything about you."

Todd was quiet for a few seconds. "You didn't tell them about me?"

Nan shook her head. "I only told one person. And she will kill me if she finds out you're here and she didn't get to see you."

That evening, Maddie stood in their kitchen, the only person tall enough to look Todd level in the eye, and said, "Oh, my gosh, I held you right after you were born. You fit in my two hands. I can't believe this... you're all grown up." She looked him up and down. "You're still bald, but you looked different naked."

Todd snorted with laughter, choking on his Coke. When he could talk, he looked from Maddie to Lyn and asked, "So, are you two...?"

"Yes," said Lyn, coming over and wrapping her arm around Maddie's waist. "We are."

"Cool," he grinned. "My parents would so freak out," he said, sounding very happy at the thought.

Dinner conversation was especially animated that evening as Todd had them all in stitches with his stories.

"What a great kid," Lyn said later as she wrapped leftovers and put them in the refrigerator.

"Leisa thinks so, too," Nan said.

"You don't?" Lyn asked in surprise.

"No, it's not that," Nan said quickly. "But I think she keeps looking at him and wishing he was ours. I think she identifies with him in a lot of ways, like not looking like the rest of your family." Her expression shifted suddenly as she thought of something. "I'll be right back."

She went to the den and opened the cupboard at the base of the built-in bookshelves there. "It's in here somewhere," she muttered to herself as she sifted through the files and records stored there. At last, she pulled out a large leather folio fastened with a leather strap. The flap was embossed with an ornate T.

———————

"Come here," Nan's grandmother said, calling Nan into her bedroom which was normally off-limits to the grandchildren. Nan sat in one of the two chairs there, upholstered in the same formal black toile as the wallpaper, while her grandmother sat in the other, holding a large album in her lap.

"Has your mother ever told you about your grandfather or great-grandfather?" she asked, looking at Nan through her wire-rimmed glasses. She scowled when Nan shook her head no. "I'm not surprised, though I don't see where your mother gets the idea she has the right to put on airs just because she married a lawyer."

She flipped open the album. "It's time you know what kind of people you come from."

Nan loved spending time with her grandmother. "She really talks to me. She asks me what I think, like I'm a grown-up," she sometimes longed to brag to Bradley and Miranda, but she was afraid they would ruin it somehow.

Nan leaned over so she could better see as her grandmother showed her an old photograph of three young men. "This is your great-grandfather," she said, pointing to the middle of the three with her knobbly, arthritic finger, "and these are his brothers. Together, they started a logging company and sawmill near Mt. Hood." She flipped the pages of the album as she talked, showing Nan more photos of the brothers and other men in their logging camp, floating logs down a portion of the Columbia River to their sawmill.

"And this," she said, turning another page, "is your grandfather, just as he looked when I met him." A small smile softened her sharp features. Nan recognized a photo of her grandfather as a young man, standing next to a felled tree whose diameter exceeded his height by two or three feet. "Your grandfather had the smarts to realize that after the war people wouldn't just need lumber for houses, they would need stores that sold everything to build houses. That's when he started Tollin Building Supply. Before long, he had five stores all around Portland. We ran those stores together," she said proudly, her eyes misting a little. "But your mother," she said sharply, sounding much more like her usual self, "seems to think there's some shame in having parents who were shopkeepers. Your grandfather was a good, honest man," she added, turning to a professionally done portrait of him in a suit and tie. "If you can find a man like that, you'll be happy."

———————

Nan smiled now, remembering that misguided bit of advice as she flipped through the album. This had been the sole thing bequeathed to her at the reading of her grandmother's will. It came with a note that read, "This is the most valuable thing I can give you." Miranda had smirked in derision when the attorney handed it to her, clearly embarrassed as he proceeded to read aloud the remaining bequeathals, which consisted of varying amounts of money and stocks. Nan had held the folio tenderly as Miranda leaned over and whispered delightedly, "Still love the old bitch?"

Having found the photo she was looking for, Nan gently pried it loose and got to her feet. She found Todd in the living room where everyone had gathered.

"I found something you might want to have," she said, suddenly feeling a little emotional. She held out the formal photo of her grandfather.

Todd took it curiously and his jaw dropped. Even given the current changes in his physical appearance, Todd was looking at someone who could have been a slightly older version of himself.

"Your great-grandfather," she said.

As the others gathered round to look, exclaiming over the resemblance, Todd glanced up at Nan with a look that said more than any words.

When he tried to hand the photo back to her later, she shook her head. "You keep it. If you have kids someday, you pass it on to them. If not, well, have your parents return it to me."

Later that evening, she was back in the den trying to stuff the bulky album back into its leather folio when a sheaf of papers fell out. Curious, she gently shook the album and more papers fell out. Picking them up, she saw they were stock certificates and statements from various financial institutions with her name as co-holder of every account. "Old bitch indeed," she said softly.

———◆———

"Todd got back to Georgia okay?" Maddie asked Leisa a week later when they ran into one another in a corridor.

"Yeah," Leisa answered. "He sent a text, but we haven't talked."

"Was his father angry?"

"Well, it probably helped that he had a few extra days to cool down," Leisa replied, smiling. "But he didn't want to come back to our house. He insisted on Todd meeting him at the airport with the car so they could head back right away."

She had driven the Mini while Nan rode with Todd to the airport where they both waited with him until his dad's flight got in. As Mr. Taylor entered the terminal, Todd had given Leisa and Nan each a tight hug.

"Remember, cars are great places to talk," Leisa whispered. "He can't get away."

Todd grinned at her before turning to face his father who did not look happy about being there.

"All we've heard so far is that they got back home," Leisa said.

"How are things with your mom's house?" Maddie asked.

"Good. The real estate agent has been through the house with us and thinks it's ready to go on the market as is," Leisa replied.

Maddie looked closely at Leisa. "You okay?"

"Yeah," Leisa sighed. "I'm kind of torn. I don't want this to drag on now that I've decided to sell, but it's going to be hard to see anyone else in that house."

Maddie gave her shoulder a sympathetic squeeze before parting. "I'll see you tonight."

Leisa continued downstairs to her cubicle. Despite her mixed emotions about selling the house, life felt more settled than it had in a very long time. Nan was keeping a light schedule and they were home together each evening. In many ways, it felt like it had when they were first together, except there was a constant haze of sadness, like a mist hanging over everything.

———◆———

"Does it ever go away?" Leisa had asked her mother as they baked cookies together the second Christmas after Daniel's death. Nan was at work and Bronwyn was lying in wait under the kitchen table, watching attentively and ready to pounce on any dropped crumbs of cookie dough.

Rose, long accustomed to Leisa's seemingly extemporaneous comments and questions, smiled. "Not completely," she replied as she sprinkled cinnamon sugar on a sheet of snickerdoodles. "You forget for brief bits of time, but it always comes back. More so at special times like holidays and birthdays, but you never feel completely whole again." She paused, looking out the kitchen window at the snow falling softly. "There are still times when I miss my mother terribly and it's been almost thirty years."

Leisa thought about this as she transferred a finished batch of chocolate chocolate chip cookies from the cooling rack to a Tupperware container. "Have you - I mean, if you ever met someone, and you know, wanted to date or maybe get married again... it would be okay with me." This felt like a very strange conversation to be having with her mother.

Rose smiled again as she rolled out more cookie dough. "Thank you for saying that, but I don't know... I guess I should never say never, but I can't imagine ever loving another man as much as I loved your father."

"It doesn't have to be a man, Mom," Leisa teased.

"Oh, that's right," Rose responded, looking surprised. "I keep forgetting there's another whole team I could play with."

"Play for, Mom, for, not with."

———

"Are you all right?" Nan asked softly, reaching over for Leisa's hand later that evening as they sat in the back seat of Maddie and Lyn's Explorer on their way to St. Michael's for the weekend.

Leisa squeezed her hand. "I'm fine."

They had left right after work, and by seven were pulling into the parking lot of their bed and breakfast, a charming Victorian house once owned by a sea captain and his wife, according to the brief history posted on the inn's website. As they checked in, the inn's owners told them they were the only scheduled guests for the weekend. They deposited their bags in their rooms and walked through town toward a restaurant.

"There!" said Lyn, pointing to a darkened building. "That's the gallery that agreed to do a small exhibit of some of my paintings. I'll bring them by tomorrow."

When they were seated at the restaurant and had placed their orders, Lyn asked, "So, Nan, what did Bruce say about your grandmother's papers?"

"Well... apparently, the financial advisor he spoke with told him the various accounts' current total value is about five hundred thousand."

Lyn stared at her. "As in half a million? Dollars?"

Nan chuckled. "About five times what she gave everyone else. I think that's why she did it that way, hid the statements inside the photo album. She knew there would be hell to pay if they found out." She took a sip of her iced tea. "But you know, I think I liked the album better before, when I thought that was all she meant by 'this is the most valuable thing I can give you'."

The weather forecast for the weekend was ideal, sunny days in the seventies, nights cool enough for a sweater. On Saturday, Lyn delivered her canvases to the gallery. She had chosen mostly seascapes, which she thought would sell well at this location. After lunch, they rented a boat and went on a cruise of the Chesapeake Bay, exploring some of the inlets and watching fishermen haul up crab traps. Dinner that evening was a feast of crab cakes and shrimp with a few bottles of wine.

"Good thing we walked," Lyn giggled as she wove a trifle unsteadily on their way back to the bed and breakfast.

The inn had a private patio with a beautiful view of the bay. They sat and talked, Leisa's head resting contentedly on Nan's shoulder as they watched the moon come up, reflecting brightly on the water. Nan could finally let herself breathe a sigh of relief that the monsoon was over. Leisa was back where she belonged and they were together and whole again. She caught Maddie's eye and smiled.

That night, she and Leisa made love and it was like coming home. Leisa's mouth and body welcomed her. They fit together the way they used to, reading each other and pleasing each other without the need for words. Afterward, Nan spooned in behind Leisa, fighting sleep, not wanting to lose a moment of this perfect time. She could feel Leisa's breathing slow and grow deeper as she drifted off. As Nan grew drowsy, she tried to remember how recently it had felt as if her life was falling apart. "We survived," she whispered.

—————◆—————

The next morning, the four of them went down for breakfast, where the innkeepers had small bouquets of wildflowers at each place at the table.

"Happy Mother's Day," the wife said with a smile as she poured coffee for each of them.

Maddie, Lyn and Nan all turned to stone. The woman, looking puzzled, returned to the kitchen.

"It's okay," Leisa offered. "You guys are horrible secret keepers. I know it's my first Mother's Day without my mom, and you were trying to help me forget, but it's been a great weekend." She reached over for Nan's hand.

"Well, since you feel that way," Maddie said uncertainly. "I wasn't sure how I was going to handle this, but..." She placed two cards on the table, each made of brightly colored construction paper and decorated with their names spelled out in bits of colored paper and crayoned writing. "I was asked to give these to you this weekend."

Puzzled, Nan and Leisa opened their cards. Inside each was scrawled, "Happy Mother's Day! Love, Mariela."

Chapter 23

"I STILL CAN'T BELIEVE the house sold its first week on the market," Jo Ann said from inside the refrigerator as she scrubbed.

"I know," said Leisa where she was boxing up all the cleaning supplies under the kitchen sink.

From the dining room Nan called out, "Bruce said it would sell fast." She came back into the kitchen. "I've got all the good china stacked on the dining room table, and the hutch is empty."

Together, they were trying to have the house ready for an estate auction in a couple of weekends. "It's so tempting to hold on to everything," Leisa bemoaned. "It all has memories attached to it."

"That's why it's easier to let a stranger handle it," Bruce had advised. "Mr. Jansen will get you the best price for everything, and then it will all be over. Just make sure you take anything you want before he comes for a final inventory, or you'll have to bid on it to get it back."

"At least the young family that bought the house seems very nice, honey," Jo Ann observed. "This old place will have a new life to it with children in it again."

"I know," Leisa said wistfully. "I keep remembering my childhood here. All the Christmas mornings, trying to sneak down the stairs to catch Santa Claus laying out my presents, but those squeaky stairs always gave me away." She grinned. "Learning how to climb down from my bedroom window using the downspout and shutters."

"What?" Jo exclaimed, clutching her chest in mock distress. "It's probably a good thing I never had children. I'm not sure I could have survived all the things they would have done."

Leisa chuckled. "You would have been a great mom," she said with a hug.

"So would you," Jo said. "And Nan," she added in a very loud whisper.

They had both noticed Jo Ann's hints – "and she is not subtle," Nan said ruefully – ever since Easter that Mariela would be a welcome addition to the family.

"I can hear you, you know," Nan said.

"Good," Jo Ann shot back.

Leisa just smiled.

Only a couple of days ago, she had replied, "she's not getting angry and she's not walking out" when Lyn asked how Nan was handling the closer ties to Mariela. "That's enough for now. And believe it or not, I think Todd is mostly to blame."

Todd had e-mailed and texted both of them several times since his parents calmed down after his return to Savannah. It sounded as if he hadn't shown them the photo of his great-grandfather, preferring to keep it to himself for now, "kind of like a talisman against the relatives," Nan guessed.

But Leisa knew. She knew the real reason he hadn't shared it was because it was a connection he wanted to preserve privately with Nan, with his roots, without having to defend it or explain it to his parents.

They spent nearly every remaining evening and weekend day before the auction cleaning, sorting, trying to group things in lots for the auctioneer. Leisa took a break to meet the new owners at Bruce's office a couple of days before the auction so they could close the sale on the house.

"Normally, we wouldn't close until the house was empty and ready for the buyers to do a walk-through, but they have to go back to New Jersey to close on their house up there. They agreed to do things this way. I assured them you were trustworthy," Bruce grinned as he left her in the care of his partner.

Leisa was prepared to thoroughly resent them, but this young family was ecstatic to have found such a perfect house and they thanked her so profusely that she couldn't help liking them. Their two children, a girl of seven and a boy - "I'm almost five," he corrected indignantly when his sister told Leisa he was four - couldn't wait for Christmas with a real fireplace. Leisa leaned toward them and whispered, "I almost caught him going up the chimney, twice." Their eyes got huge as they squirmed in their seats.

All the same, it was heartwrenching to watch Bruce's partner hand them a set of keys after all the papers had been signed.

Apparently, the auction people did a good job of advertising, because the streets for blocks around were lined with cars by seven a.m. on the Saturday of the sale.

"Go home," Nan urged anxiously by mid-morning as Leisa looked ready to cry nearly every time an item sold. It didn't matter whether they sold for a little or a lot, they were all treasures to her. "I'll stay here and help out as much as I can. Bruce and Jo Ann are here, too. We can keep an eye on things."

Leisa finally agreed when the dining table and hutch sold and all she could think of were all the family meals they had shared around that table. "You're right," she admitted, blinking back tears. "I've got to get out of here."

She went home and tried to busy herself with some cleaning that had been neglected while they were working on the other house. She had the front door open and saw the mail carrier come onto the porch.

"Thanks," she said as she went out to meet the mailman and collect the bundle. She sat down on the top step of the porch and sorted through it. There, amidst the catalogs and credit card offers, was an envelope from the Syracuse hospital that did the transplant.

It looked like a bill. Frowning, she opened it. All of her expenses were to have been paid with no out-of-pocket from her.

She shook out the papers inside, and stared at them for several minutes, trying to make sense of them. It was a bill, but not for her. It was for Donald Miller, totaling over seventy-eight thousand dollars. The other paper was a financial form listing her and Eleanor as the responsible parties. At the bottom was her signature, except it wasn't quite. The form was dated three days ago. Her hands were trembling in anger as she tried to think calmly. Forgetting to lock the front door, she carried the papers with her back over to her mother's house.

Wandering frantically through the house, she searched the sea of faces for Bruce, Jo or Nan. She found Jo Ann first.

"Leisa, honey, you're white as a ghost," Jo said worriedly. "What is it?"

Mutely, Leisa held out the papers. Jo Ann's face became a livid red and her lips pursed until they disappeared entirely. "Go find Nan. I'll find Bruce and meet you on the back porch," she said.

A few minutes later, they were all huddled over the forms. Bruce expelled a disgusted breath. "I was afraid they might try something like this."

At Leisa's puzzled look, he explained, "Real estate sales are public record. All they had to do was keep an eye on the Internet and do a search for your name. They know exactly how much you sold the house for."

"He can't get away with this, can he?" Jo asked in alarm.

"No, of course not," Bruce said calmly. "But it is a pain in the neck. The hospital has your social security number from your admission paperwork?" Leisa nodded. "We'll have to prove it's not your signature and that you have no legal connection to him, but they could make things difficult with your credit in the meantime." He laid a reassuring hand on Leisa's shoulder. "Don't worry. I'll have my partner draft a letter and place a phone call first thing Monday morning."

Leisa shook her head in total disbelief. "I just didn't think they were capable of this," she said in dismay.

One of the auction workers ran up just then to ask a question about an upcoming item. Bruce and Jo Ann went with him.

"Are you all right?" Nan asked, watching Leisa carefully.

"I'm fine," Leisa answered in disgust.

"You couldn't have known," Nan told her firmly. "You had no reason to suspect them."

"I could have listened," Leisa said as her jaw hardened. "You all tried to warn me."

"You had no more reason to distrust them than Todd and his parents had to distrust me," Nan reminded her.

"I guess," Leisa admitted, looking at the papers again and shaking her head.

———

Father Linus leaned his elbows on the windowsill, watching the kids out on the playground. Both basketball hoops were surrounded by boys shooting baskets, only a few intrepid girls brave enough to push their way in uninvited; a few groups of girls were jumping rope, creating their cliques as only girls can do, the outsiders sitting and watching wistfully, hoping to be invited to join in; the swings and slides were all occupied; a few loners were scattered about on the outskirts of the playground, mostly the odd kids, the ones the other kids thought weird, the ostracized ones. And then there was Mariela, an exception to every one of those social roles.

Maddie joined him at the window. Linus pointed Mariela out.

"She is amazing," he said. "I've been watching her ever since her mother's funeral. She enjoys being alone, but it's always her choice. The other kids all like her. They ask her to play, and sometimes she does. Then other times, she deliberately seeks out the oddballs and invites them to play. It's like she can tell when they're feeling hurt or lonelier than usual."

Maddie nodded. "She's a good egg."

"What?"

Maddie smiled. "One of my psychology professors believed that some people are 'good eggs' and some people are 'bad eggs', and most of us are somewhere in between. The bad eggs are the ones who seem to have no conscience. They're cruel and violent, with no empathy for other people. They can come from anywhere - good families or bad, or places like this. Then, there are the good eggs, the ones who would flourish in a nurturing environment, but who still find a way to not just survive, but thrive, in a bad environment. These are the kids who climb their way up from horrible conditions to become doctors," she glanced over at Linus, "or priests."

He grinned. "I think you're right. Mariela is a good egg." He cleared his throat. "She came to me last week."

"What about?" Maddie asked in surprise. "If you can say," she added hastily.

"Yeah, it wasn't anything confidential. But she wanted to know if God could answer any prayer, even if it meant someone else had to do something to make it come true."

"She worded it like that?" Maddie asked, frowning.

Linus nodded. "Yes. I told her God can sometimes touch someone's heart and help them see something they were missing or help them realize they feel something they didn't even know they were feeling. And sometimes it answers someone else's prayer when that happens."

Maddie closed her eyes for a moment. "What did she say to that?"

Linus smiled. "She said she was going to go pray."

"Do you know what that was about?" Maddie asked.

Linus gave her a knowing look. "I think we can both guess."

"Leisa."

Linus nodded. "How is Leisa?" he asked casually. "She seems... wounded. I've tried talking to her, but she always avoids getting into it, whatever it is."

Maddie sighed. "She's been through more in the past few months than most people go through in decades."

"So has Mariela," he reminded her.

"Always assume the best of people," Daniel used to say. "Then, if they prove you wrong, shame on them. But don't ever get to the point where you assume the worst right from the start. If you look for the bad, you will find it."

Leisa tried to remember that advice as she waited for a response to the legal correspondence on her behalf. Bruce's partner had called the hospital Monday morning, and asked to speak with a patient account supervisor. He learned that the bill had come to Leisa because no payment arrangements had been made on the account to date. He informed her that Leisa was fraudulently listed as being responsible for the bills, and that he would initiate legal action if necessary. He followed up with a letter to them and another to Donald and Eleanor Miller advising them that they could all be subject to legal action if any collection activity against Leisa was pursued.

"Just when it seemed like we might be able to relax," Leisa griped to Lyn and Maddie. "I was looking forward to a bit of nothing, now that the house is sold and the auction is over."

"Well, how about our trip to the zoo this weekend?" suggested Maddie. "It will take your mind off things, and Mariela has been waiting for us to come up with a date."

How is it, Nan would wonder, that she could have lived her whole life feeling a certain way or believing certain things, and then realize, suddenly, that she didn't feel that way anymore? "It wasn't sudden," Maddie was to say afterward, when Nan talked about this. "It's been changing bit by bit over a long period of time, you just didn't see it."

"No, it was God," Mariela would have said.

How could it feel so natural, so right to have Mariela holding her hand as they walked to the ape enclosure at the zoo, or climbing into her lap to watch the snakes because they scared her? She watched Mariela's freely offered affection with Leisa, and even with Maddie, though she was a little more shy with Lyn, and "she's so resilient, so trusting," she said to Leisa later, "even after everything she's been through."

217

At one point, they were all at the elephant compound, where there were two baby elephants gamboling about. Nan glanced down and realized that Mariela wasn't watching the elephants. She was scanning the crowd as she clung to Leisa's hand.

Squatting down next to her, Nan asked quietly, "Is this where you were when he took you?"

Mariela nodded, her dark eyes wide and frightened.

"He's still in jail, and this time, we're all here to look after you," Nan reassured her. She directed Mariela's attention to the elephants. "See how the big elephants protect the little ones? Watch, that baby is getting too far away and the grown-up is nudging her back where she belongs. That's us. We won't let anything happen to you."

"Excuse me?" Maddie asked indignantly. "Are you saying I'm as big as an elephant?"

For some reason, Mariela found this hilarious and giggled contagiously.

A little while later, as they walked along to the next enclosure, Leisa leaned close to Nan and murmured, "I really love you."

Later that evening, after they had left the zoo and stopped for burgers and shakes for dinner, Mariela fell asleep in the back seat of the Explorer. When they pulled into St. Joseph's, Leisa said, "I'll carry her up to her dorm. Be right back."

Watching them go, Nan asked Maddie, "Has Leisa said anything more about Mariela? About adopting her?"

"No, she hasn't," Maddie said.

"So, hypothetically speaking, how would it work if someone was thinking about adopting someone?"

Lyn bit her lip and turned her face away to hide her smile as Maddie replied, "Well, most people start with a few overnight visits on weekends, just to see how everyone handles being together for twenty-four to forty-eight hours. You never know how it's going to go, but that's a fairly good way to see how compatible everyone is."

She turned in her seat to look at Nan as she said seriously, "But I wouldn't authorize anything between you guys and Mariela right now."

"Why not?" Nan asked, caught off-guard.

"You know how much I love you two," Maddie said, "but that little girl has been through hell. And so have you and Leisa recently." She quickly considered whether to tell Nan about her conversation with Linus and decided not to. "I won't risk pulling the rug out from under Mariela when you and Leisa still have so much healing to do. It wasn't all that long ago that Leisa was on the edge of a breakdown. You're still trying to get back on solid ground and until you are, I can't take the chance it wouldn't work out."

"But," Lyn spoke up hesitantly, "wouldn't it help the healing to have someone like Mariela to love?"

Maddie weighed her words carefully and said, "That's not a child's role. Not anymore than when people think having a child will save a marriage. Solid relationship first, then a child. Not the other way around."

The vehicle was filled with a very heavy silence when Leisa got back in. She quickly glanced from Nan to Lyn to Maddie. "What?"

"It's probably a good thing you didn't tell me about that conversation then," Leisa said later when she found out. "Because Maddie was right."

"How ironic is it," she could have said, "that just as Nan is starting to believe she could be a parent, I'm questioning whether I should be one? Look at what I come from. I know, I was raised by wonderful people, but we've all seen that you can't ignore genetics. We're all a combination of both and you can't ignore one side of who you are just because you don't like it. I'm part of Eleanor, whether I like it or not." That was the part that tormented her.

A week after the zoo trip, Leisa was surprised at work by an e-mail from Eleanor, also at work, saying they needed to talk and asking Leisa to call her over their lunch break. For the remainder of the morning, Leisa was distracted, wondering whether she should call Bruce first, and wondering what on earth Eleanor could have to say.

Nervously, she punched the numbers into her cell phone a little before noon. "Eleanor," she said coldly when the phone on the other end was answered.

She could hear the tremor in Eleanor's voice as she said, "Thank you for calling."

Leisa didn't respond, but listened to Eleanor breathing and nervously clearing her throat. "You must... you must think..." She started crying. "I didn't know," she sputtered. "I didn't know he did that. I know you don't have any reason to believe me..."

"No, I don't," Leisa replied, surprising even herself.

"It's just, I'm so scared," Eleanor gasped, still crying. "I don't know how we'll find the money. I don't have that kind of money..."

Leisa felt her resolve wavering just a bit. She sighed. "It's probably too late to change him," she said, "but you created this. He is arrogant, selfish, lazy - I could go on and on. He's a user, Eleanor, and you have allowed him to use you all his life. You've never made him be accountable for anything. He is healthy enough to get a job now. He could help pay those bills. And don't make excuses for him. I'm done listening to them."

"You're right," Eleanor admitted in a small voice. She cleared her throat again. "We'll work it out somehow. But I wanted to tell you... I hope you know, I really did want to find you, just to know you're okay, and that you grew up happy. I wanted you to know that," she finished softly.

Leisa swallowed hard. "Thank you," she said.

Leisa hung up and pressed her forehead against her hands, her elbows propped on her desk. "Why couldn't you include me, just a little bit?" she longed to have said. She knew it didn't make any sense to feel that way. "I want it, and I don't - all at the same time." Looking at how Donald turned out, she was more grateful than ever that she'd been raised by her parents, but a small piece of her couldn't help wishing Eleanor had wanted her, too. *Or wanted more of me than just a kidney*, she corrected herself.

Chapter 24

"HEY," SAID LYN'S VOICE when Nan answered the telephone at her office. "Am I catching you at an okay time?"

"Yeah, this is fine. I'm in between clients," Nan said.

"Oh, good," Lyn said, sounding relieved. "I always hate to call you at work, but there's something you need to see down at the gallery. Any chance you can come by after you finish?"

Nan glanced at the clock. Her last client was late. Looked like a no show. A good way to start Memorial Day weekend. "I could probably be there within half an hour. Are you there now?"

"Yes," Lyn replied excitedly. "I'm working here all weekend. Just get here as soon as you can. I'll be waiting."

Puzzled and curious, Nan began gathering her things and closed up the office. About twenty minutes later, she was parking down near Fell's Point. Lyn was waiting for her when she entered the gallery. She grabbed Nan by the hand and led her back to the office. There, in a small crate was a corgi puppy.

Lyn was wringing her hands, looking excited and apprehensive at the same time. "I know, I know," she said. "But someone returned him to the breeder and they need to find a new home for him. I wouldn't normally do this, but I thought I'd better show him to you first. If you don't like him, I'll take him back to the breeder. She's a customer of ours, someone we all know." Lyn rattled all of this off so fast, Nan couldn't get a word in edgewise.

"Lyn!" she said finally, and Lyn nervously fell silent.

"First of all, why did they return him?" Nan asked.

"For some reason, they thought getting a puppy to go with their new baby would be a really good idea," she said sarcastically.

"How old is he?" Nan asked, squatting down to get a better look at the small creature watching her.

"Four months," Lyn replied, watching as Nan opened the door of the crate and the puppy come bounding out. He was still covered in puppy fluff, tri-colored, with huge ears that looked three sizes too big for him.

He let Nan pick him up, licking her face and becoming surprisingly calm when she turned him on his back, cradling him to her.

"Is it too soon?" Lyn asked worriedly. "I know how much you and Leisa miss Bronwyn, and I wouldn't have interfered normally, but this puppy literally fell out of nowhere."

"Sometimes, those are the ones that are meant to be," Nan murmured, watching the beautiful brown eyes staring up at her.

"So?" Lyn held her breath. "Do you think this is someone you might want to take home, just to see what Leisa thinks? If she doesn't want him, I will come get him tonight and bring him back to the breeder," she promised.

Nan looked up at her, and then back down at the puppy. "We might as well see what she says."

When she pulled up in front of the house, Nan wisely set the crate down in the front yard to let the puppy out before taking him into the house. After he had emptied his bladder, she carried him inside. "Leisa? Where are you?"

"I'm back in the den," Leisa responded.

Nervously, Nan walked partway down the hall and set the puppy down, letting him enter the den on his own. From inside, she heard, "What –?"

Nan peered around the edge of the door and froze.

"Surprise," Leisa smiled, sitting on the floor with the puppy in her lap.

There, where a chair and lamp used to be near the window, sat a piano.

"What –?"

Leisa watched her anxiously.

Nan walked over and ran her hands over the smooth walnut. Sitting at the bench, she touched the keys, but didn't depress them.

"You won't hurt it, you know," Leisa said from the floor. "If you don't like it, it's returnable, or we can exchange it for one you like better. I don't really know anything about pianos, so I wasn't sure what you would like."

Nan looked over at her, the puppy gnawing playfully on her fingers. "And Lyn promised he could be returned to the breeder if you don't think it's time. He's an orphan."

"He's beautiful," Leisa murmured, picking him up and cradling him under her chin. "Play us something," she suggested, shifting so her back was against the couch, letting the puppy down to explore.

Turning back to the piano, Nan tentatively hovered her hands above the keys, and then, slowly, softly, began to play a long-ago memory. Entranced, Leisa listened, and she realized the puppy was listening also as he sat, his head tilting from one side to the other as the notes reverberated in the air.

"That was beautiful," Leisa said when Nan stopped. "What was it?"

Nan smiled. "Something I learned for Marcus." She came over and sat next to Leisa on the floor. "I don't know how to thank you," she murmured, taking her hand. "It's like a whole piece of me has been locked away all these years, ever since the church mob forced Marcus to leave." She shook her head. "Marcus, Todd. I've lived too much of my life walling off parts I didn't want to think about. I don't want to do that anymore."

———◆———

The next evening, Nan and Leisa and the puppy, along with Jo Ann and Bruce, were invited to Maddie and Lyn's for a cookout.

"Lyn will be home soon," Maddie said as she picked the puppy up and snuggled him. "He is adorable. What's his name?"

"Gimli."

"Really?" Maddie chuckled as set him down and handed out drinks.

"Gimli? What kind of name is Gimli?" Jo asked.

"It's perfect." Bruce smiled as he played tug of war with the puppy, who was growling as fiercely as he could through a mouth filled with rope toy. "Doesn't 'corgi' mean 'dwarf dog' in Welsh?" he asked.

Leisa grinned. "Exactly."

Lyn came in a short while later. "Oh, my gosh," she moaned as she dropped, exhausted, into a kitchen chair. Leisa handed her a Corona with a slice of lime pushed into the mouth of the bottle. "Thanks," Lyn said, closing her eyes and taking a long pull on the bottle. "I don't know what I was thinking when I said I would work Memorial Day weekend."

"Was it not worth going in?" Nan asked. Her eye was caught by Puddles' positioning herself safely on a kitchen chair, her back to the puppy. She watched as the cat deliberately let her tail drop over the edge of the seat, twitching the tip like a wriggling worm luring a fish. Gimli sat down, snapping his jaws, trying to catch the tail with each twitch.

"It was packed!" Lyn exclaimed. "We probably sold more paintings this weekend than we have all year, but I didn't expect it to be that busy."

"That's why we don't go to the beach any more on this weekend, remember? Any place near the water is going to be nuts," Maddie reminded her as she sprinkled seasoning on the hamburgers and chicken. "You relax; we've got dinner almost ready."

Lyn looked down at Gimli, who had gotten bored with the aloof cat and was now tasting her sandal straps and deciding he liked them. She picked him up and held him, rubbing her cheek against his soft fur. She looked at Leisa and said, "I think this is just what you guys needed."

———

Leisa and Nan came in from a walk with Gimli. Exhausted, the puppy walked into his open crate in the kitchen and promptly fell asleep. Leisa turned on the television, and Nan went to the den. A short while later, Leisa heard the sound of the piano. She smiled. Nan had spent some time almost every evening playing, usually by herself with the door closed.

"It seems to calm her," Leisa had said to Maddie and Lyn after Nan finally showed them the piano, something she was reluctant to do at first.

"I don't want to play for anyone," Nan warned Leisa before she would agree to tell them.

"It's probably like meditation in some ways," Maddie suggested.

"Did you know she played?" Lyn asked curiously.

Maddie shook her head. "No," she said thoughtfully, "but it doesn't surprise me. I think with Nan, you could know her for a lifetime and still not know everything."

Leisa was startled now by the ringing of the telephone. "Hello?"

"Hello," came a Southern accent Leisa recognized immediately. "This is Georgina Taylor. Is Dr. Mathison at home, please?"

"Yes, Mrs. Taylor. Just a moment." Leisa carried the phone down the hall and knocked softly. "It's Todd's mother," she said. She handed the phone to Nan and went back to the living room, her heart pounding as she prayed they weren't going to get bad news.

Nan came in several minutes later and sat on the couch.

"Well?" Leisa prompted, her heart sinking when Nan didn't say anything right away.

Nan looked at her and said, "Todd's fine. Health-wise. But apparently, he's staging a little rebellion. He's refusing to go to their family reunion, he says he won't have any more chemo," she paused, "and he says he wants to come live with his real mother."

"Oh, crap."

"Yeah."

"What did you say to her?"

Nan shrugged. "I said all the things a good psychologist should say - that he's just acting out, he's angry, it's a phase, it'll pass. I reassured her that I am not going to agree to his coming up here to live. She thinks he'll try calling me soon."

"Has he called yet?" Lyn asked a couple of nights later.

Leisa glanced at Nan. "He called last night," she said when Nan didn't reply immediately.

Maddie looked up. "What did you say?"

———

"You understand me so much better than they do," Todd said. "You and Leisa both."

He hadn't come right out and said it. Yet.

"Todd, it often feels like other adults understand you better than your parents, because it's temporary. They're only around for the good stuff, and they don't have to discipline you," Nan said. "But your parents are still your parents."

"No, they're not," he burst out angrily. "They adopted me, but you're my real mother."

There it was. Nan closed her eyes, steeling herself.

"I am not your mother," she said icily. "You were an accident. I didn't want a kid then, and I sure as hell don't want a kid now. Whatever is going on with you and your family is not my problem and not my responsibility. You need to deal with it." She listened to the deafening silence on the other end of the line. "I have to go now."

———

"What did you say?"

Nan pushed away from the table. "What I had to," she said, calling the puppy to go outside.

"I'm sorry," Lyn said, berating herself for asking.

"It's okay," Leisa reassured her, filling them in on Nan's conversation with Todd.

"Is she all right?" Maddie asked, looking out the kitchen window at where Nan stood, arms crossed as she stared at the ground, oblivious to the fact that Gimli was happily rolling on his back under one of the trees.

"Not really," Leisa replied. "She said she thought the monsoon was over, but it feels like we keep getting battered over and over again."

"You know," Maddie mused, her eyes narrowing as she tried to recall, "I can remember the old Indonesian woman telling us that after the worst monsoons, victims would still be found months, even years later, and some people were washed away and never found. It was something they had to learn to live with."

Nan suddenly burst into the kitchen, holding the puppy at arm's length with her face screwed up. "Poop. He was rolling in poop," she growled as she carried him to the bathtub.

"Well, that certainly puts things back in perspective, doesn't it?" Maddie said as Leisa and Lyn cracked up laughing.

———◆———

Maddie buzzed down to Leisa's office. "No big hurry, but could I talk to you when you have a few minutes?" she said.

"Sure. I can be there in twenty or thirty minutes?"

"That's fine."

Leisa finished writing a social history on a new child who had just come to St. Joseph's, and then went up to Maddie's office.

"Come on in, and close the door," Maddie said.

Leisa did as she was bidden and sat down.

Maddie cleared her throat then said nothing. She cleared her throat again before saying, "I've been thinking about you and Nan and Mariela." She paused again.

Leisa frowned. Maddie never had this much trouble expressing herself. "What about us?" she asked.

Maddie looked her in the eye and said, "If you and Nan are ready to seriously consider adopting Mariela, I will allow weekend visits."

"What changed your mind?"

227

———

Lyn had come into the living room, and picked up the remote to turn the television off.

"What is it?" Maddie asked as Lyn sat down beside her on the couch, tucking her legs under her.

"You know that I never interfere in your work, or the decisions you have to make," Lyn began. Puddles jumped up onto the back of the sofa, placing herself easily within reach of some petting. "But this time, I think you're wrong."

Maddie turned to her. "About what?"

"About Nan and Leisa. And Mariela. I know they've been through a rough patch, but they're back together. They seem to be through the worst of their problems." She placed a hand on Maddie's knee. "They both risked their lives to save her. They could easily have been killed that night, and they did it willingly. I don't know why I feel so strongly about this - maybe it's seeing Nan warm up to a child for the first time; maybe it's Mariela herself. There is just something special about that little girl."

Maddie thought about this. "There is something about her." She sighed. "I think maybe you're right. Watching Nan do the right thing with Todd, hard as it was, made me wonder if I'd done the right thing."

"They'll have Jo Ann and Bruce, and us, as extended family," Lyn reminded her, relieved that Maddie had already started to reconsider her decision.

Maddie smiled and placed her hand over top of Lyn's. "Are you ready to be an aunt?"

———

"What changed your mind?"

Maddie pursed her lips for a moment. "You and Nan mostly. Mariela partly. Lyn some."

Leisa grinned. "Feeling a bit besieged?"

"A bit," Maddie replied, grinning also. "But," she added, her grin fading, "I do want you and Nan to talk seriously about this. I don't know if I should tell you or not, but Mariela has been praying for this. She even asked Linus for advice. It would break her heart if this started and then ground to a halt for some reason."

Leisa nodded. "I couldn't do that to her. If we can't go into this ready to make a commitment, we won't start."

———

The doorbell rang and Gimli scrabbled to get to Jo Ann who was coming in carrying a large shopping bag.

"No," she said, laughing as she bent down to pet him. "This isn't for you."

Leisa came into the foyer. "What's all this?"

Jo pulled from the bag a stuffed bear and some children's books. "I didn't know what grade level she's reading at, so I got a few classics for her library."

"Her library."

Jo and Leisa turned around to see Nan who looked ill.

"What's the matter?" Jo Ann asked. "Are you sick?"

Nan shook her head and went back to the kitchen.

"Jitters," Leisa said. "She sat down and looked at our finances and started panicking about what it will cost to send her to college."

Jo's eyebrows shot up. "Don't you think you should bring her home for her first visit before you start planning for her college expenses?"

Leisa smiled. "Yeah. Most people would do it that way, but I think Nan is trying to brace for this by having everything planned out ahead of time."

Jo laughed. "If she figures that out, tell her to write a book."

They walked back to the kitchen where Nan was sitting over a cup of tea. Jo sat and laid a calming hand on Nan's arm.

"I only got to share long-distance in my sister's anticipation of bringing Leisa home," she said to them. "But I know she and Daniel had all the same fears of doing something wrong, not being able to give her everything they wanted to, but they figured out - and you will too - the only thing you can control is the love you give her. Love is always enough."

229

———

"Love is always enough."

Nan repeated that to herself Saturday night as she stood leaning against the doorjamb, peering into the guest room where Mariela was sleeping.

Leisa had brought her home after work on Friday and introduced her to Gimli. They'd had a quiet dinner, just the three of them and had watched some television before putting Mariela to bed.

"Will you be okay in here by yourself?" Leisa asked as she tucked Mariela in.

Mariela nodded.

"If you need anything, our room is right next door. You come get us, all right?"

Nan got up three times that night to check on her.

"I think she'll be fine," Leisa whispered sleepily as Nan got back into bed.

"I know."

"So will you. Now go to sleep."

Most of Saturday was spent over at the Gallagher house. Jo Ann and Bruce were ecstatic to have Mariela with them for the day. They invited Maddie and Lyn over for dinner and played Go Fish and Old Maid most of the afternoon. Gimli entertained himself with a new squeaky toy.

"I didn't even remember these games existed," Nan said after losing her fourth hand of Old Maid.

"These were Leisa's old sets of cards from when she was little," Jo said nostalgically. "I never thought we'd have another child here playing with them."

Mariela hugged Jo and Bruce when it was time to leave. "What time is church tomorrow?" she asked Leisa and Nan as they walked home.

"Um," Leisa stammered as she and Nan locked eyes. "How about if we go to Father Linus's Mass?"

"I couldn't tell her we don't go to church," she whispered to Nan a few minutes later when they got home and Mariela was playing in the bathtub. "Linus is the only priest I think I could stand. But I don't even know what time his Mass is."

"Hang on," Nan said grimly. She picked up the phone and dialed Lyn and Maddie's house. "All right. We now have a - hold on," she said, turning to Leisa. "How old is she anyway?"

"Um, we're not sure, exactly. The doctor thought she was five or six."

"Okay, we have a six-year-old kid who expects us to go to church tomorrow. I'm not even Catholic. What are you going to do about it?"

Leisa could hear the laughter from where she sat.

"Yes... okay... all right." Nan hung up and turned to Leisa. "They're picking us up at eight-thirty."

Chapter 25

DURING A BREAK IN between clients, Nan checked her cell phone to see a missed call from her parents' number. Apprehensively, she called them back.

"Dad? I saw you called. What's up?"

"It's your mother," Stanley said.

"What about her?"

"Well, a couple of months ago, she was stopped by the police."

Nan closed her eyes. "Again? What was her blood alcohol level?"

Stanley didn't answer immediately.

"Dad?"

"Point two."

Nan's mouth opened and closed a few times. "Point two? I wouldn't even be able to stand up at point two. Did she hurt anyone?"

"No," he said quickly. "She just hit a curb. Anyway," he pressed on before Nan could say anything further, "the judge ordered her to rehab."

"You didn't get her off this time?"

She could hear her father breathing. "I couldn't," he said, but she knew he had tried, like he had done a half-dozen times before. "Anyway, she's been there for a week, and I thought maybe you would want to come home and –"

"No!" Nan pressed her hand to her eyes. "She's starting to call you, isn't she? Begging you to bring her home." She took his silence as confirmation. "Dad, she needs to stay there the entire prescribed period. I'll be here if you need to talk, but I am not coming home."

"He'll give in," she said to Leisa a few hours later when she got home and repeated the story to her.

"Your mom has been in rehab before?" Leisa asked, looking up from an array of papers spread out on the kitchen table.

"A few times," Nan said, reading the papers upside down. "But he always caves and gets her out early. What are you doing?"

"The home assessment," Leisa sighed. "Maddie arranged for another agency to do it. Since I work at St. Joe's, they can't assess us."

"How can I help?" Nan asked as she sat.

"Funny you should ask," Leisa smiled. She held out a form. "Your family history." Nan made a face. "Maybe it's a good thing they're three thousand miles away."

"Speaking of which," Nan said as she accepted the form from Leisa. "How much are you going to divulge about the biologicals?"

It was Leisa's turn to grimace. "I don't know. I'm not sure I really need to include them at all since we don't have contact with them."

Nan noticed for the first time what Leisa was wearing. "Did you go to the gym today?"

"Yes, on my way home."

"I keep meaning to ask you how things are with Sarah since your talk with her," Nan asked casually, pretending to be concentrating on the form she was filling out.

"And I keep meaning to tell you, I haven't seen her," Leisa replied, not fooled at all by Nan's nonchalance. "At first, I thought we were just there at different times, but then I overheard one of the staff telling a member that she's gone to another gym."

Nan looked up in surprise. "Do you think it was because of you?"

Leisa smiled guiltily. "I hope so."

The telephone rang, and Leisa reached for it. *How many times,* she wondered later, *is our life going to be disrupted by this damn machine?* She seriously considered unplugging every phone in the house.

"Leisa?"

It was Eleanor.

"Yes?" Leisa responded warily.

"How are you?"

"I'm fine," Leisa answered, more suspicious than ever. "What do you want?" she asked, deciding to take the initiative.

"Well, I wanted to see how you were doing," Eleanor said lamely.

Leisa thought she heard Donald's whisper in the background. It gave her the courage to say, "The only time you and Donald care about how I'm doing is when you want something from me."

A very long, tense silence followed. Leisa resisted the urge to fill it, and let it drag on.

"The hospital... they're... they've turned us over to a collection agency," Eleanor stammered. "I'm not asking you to pay the bill," she added hastily. "I know that's our responsibility, but... my car broke down. It needs a new transmission, and I don't have that kind of money, and... I can't get a car loan with my credit right now, and... I was wondering if you could lend me money for a car? I'll pay you back, I promise," she blathered.

Leisa was torn. She knew she could easily afford to lend them the money, but "where will it end?"

———◆———

"Please, please, please," Leisa begged. "Couldn't you lend me the money?"

The summer after eighth grade, she had fallen in love with a bright orange ten-speed bicycle. It cost a hundred dollars and she only had thirty-five saved up.

"I know you won't let me touch my college money, but I promise I'll pay you back," she said to her parents. "If I have to save all the money first, the summer will be over, and I'll hardly get to ride it."

Rose and Daniel looked at one another in that non-verbal communication that parents share.

"We will lend you the money," Daniel said at last. "But it is a loan, and you will pay us back."

Leisa honestly couldn't recall later if she actually thought they wouldn't hold her to it, but they did. There were little slips of paper every now and then, for July fourth or Labor Day, that forgave five or ten dollars of her debt, but they kept an account, posted on the kitchen bulletin board, of what she had borrowed and each payment she made until the entire loan was repaid. She never mowed so many yards or babysat so many kids as she did that summer trying to earn money. She was so busy, she hardly had time to ride her new bike, but she loved that bicycle. She polished it and lubed it. She could still remember the pride of making that last payment.

"Thank you," she said to her parents years later. "For making me pay for that bicycle. It wouldn't have meant nearly as much if you had given it to me."

———◆———

As Leisa teetered on the verge of giving in, she heard Donald whisper in the background, "Say we're family."

Instantly, she came crashing back to earth.

"You know," she said to Nan afterward, "I know they don't understand that I gave the kidney because I couldn't have lived with myself if I hadn't, but when I heard him say that... Am I so pathetic that he knew to use that to get to me?"

What she couldn't admit, even to Nan, was how much she wanted to say, "How come I wasn't family when you had your picture taken in the hospital?" but it would have sounded petty and childish.

What she did say was, "No. Tell Donald we are not family." She looked at Nan, her eyes bright with the strength of her emotions. "I have a family, a wonderful family of people who love me without wanting anything from me. I will not lend you money. I gave you a pound of flesh. Literally. It's more than you deserve and it's all you're going to get. Please don't call me again."

———◆———

That moment of clarity, when she realized she had always had all the family she needed, would stay with Leisa for the remainder of her life. Like being there as her father drew his last breaths, or feeling Nan's arms around her the night Bronwyn died, or seeing the trust in Mariela's eyes as she lay down that first night in the police station. These were moments the memory of which never faded in intensity no matter how much time went by. "I was so blind," she would say to Nan later. "Like Dorothy in Oz, it was right there in front of me all along, perfectly visible, but it wasn't until someone challenged me and I was faced with either losing it or claiming it, that I could see it." Donald's attempt to manipulate her by using a family connection helped her to see the truly unconditional nature of the love extended to her by those who surrounded her. That realization became the shield that protected her during those moments, ever rarer, when the shadows threatened to overtake her.

Maddie helped to solidify that feeling when she came to Leisa's cubicle a couple of weeks later, informing her that the home assessment had passed with no problems.

"So soon?" Leisa asked, astounded.

Maddie smiled. "Well, there were extenuating circumstances," she said. "You knew what they needed in the paperwork, they know you, and... I asked them to give this priority."

"Thanks," Leisa smiled gratefully.

"But, since it is summer time, and Mariela's not in school, we will have to wait to place her with you until you or Nan can take some time off to be home with her," Maddie pointed out.

Leisa's brow furrowed as she considered. "What about Jo Ann? Could she be one of the caretakers as well, so we can rotate time off?"

"I hadn't thought of her, but I don't see why not."

"Wow," Leisa said as the reality of the situation hit her. "We need to go shopping."

"Wow," echoed Nan that evening when Leisa told her they were approved. She expelled a deep breath. "This is really real." She looked over at Leisa. "Maddie said that Mariela wants this, but have you spoken to her yet?"

"This weekend?" Leisa asked hopefully.

"This weekend," Nan agreed. She looked down at Gimli who was enthusiastically ripping the stuffing out of a toy, trying to get to the squeaker. "A puppy and a little girl. What were we thinking?"

On Saturday morning, they got in the car to go pick Mariela up for the weekend.

"Are you okay?" Nan asked as she drove. "You seemed like you had a really restless night."

"Just some strange dreams," Leisa answered, rubbing her eyes tiredly. "Sorry if I kept you awake."

Nan reached over for her hand. "Ready for today?"

Leisa forgot all about being tired as she smiled. "Yes. How about you?"

"Yes," Nan said slowly. "I cannot believe I'm saying that."

A little while later, they were back home with Mariela. As usual, the first thing she did was sit on the floor and let Gimli climb all over her, licking her face and nibbling on her ears as she giggled.

When she got up, Leisa said, "Mariela, we would like to talk with you."

Mariela sat at the kitchen table.

"Do you like coming here to our house?" Leisa asked.

"Yes," Mariela nodded. She looked from Leisa to Nan and back again. She must have seen something in their expressions that alerted her because she asked, "Have I done something bad?"

"No," Leisa and Nan both replied at once.

"We wanted to talk to you," said Nan, "to see if you would like to live here with us, all the time."

Mariela's face, instead of bursting into the ecstatic expression they had anticipated, became wary. "What do you mean?"

Leisa leaned forward. "We would like to adopt you," she said. "But only if that's what you want, too."

Mariela looked back and forth, from one face to the other, still guarded, and asked, "For how long?"

"It broke my heart to see her that cautious and defensive," Nan admitted later, but, "Forever," is what she said to Mariela. "We want

238

you to be part of our family forever."

When Mariela still didn't respond, Leisa said hesitantly, "But if that's not what you want, we can still be friends, just like we have been."

"Excuse me," Mariela said, sliding off her chair and leaving the kitchen.

Leisa and Nan exchanged puzzled looks. "That wasn't the response I expected," Nan said, nonplussed.

Together, they tiptoed out to the living room where Mariela was kneeling in front of one of the chairs near the fireplace. "Thank you for giving me what I asked for," she whispered. "Please help me be good so they'll always want me."

Leisa reached for Nan's hand, squeezing it hard. She went in and sat on the floor next to Mariela while Nan sat on her other side. Mariela rocked back on her heels and looked at them.

"This is what you want then?" Leisa asked softly.

Mariela nodded, smiling now.

"You don't have to be good so we'll want you," said Nan. "We will always want you."

"That's what mothers do," Leisa said.

"Mothers?" Mariela asked.

"We're not trying to take the place of your mother," Nan said quickly, "but –"

"But we would like to be your new mothers if you're ready for that," Leisa finished.

This time, Mariela's face lit up as she hugged each of them.

Later that day, when they asked her what she would like to change in the guest room to make it feel like hers, Mariela couldn't tell them anything she wanted to have changed. "I like it the way it is," she kept insisting.

"Well," said Nan that night as she and Leisa lay in bed, "if everything else goes this well, this is going to be a piece of cake."

"I should have known better," Leisa would say later.

Chapter 26

LEISA WOKE FEELING DISORIENTED as she looked at the shadows of her own room. Damn. She needed to get some sleep. Some real sleep. These dreams were coming almost every night now, and becoming more detailed. They started at her mother's house where she wandered pointlessly from room to room, searching for... she didn't know what. Sometimes the house was as she remembered it with all the furniture, other times it was empty, but still she searched. Whatever it was, she wanted to find it, but dreaded it at the same time. Sometimes, she left the house, but the dream always evaporated if she did, waking her with a start. Other times, she seemed stuck going through the house again and again for what felt like the whole night.

She glanced over at Nan's dark silhouette next to her and listened to her calm, even breathing. She shifted a little closer, just enough to feel the warmth of Nan's back pressing against her arm, comforting her enough to allow her to fall back asleep.

They were rotating days off to stay home with Mariela, with Jo Ann helping out once or twice a week. Mariela's greatest discovery thus far had been the library.

"I never saw so many books!" she exclaimed.

They were soon going to the library for a fresh supply of books every couple of days as she voraciously read all the ones she brought home. She was soon bored with first grade books and began checking out second and third grade level books. Once home, she was content to read for hours.

"We're all reading more," Nan told Maddie as they kept an eye on the grill. "We hardly ever have the television on lately."

Lyn and Maddie had invited them over for dinner, where Lyn put Nan and Maddie in charge of barbecuing the chicken while she and Leisa worked in the kitchen.

"And how are you doing?" Maddie asked knowingly as she and Nan watched Mariela playing with Puddles on the back patio while Gimli was corralled inside to give the cat some peace.

Nan smiled wryly. "Better than I expected," she admitted. "I know we're lucky that she is not more profoundly affected by everything she's been through, but..." she hesitated.

"But what?" Maddie prodded as she lifted the lid on the grill and turned the meat.

"This sounds bad, but, it's kind of like getting Gimli at four months old. I know the puppy, or I should say, baby stage is cute, but it's so much easier when they're a little older."

"Then why does Leisa look so tired?"

"No offense," Lyn was saying to Leisa in the kitchen at that moment, "but you look awful. What's up?"

"I'm not sure," Leisa replied honestly as she set the table. "I'm not sleeping well. I've been having some really bizarre dreams. Almost every night."

Lyn looked up from the potato salad she was making. "Are you having second thoughts about Mariela?"

"No," Leisa said emphatically. "At least, not consciously. In all these dreams, I'm wandering around Mom's house. Around and around. I don't know, maybe I'm having a delayed reaction to letting it go."

"How is Mariela adjusting to being part of a normal household?"

"Really well," Leisa answered. "She's curious about everything – cooking, cleaning. You don't realize how many things we're exposed to as kids and don't even think about. She thinks vacuuming and washing dishes is play."

Lyn laughed. "You'd better hope she keeps thinking that."

Leisa's expression darkened. "She's also starting to ask questions about her mother," Leisa added.

———

"Was my mama bad?" Mariela asked unexpectedly one evening at the dinner table.

Leisa and Nan exchanged a quick glance. "Why would you ask that?" Nan asked.

Mariela said, "I heard kids talking at the other place, at St. Joseph's. They talked about their mothers or fathers being in jail because they did bad things, and that's why the kids had to go there. My mama was in jail."

"Yes, she was," Leisa said carefully. "And it's true that some of those kids were at St. Joseph's because their parents were sent to jail. Some were taken away because their parents weren't taking good care of them."

Mariela looked hard at her. "My mama didn't take care of me." It wasn't a question.

Leisa leaned forward. "Your mother was sick. When people need drugs, they can't think of anything else. Your mother took the best care of you she could, but you're right. She didn't take very good care of you."

Nan spoke up. "But that doesn't mean she didn't love you. Even if she couldn't take care of you the way she should have, she loved you."

Mariela poked at her food, pushing it around on her plate. "She lied to me. Mothers aren't supposed to lie."

Leisa blanched a little and sat back.

"We won't lie to you," Nan said firmly, with a worried glance at Leisa.

"Promise?" Mariela demanded.

"We promise," Leisa murmured.

It wasn't until hours later, after Mariela was asleep, that Nan had a chance to ask, "What happened earlier, at the dinner table?"

"Nothing," Leisa said. "It's just hard to listen to a child questioning why her mother didn't love her enough to take care of her."

But it didn't escape Nan's notice that Leisa didn't look at her as she answered.

"Leisa!"

She turned to see Linus running up the stairs after her.

"Hi," he gasped. "Whew, I gotta get more exercise than just playing video games."

"What's up?"

"I haven't had a chance to congratulate you and Nan on becoming mothers," he said, holding out a wrapped package. "It's nothing much," he added as she accepted the parcel. "A couple of books of bedtime stories and some pouches of cookie mix." He shrugged. "Just some things I thought you guys could do together, as a family. Things I remember from when I was a kid, before..."

"Before you were placed in foster care? Thank you," Leisa said, giving him a hug. "We'll invite you over to help with the cookies."

"Really?"

Leisa laughed. "Yes, really."

"That would be great."

They continued up the stairs.

"How are you doing?" he asked. "I mean, you've been through a lot from what Maddie says."

Leisa didn't answer immediately. "I think it's calming down at last. I hope we can just settle into a normal life as a family now," she smiled, hefting the package.

"I hope so, too," Linus said. "Say hi to Mariela for me."

When she got home that evening, Nan and Mariela were already home, waiting for her.

"What's that?" Mariela asked immediately.

"It's from Father Linus," Leisa said. "For you."

"And this came for you," Nan said in a low voice as Mariela tore the wrapping paper off Linus's package. She held out a small box. "It's from Ithaca."

Leisa's face hardened. "Even then," she would tell Nan later, "I was stupid enough to think maybe it was a belated thank-you present." But, "It's my baby book." She turned away, not wanting Nan to see the disappointment on her face. "I guess she really is done with me."

Nan flipped the book open and, looking through the photos, came upon a blank page smudged with the imprint of an old photo. "Maybe not completely."

———

Leisa's dream shifted as for the first time she walked out her mother's front door and found herself outside the funeral home. She didn't want to go in, but the doors were propped open, beckoning her inside. Reluctantly, she entered. As she walked down the main corridor, all of the small parlors were filled with people who turned to watch her as she passed. At the end of the hallway was one last parlor, which was empty. She entered and sat down, waiting. She could smell the lingering odors of flowers and candles. After a while – it could have been minutes or hours – Rose came in and sat next to her.

"You've been looking for me?" Rose asked.

And though Leisa hadn't expected her, she knew then that all the nights of wandering through her mother's house had been just that. She nodded.

"You want to know why I never told you about the note?"

Leisa nodded again.

"I should have, I know," Rose said. She looked at Leisa with an expression of unutterable sadness. "But I was afraid."

"Of what?" Leisa asked, speaking for the first time.

"If she kept you once, maybe she would try again. I lived with the constant fear that she would change her mind and try to take you back," Rose confessed. "And... I suppose I was also afraid that if you met her, you might wish she'd kept you."

"I would never -" Leisa began, but thought how she would feel if Florida Gonzalez were alive, what it would be like to live with the apprehension that she might come back into Mariela's life. She looked at Rose and saw, not her mother, but a woman, imperfect and frightened as she admitted her deepest fears. "But I can understand why you felt that way," Leisa said.

"The longer we went without talking about it, the safer it felt. And... it was easy to say it was okay as long as you didn't want to know anything about her. Of course, it wasn't fair to put that on you. Your father wanted us to sit you down and show you even if you weren't asking, but I kept saying, 'when she's older.' Only, it didn't get any easier as you got older, and it seemed best just to keep it shut away."

Leisa sat there, thinking about this. "I met her, you know."

"I know."

Leisa's throat burned as she said, "She only wanted to find me because she needed something from me."

"Maybe," Rose said, "but I think she always wondered if she did the right thing."

Leisa shrugged. They sat in silence for a while.

"You won't say it, will you?" Rose said.

"Say what?" Leisa asked uneasily.

"How angry you are with me."

"I'm not."

"You should be," Rose said softly.

"It... it was just... when I found it, you and Dad were gone. I couldn't ask you," Leisa said as she began to cry.

"I know," said Rose, her eyes beginning to tear up as well. "What can I do for you?"

"Hold me." Leisa turned to her and sobbed as Rose wrapped her arms around her.

Nan woke to the sound of Leisa crying. She turned to her and took her in her arms, holding her as she cried. She couldn't tell if

Leisa ever woke, but she eventually quieted and fell asleep, still lying in Nan's embrace.

Ellen Cavendish was again Nan's last client of the day. "I like knowing that if I'm really bonkers, I can pay you extra to run over," she often joked. She reached down for her purse. "How are you, Nan?" she asked.

Nan stopped writing next week's appointment in her planner and glanced at Ellen. "Why? How do I seem?" she asked cautiously.

"Relax," Ellen smiled. "I only ask because you seem to be in a very different place from where you were just a couple of months ago."

"I am," Nan said simply, not offering any further explanation.

"How do you... how do you *be* so happy?" Nan had asked Maddie years ago when they were working on their doctorates, working part-time – Nan in a mental health clinic and Maddie at St. Joseph's – and going crazy. Or at least Nan was going crazy. Maddie seemed to sail along with whatever came. Nothing fazed her, where Nan was so easily frustrated by the ups and downs of their schedule, so much of it beyond their control. That was what bugged Nan the most, not having control.

Maddie smiled as she thought about Nan's question. "I be happy," she mused. "I should have that made into a bumper sticker." She shrugged. "I don't know. Part of it is deciding to be happy instead of dwelling on the crap. It's not that there isn't crap in my life, or that I don't notice it, but I don't want to become one of those people who are addicted to misery."

"Are you saying –"

"I did not say that's what you are," Maddie interrupted, anticipating Nan's protest. "Although, you do have a slight tendency to dwell on the negative," she pointed out tactfully. The other part," she continued, before Nan could argue the previous point, "is finding a way to accept that there will be things you cannot control. The world will not end; your life will not be totally ruined; there will be no truly serious consequence to most of what makes you angry. You need to learn how to step back and get some perspective, really see the big picture and let things go."

———

Nan smiled as she followed Ellen out the door. It had taken the collapse of her world and the near ruination of her life for her to learn that lesson. "You always did learn things the hard way," Maddie would have reminded her.

When she got home, Leisa and Mariela were already there. Mariela was now going to day care, where she was getting some review prior to the start of first grade in a little over a month.

"I could keep taking care of her," Jo Ann had protested.

"We know you could," Leisa said fondly, "and we may take you up on that sometimes, but this is good practice for school. And this way, you're not tied down when you've got other things to do."

Leisa helped Mariela get Gimli outside so they could play in the backyard. "How was your day?" she asked as Nan flipped through the mail on the kitchen counter.

"It was –"

Leisa turned to see Nan staring at a manila envelope in her hand.

"What is it?" Leisa asked, coming over to her.

"It's from Savannah," Nan said quietly.

———

"Todd's mother wrote a very nice letter," Leisa told Maddie and Lyn on the telephone later that evening after Mariela had been put to bed. "When Todd went back into the hospital a couple of weeks ago, he asked her to return the photo of Nan's grandfather. He must have known he wouldn't be going home this time."

Lyn, speaking on a second extension, sounded as if she was crying as she asked, "How is Nan?"

"I'm not sure," Leisa said softly. "She's back in the den. She wanted a little time alone."

"She never got to speak to him again after she told him he couldn't come up here, did she?" asked Maddie heavily.

"No," said Leisa, her own throat tightening painfully. "I think that will be the hardest part, that she never got to say she didn't mean it."

When Leisa hung up, she went back to the den. Nan was watching *City of Angels*. Leisa sat down next to her on the couch, putting an arm around her shoulders.

"I hope his angels were with him," Nan whispered as her eyes filled with tears.

"I know they were," Leisa said, holding her tightly.

Chapter 27

MARIELA'S FACE WAS SCRUNCHED up with her intense concentration as she took a mighty swing and... hit the whiffle ball to the far end of the yard. Amidst the cheers and claps, she heard Leisa yelling, "Run!" Still carrying her bat, she took off for the paper plate serving as first base. "Keep going!" Leisa yelled again and Mariela kept running, Gimli nipping at her heels as she rounded second and kept going to third while Bruce fumbled about in the azaleas for an extraordinarily long time trying to get his hands on the ball. "All the way!" Leisa called out, and Mariela ran towards home plate, beating Bruce's feeble throw in to home.

"I did it! I did it!" Mariela squealed happily, giggling as Leisa picked her up and swung her around.

The game broke up as Gimli grabbed the whiffle ball and ran away with it, his huge ears folded flat against his head as he was chased by Mariela who thought this was as much fun as the puppy did.

"I haven't heard this much laughter in your house in a very long time," Maddie said, leaning toward Nan as they sat at the table on the patio, watching the goings-on.

Nan smiled. "You're right."

Maddie watched Nan's face shrewdly as she asked, "How are you?"

Nan thought about her answer as she watched Mariela and Gimli who were now playing tug of war with a stick. "I'm doing better than I would have before."

They were interrupted by Leisa calling through the kitchen window, "Nan, could you get the grill started, please?"

That was the signal for everyone to pitch in and help with dinner preparations. Mariela was learning how to husk corn outside with Jo Ann and Bruce; Lyn and Maddie were putting together a huge salad while Leisa sprinkled seasoning on the steaks and hamburgers.

"Give me something to do," Nan pleaded.

"It's your birthday," Leisa said. "You take it easy."

Nan went back outside to help with the corn. She sat down next to Mariela who was wearing a large number of corn silks - all over her lap, in her hair, everywhere.

"When's my birthday?" Mariela asked out of nowhere.

"Ask your mother," Jo Ann said.

"Which one?" Mariela asked.

Nan stared hard at the ear of corn she was husking. "You better ask your other mother," she said quietly.

"I am so sorry," Jo whispered when Mariela had left. "It just came out."

"It's okay, I just... Wow. Hearing that for the first time." She shook her head.

Mariela went to find Leisa who was in the kitchen with Lyn and Maddie. "Mom, when's my birthday?"

Leisa's only sign of shock was dropping the steak knives in her hand. "That could have been dangerous," she muttered under her breath. "Um," she stalled, with a quick glance over to Maddie who shook her head. "We don't really know."

"Do you remember your mama ever celebrating your birthday?" Maddie asked. "She might have called it *cumpleaños*."

Mariela shook her head.

"Well," said Leisa slowly. "I came to the police station to get you on January 16th. How about we make that your birthday?" she suggested with a shrug, glancing at Maddie who shrugged also.

Mariela thought about this. "Okay," she said, and went back out to shuck more corn.

Soon, they were all seated at the table, eating and laughing their way through Nan's birthday dinner. After dinner, a large cake with thirty-eight lit candles was produced as they sang to her. "Thirty-eight?" Mariela counted with a gasp, as if she couldn't comprehend such a large number.

"Thanks a lot," Nan grumbled jokingly.

Mariela seemed to be impatient for everyone to finish their cake. "Is it time yet?" she whispered dramatically to Leisa.

"Yes," Leisa whispered back. "It's time."

Mariela leapt out of her chair, taking Nan by the hand, and dragging her from the kitchen. "Come on," she urged.

"Where are we going?" Nan laughed as Mariela pulled her down the hallway toward the den. "I haven't been allowed in here for two days," Nan said suspiciously as they approached the closed door. "What have you been up to?"

"Open it," Mariela commanded.

Cautiously, Nan opened the door of the study and entered. There, one entire wall had been converted to a huge collage of photos. Some of them Nan recognized as ones that had been in Rose and Daniel's house, the ones Leisa had packed away. But there were others as well – there were pictures of Maddie and Lyn, Bruce and Jo Ann, Jo and Rose. Many of them Nan had never seen. In the center was a recent snapshot of Mariela with her arms wrapped around Leisa and Nan's necks.

"It's our family!" Mariela said proudly.

Nan stepped closer and saw an early photo of Florida Gonzalez, before drugs and a harsh life had taken their toll on her beauty. There were photos of Bronwyn, and a few of Gimli. And there, in the middle, was Nan's grandfather next to Todd's high school photo. Leisa stepped close and wrapped her arm around Nan's waist as everyone else came closer as well, laughing and pointing to various pictures.

Nan turned to Leisa. "Our family," she murmured. "Thank you."

"Play for us?" Leisa asked.

She could see the hesitation in Nan's eyes, but then, to her surprise, Nan went to the piano and sat. Everyone stopped talking and turned as she began to play. Leisa recognized it as one of those pieces Nan said she'd learned for Marcus many years ago, a wistful, haunting composition.

———

"If people know the monsoon is coming, why don't they flee?" Nan asked, perplexed.

The old woman peered at her with her stony black eyes. "Would you flee life? Yes, monsoon brings flooding and death, but without monsoon, there is no life. All becomes stagnant and still. Only after the destruction can life begin again. Without the rains, the floods, all would wither and die. Nothing could grow. We fear monsoon, but we need it as well."

Nan had never understood what the old woman meant. Life was tough enough without putting yourself in harm's way, but "she was right," Leisa would have said. "I would give anything to have Mom and Bronwyn back, but now, knowing how easily it can all be taken away, knowing what it feels like to be so utterly lost... everything feels more real, more precious... just more."

"So, you thought of me as a monsoon?" Mariela asked years later when they spoke of this.

"Not you," Nan said, smiling indulgently. "But all of the things that coincided with you coming into our lives? Yes. You blew in with the monsoon. The deaths, the loss, the threat of losing everything we held most dear. But, without that, I don't think my heart could have opened enough for all that came later."

In her mind's eye, she could see the old woman nodding her approval. "Now you understand."

THE END

Author Biography

Caren was raised in Ohio, the oldest of four children. Much of her childhood was spent reading Nancy Drew and Black Stallion books, and crafting her own stories. She completed a degree in foreign languages and later another degree in physical therapy where for many years, her only writing was research-based, including a therapeutic exercise textbook. She has lived in Virginia for over twenty years where she practices physical therapy, teaches anatomy and lives with her partner and their canine fur-children. She began writing creatively again several years ago. She is an award-winning author of several novels, including *Looking Through Windows*, *Miserere*, *In This Small Spot* and *Neither Present Time*. Look for her books on Amazon, Smashwords and other booksellers.

Made in the USA
Charleston, SC
02 March 2014